**"A wager that if you fail to seduce the delectable Mrs. Lansbury before Christmas—"**

"And why should I want to seduce her?"

"To prove that you can—that you haven't lost your touch."

The challenge was thrown lightly, and Maxim teetered on the brink of accepting when caution reared its head. Seducing any woman who was reluctant to be seduced was not his thing, but the lovely Eve Lansbury had captured his attention and he found the challenge was intriguing. Besides, her parting words, that they would never be anything more than neighbors, was a challenge in itself. If his conscience pricked him at all at the calculating way he was considering the wager, he ignored it.

She was the most fascinating, beguiling creature he had come across in a long time, and for all his sins, she fascinated him. The memory of her fury would not leave him, and her angry words and cold manner didn't make her any less desirable to him. In fact, he found that her very dislike of him aroused the hunter in him. It was difficult for him to set aside thoughts of her. He was a man who must win, whatever the odds stacked against him. Whenever he set his mind on having something, he was not easily dissuaded.

## Author Note

Imagine being on the receiving end of a wager between two gentlemen. Imagine how a lady would feel should something like this occur—horrified, furious, humiliated and deeply hurt—especially if the lady in question thought she knew the gentleman, trusted him implicitly, even.

Such a thing would take some forgiving—more so if the lady happened to be in love with the gentleman who agreed to the wager—to seduce the lady before a certain time or his house would be forfeit. It would certainly take some explaining.

So, does the lady forgive him or send him on his way? You won't be disappointed when you read *The Earl's Wager for a Lady* and find out the answer.

# HELEN DICKSON

---

## The Earl's Wager for a Lady

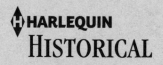

**HARLEQUIN®**
**HISTORICAL™**

Recycling programs
for this product may
not exist in your area.

ISBN-13: 978-1-335-72343-7

The Earl's Wager for a Lady

Copyright © 2022 by Helen Dickson

For questions and comments about the quality of this book,
please contact us at CustomerService@Harlequin.com.

Harlequin Enterprises ULC
22 Adelaide St. West, 41st Floor
Toronto, Ontario M5H 4E3, Canada
www.Harlequin.com

**Printed in U.S.A.**

**Helen Dickson** was born and still lives in South Yorkshire, UK, with her retired farm manager husband. Having moved out of the busy farmhouse where she raised their two sons, she now has more time to indulge in her favorite pastimes. She enjoys being outdoors, traveling, reading and music. An incurable romantic, she writes for pleasure. It was a love of history that drove her to writing historical fiction.

### Books by Helen Dickson

### Harlequin Historical

Visit the Author Profile page
at Harlequin.com for more titles.

# *Chapter One*

*Surrey, 1810*

With yet another busy day ahead of her, protected from the sun by a broad straw hat covering hair the colour of ripe corn, and wearing a cornflower-blue dress that had seen better days, Eve left the house and headed for the fields beyond the walls that surrounded The Grange—a beautiful old house encircled by stately elms. The sky was soft with sunrise washing the land in its golden light. Swallows swooped above the poppies edging the field, crimson against the golden corn.

Eve sighed, pausing to let her gaze take everything in. This was her favourite time of day, the quietness soon to be broken by the day's back-breaking toil to get in the corn before the weather broke.

Suddenly a gunshot pierced the air. A flock of birds rose up into the sky, flapping their wings and squawking furiously at being disturbed. Alarmed, Eve set off towards where the sound had come from to investigate, covering the ground at a run. She reached the road that threaded its way through the density of the woods on either side. The sight that met her eyes halted her in her tracks. Quickly she assessed the scene and the situation. A man was lying on the dew-soaked grass with blood oozing from a shoulder wound. His terrified horse stood trembling close by. But what held her attention the most was her brother, Robert, standing some distance away holding a rifle, a look of abject horror on his young face.

'Robert! What have you done?'

'I—I didn't do anything. I was out hunting rabbits and… Is—is he dead?' he asked.

Immediately Eve sprang into action, falling to her knees beside the recumbent man. Placing her hand on his jacket, she uttered a sigh of relief on feeling the rise and fall of his chest.

'No, thank God, he's still breathing.'

'That's a relief,' the man uttered, opening his eyes and fixing them on her face, lowered over his.

Eve fell back on her haunches, staring at him, unable to comprehend for the moment what could have happened. The man's voice was firm and sure. His face was handsome, recklessly so, lean and hard, his jaw uncompromisingly square. He had fine dark brows that curved neatly and a firm but almost sensuous mouth. His clothes beneath the dust were of the finest quality that could only have come from one of London's foremost tailors, indicating that he had ridden far. He'd shed his hat in the fall and his dark hair was tumbled and gleamed beneath the morning sun slanting through the trees. She gazed down into two crystal-clear eyes beneath winged black brows. There was a vibrant life and intensity in those eyes, silver-grey and brilliant.

'You are wounded,' Eve said, her gaze drawn to the shoulder of the man's jacket, seeing blood seeping through. 'Let's hope it isn't serious.'

He raised himself up with difficulty, wincing as a piercing pain shot through his shoulder. Propping himself against the stout trunk of a tree, he closed his eyes and rested his head back, breathing heavily.

Without more ado Eve briskly unfastened his blood-soaked jacket, loosened his neck cloth and waistcoat and opened his shirt, her expression schooled to impassivity as she examined the wound. Getting to her feet, she pulled up her skirt and ripped a strip off her petticoat. Folding it into a wad, she pressed it against the torn flesh to staunch the bleeding.

'It's a superficial wound, so you've been lucky.'

'Lucky?' he retorted sarcastically. 'I'm glad you think so.'

'Here.' Taking the man's hand, she placed it on the cloth over the wound. 'Press hard,' she commanded. 'We'll go to the house and I'll dress it properly.'

There's no need for that. Help me to my horse and I'll be on my way. My physician will take a look at it.'

'Please don't argue. You are in no position to object. The house isn't very far.' Getting to her feet, she turned to Robert. 'Give us a hand, Robert.'

'I take it this is the young man who shot me.'

'It would appear so,' Eve replied, unable even to consider the consequences of what Robert had done or how such a thing could have happened when he had left the house earlier to hunt rabbits. 'I'm sure all will be revealed later, but for now your wound needs tending. If the shot is still in there, it will have to be removed, but I think we'll find it's just a flesh wound.'

Together they helped him to his feet. He swayed, supporting himself against the tree. 'Help me to my horse, will you?'

'It would be inadvisable and foolish of you to ride after sustaining a wound like that. There is every possibility that you would fall off and incur a more severe injury, which could very well incapacitate you for some time.'

'Perish the thought,' the man uttered dryly.

'Precisely. Robert, take the horse. Now, come along,' Eve said to the stranger, handing Robert her hat. Taking the man's arm, she draped it about her shoulders. 'If you lean on me, we will be at the house in no time. Keep your hand pressed over the wound.'

'I am impressed by your efficiency, Miss…?'

'Mrs,' she provided. 'Mrs Eve Lansbury.'

'Ah—Matthew Lansbury's wife.'

'Widow,' she corrected.

He paused and looked at her closely. 'Yes, of course. I'm sorry for your loss, Mrs Lansbury.' He hesitated and closed his eyes as a wave of haziness seemed to sweep over him. 'What in damnation has happened to me?'

'You've been shot—and please don't swear,' Eve rebuked. 'There is a time and place for obscene language, and this is not it, so I would be grateful if you would keep a tight rein on your tongue.'

His lips twitched as he looked down into her up-turned face and managed to suppress a smile. 'I apologise. I quite forgot myself and stand rebuked. I did not mean to be disrespectful.'

'Thank you. Now, come along before you bleed to death.'

Without another word, she walked him unceremoniously back to the house. Halfway there, she was sure he was capable of walking by himself, but he seemed content to let her take some of his weight. Having made a quick assessment of his character, she thought here was a man who inspired awe in all those he met, that he was unreadable and single-minded. This was as close as she had been to any man since Matthew had died. With the man's arm draped about her shoulders, she could feel the heat of him, the vigour of him, the toughness, the power of his arm and the fine aroma of cigars and brandy on his breath that fanned her cheek.

On reaching the house, with one hand she raised her skirt to climb the steps, revealing the stout boots she wore in the fields.

'That's a fine pair of boots you are wearing. The army could march into battle with such sturdy boots.'

Dropping her skirt, Eve glanced up at him. 'And you would know that, would you…?'

'Lord Levisham—Maxim Randall—and, yes, I would, although some of the boots my men had to wear were nowhere near as good quality.'

'They've seen better days, but they still serve me well enough.'

Having taken note of his identity, an odd expression crossed Eve's face as she scrutinised him, and in her eyes was a deeply rooted dislike which he noticed. He studied her, a little amused, a little curious, a little derisive.

'When I see a look like that, it tells me you've heard of me.'

'Considering you are my neighbour, give or take a few miles, yes, your name is familiar to me.'

This was true. She was also aware—as was everyone else—that, since the death of his brother in a hunting accident, he had inherited his title and the Netherthorpe estate. What Eve had heard of her illustrious neighbour had given her no desire ever to meet him. Perhaps thirty years of age, everything about him was elegantly aristocratic, exuding power and a sense of force. According to the local rumour mill, he was an arrogant man who, when on respite from military duties, thought he could do as he pleased with whomever he pleased. Gossip had linked him to several beautiful women in London and his scandals were infamous. Any sensible young woman mindful of her reputation would be best advised to keep well out of his way.

Eve helped him into the house. 'There,' she said, separating herself from him. 'I think you are capable of walking by yourself now. Come this way,' she ordered, going ahead of him into the drawing room and indicating that he should sit on a sofa close to the window. Excusing herself, she smoothed down her skirts and hastened to the kitchen.

Agatha Lupton, the housekeeper of many years at The Grange, was preparing the evening meal. The sleeves of her dress were rolled up as she rolled out pastry to cover the meat pie she was making for dinner, a dusting of flour on her cheek. She glanced up at her mistress but didn't pause in her work.

'What is it that's got you into such a flap?' Agatha asked, having noted her mistress's flushed face.

'We have a bit of a crisis, Agatha,' Eve said, filling a bowl with water and gathering dressings from a cupboard that accommodated such things. 'The new Lord Levisham of Netherthorpe has been shot and needs attention.'

Agatha paused her rolling, her eyes opening wide with amazement. 'Good Lord! Lord Levisham, you say? The Earl of Levisham? Shot? Who on earth would do such a thing?'

'I'm not sure,' Eve answered, reluctant to incriminate her brother until she heard what he had to say. 'There will be time for questions later. Fortunately, the wound is superficial and not life-threatening.'

'Sal is upstairs cleaning the nursery. Shall I give her a shout?'

'No, leave her. I can manage.'

'What's he like—this new earl? Anything like the last?'

'Never having moved in the same circles as Andrew Randall, I didn't know him well enough to form an opinion. From what I remember—having only met him once, and from seeing him in church occasionally—they share a likeness, although I think the present Lord Levisham to be slightly taller than his brother. The sooner I've dressed his wound and he is on his way to Netherthorpe, the better I shall feel.'

Returning to the drawing room with water and items she would need to dress the wound, and placing the bowl on a small table beside her, Eve carefully peeled away the blood-soaked cloth from Lord Levisham's shoulder. His bare, muscled arm and shoulder gleamed in the soft light. Thankfully, the wound wasn't bleeding quite so much.

Prising the wound open to inspect it for shot, and satisfied it was clean and no danger to his life, she dipped a cloth into the water and proceeded to clean it. His expression tightened and he gritted his teeth. Her heart wrenched, having no wish to cause him pain. It was excruciatingly intimate to touch his flesh. It was warm and firm. He was strong and sleek but not gaunt, all sinew and strength, his muscles solid where her fingers touched. Her hands worked quickly and efficiently.

'I think you'll live to see another day,' she said, trying to keep her attention fixed on the raw wound, forcing herself not to think about his manly physique. 'You might wish to let your physician take a look at it but it's just a flesh wound and will soon heal.'

'I have every confidence that your ministering will be sufficient.'

'The dressing will have to be changed frequently until it begins to heal. I'm sure someone will attend to it for you. Would I be correct in thinking you have just returned from foreign parts?'

'You would. The Peninsular. It's kind of you to do this.'

'It's the least I can do,' she said, glancing at her brother hovering in the doorway still holding the rifle, noting his ashen face. 'You'd better go and lock that away, Robert, before you shoot someone else.'

'But—I didn't do it. I swear I didn't.'

Lord Levisham's eyes settled on him, calm and assessing. 'I can't believe that I've been fighting the French these past four years or more, getting shot at and escaping canon—only to come home to fall at a young man out hunting rabbits. I beg you not to spread it abroad. It will do nothing for my reputation.'

The tone of his voice was sarcastic and mocking. It did nothing for Eve's temper. 'Perhaps you should hear what my brother has to say. If he says he didn't do it, then I believe him. He is not a liar, Lord Levisham.'

Relieved to hear his sister's defence, Robert came further into the room. 'That's right. I hadn't fired my rifle all morning. Here,' he said, shoving it under Lord Levisham's nose. 'If I had, you would be able to tell.'

'Then if you didn't shoot me, who did?'

'I have no idea. The shot came from the opposite direction from where I was standing.'

Lord Levisham became thoughtful. The lines on his face and creases around his eyes made him look amiable, but his eyes were as impenetrable as stone. Then he nodded. 'Very well. I believe you.' He shoved the barrel of the gun away from his face. 'I am beginning to realise that I was the intended target, not a rabbit after all, and I mean to find out who is responsible. Did you happen to see anyone—someone acting suspiciously?'

'Yes. I saw a man disappear into the trees. I didn't see his face. He was wearing dark clothes with a hat pulled well down over his face.'

'His horse? What colour was it—brown, black?' Lord Levisham demanded.

'Dark brown—but on hearing the shot I was more concerned about what had occurred than to take note of what the man and his horse looked like.'

His expression grim, Lord Levisham nodded. 'Whoever it was must have known I was riding to Netherthorpe. He must have been waiting for me. He didn't try to rob me, so I must assume he had murder in mind. There was no warning. Nothing. If he was prepared to try once, he'll not let it alone.'

Eve paused in her work and looked at him. 'Then you will have to look to your safety, Lord Levishan, and take all due care.'

'I intend to. I'm not the sort who jumps at shadows, and nor do I run from threats. As a soldier I had to watch my back—I didn't realise I would have to continue doing so at home.'

'It would seem you have an enemy, one who hates you enough to want you dead. I'm sure Lord Levisham's nerves have taken a shock, Robert. Pour him a brandy and then go and put the rifle back. You know I hate firearms.'

Robert did as she bade, pouring out and handing Lord Levisham his brandy then disappearing.

'Robert is to leave for Woolwich shortly—to join the Royal Artillery. He's excited to be going.'

'I did my training at Woolwich. With any luck, the war in the Peninsula will be over by the time he passes out.'

'I sincerely hope so. If only the allies can beat Bonaparte, at least the war would be over.'

Eve carried on cleaning the wound, applying a healing salve when she was satisfied. 'You won't be returning to your regiment, Lord Levisham?'

'I've worn the uniform for so long it had almost become a part of me,' he said, his voice rich-textured and deep. 'But, no, I won't be going back.'

Raising her eyes, Eve looked at him steadily. 'Do I detect a note of regret?'

He nodded slightly. 'Perhaps—although, after twelve years of military service, it won't be easy adjusting to being a civilian again.'

'So, you have dispensed with your military attire,' she said, the cut and seam of his coat evidence of the tailoring only noblemen could afford. 'Your tailor must delight in the opportunity to clothe such an illustrious hero of the wars with Bonaparte. Why,' she said on a note of amusement, 'A gentleman with such expensive and stylish apparel will be the envy of every roué in London.'

'I count myself fortunate in my tailor, who has made my wardrobe for a good many years—military uniforms, mainly. Now I have retired from military life, he is delighted at the opportunity to finally outfit me with all the clothes of a gentleman.'

'Indeed. I think even that master of style and fashion, Mr Brummel, will have to sit up and take notice.' Catching his look of surprise, she laughed. 'Oh yes, Lord Levisham. I may be a country girl, and spend every minute of my time running The Grange, but I do go to London on occasion—I have family in Kensington. Even I have heard of the flamboyant Mr Brummel.'

'There are few who haven't. My tailor is a man of sober tastes, and it would go against the grain to kit me out in garish garb—and I have no desire to emulate the overdressed Beau Brummel. Besides, the last I heard was that that particular gentleman has fallen out of favour with Prince George. It is also rumoured that he is heavily in debt and no longer as stylishly garbed as he once was.' He frowned at Eve as she continued to tend his wound. 'Was your comment about my attire because you find it flawed in some way?'

'No, not at all. In fact, I must commend your tailor's abilities, although I imagine he would be terribly put out if he were to see the state of your jacket. I—I was so sorry to hear about your brother. Indeed, the whole county was shocked. It was a terrible tragedy.'

'Yes—yes, it was,' Lord Levisham said sharply, his expression telling Eve that he had no wish to discuss the matter further. 'Your workers will be busy with the harvest at this time,' he remarked on a change of subject, watching her face closely.

'We start tomorrow—at least, that is what I hope—if I can get some labour to give us a hand.'

'You have no itinerant workers?'

'No. Not this year.'

'And why is that? There is no shortage of people wanting work at this time.'

'I know, but this year is different. It's always a matter for worry during harvest that everything goes like clockwork—providing the weather holds. With everyone else round about harvesting, workers are in demand. We are usually fortunate. Those who worked here in the past often come back. This year is different.'

'What is different about this year?'

'Sir Oscar Devlin has taken them for a few shillings more than I can pay, so those who have been coming to The Grange for years have now gone to him.'

'But what of their loyalty to you?'

She shrugged. 'That doesn't count when money is involved.'

'Can't you go and see him—explain that you cannot do without them?'

She shook her head. 'Sir Oscar Devlin is the last man I would ask favours of. I would not dream of it. I cannot blame the workers. They have families to support. Every penny counts. We'll just have to manage. Every year it seems there is a curse on the harvest. If it isn't the weather that is against us, it's the yield. The harvest was poor last year and the year before that—as it was with other farmers. This year it's the lack of workers. We cannot win.'

'You work in the fields?'

'Not only do I supervise the work, I have to do my bit—even more so with the lack of labour. There's always so much to do, running a place like this, but this is an exceptionally busy time. Getting the corn in before the weather breaks is my priority.'

He surprised her by taking her hand and running his thumb over the calluses on her palm. 'I see you work hard. Field work is not for ladies.'

'I'm no wilting flower, Lord Levisham—and I am no lady,' she said, retrieving her hand. 'I know that what I do is frowned upon by those in the village. I'm talked about—something of a curiosity—but it doesn't bother me. I just get on with what has to be done and going unnoticed serves me well. The land remains the same, always. It doesn't judge. Besides, the band of field workers who usually come to The Grange at this time of year are made of women and children. Why should I be any different?'

'And your reputation?'

'What reputation? I am aware that I am a provider of entertainment in Woodgreen—with any luck it will continue to be so for years to come. It doesn't concern me in the slightest, so please don't bore me with that argument.'

'I won't.'

'That's a relief.'

Eve was silent as she applied a bandage to his wound, feeling his eyes on her all the while. How could she tell this man how bad things were? They had never been so bad. Every penny they made, she ploughed back into the business. Life was hard, and regret was useless, but it still caught in her throat and weighed her down.

'So, you have issues with Oscar Devlin.'

'A few. He wants everyone in and around Wood-green to realise that he is master—he does own most of the land. There is only the land here—and of course some of the Netherthorpe land, which belongs to you and which is beyond his jurisdiction, but he is not averse to trying to claim some of it one way or another.'

'By hook or by crook, if what I know of him is true.'

'Yes. He wants me to sell him some of our prime land to build houses for his workers and he's determined to wear me down to get it. So far I've refused to oblige.' This was true. Sir Oscar was one of the more affluent gentlemen of Woodgreen. He farmed five hundred acres and was a businessman, with employees and obligations, with an eye to expand.

'You are a fighter, Mrs Lansbury. That is obvious.'

She met his eyes directly. 'I have to be. There is no other way. When Matthew died, I was determined to succeed against all the odds. I'm never giving up, not until the last field has been cleared and the last husk of corn has been gathered up—and even then I'll plant more and start again.'

There was a glimmer of admiration in Lord Levisham's eyes. 'I salute you,' he said as his lips broke a warm-hearted smile. 'Hold your head high. Let Devlin see your determination and ambitions are not to be thwarted. But he is a powerful man—and creative and subtle in his dealings with others,' he said softly, almost to himself. 'My brother has had issues over land with him in the past, and he is persistent.'

Eve looked at him sharply and then looked away. If Lord Levisham also had issues with Sir Oscar, it was not her business. Had she not enough to contend with without taking on anyone else's troubles? 'I'm not afraid of Sir Oscar Devlin.'

'No, maybe not, but be warned—Woodgreen is a small town and everyone has to live together. Like it or not, Sir Oscar is a powerful opponent.'

'He's not used to anyone saying no to him, that's his trouble.' Having finished dressing his wound, Eve handed him his jacket. 'It's ruined, I'm afraid, but I have no doubt you have more.'

'I have indeed.' Getting up, he swallowed what was left of his brandy.

Suddenly the door swung open and a child fell in—a bundle of strawberry curls and bright-green eyes. Getting to his feet, he ran towards Eve on wobbly legs and hid behind her skirts. A young woman came in after him. Seeing him peeking from behind his mother's skirts, she rushed over to him.

'There you are, you little scamp.' The child giggled when she scooped him up into her arms and he folded himself into her. 'I'm so sorry, Mrs Lansbury. He wanted to see you and there was no stopping him.'

Eve laughed, always delighted to see her son. He was the joy, the love, of her life. Everything she did was always with him in mind. 'That's all right, Nessa.' She turned to Lord Levisham. 'Let me introduce you to Christopher, my three-year-old rascal son, Lord Levisham. As you see, he is a quite a handful.'

Lord Levisham smiled as Christopher waved a chubby fist at him, not at all fazed by this imperiously masculine stranger in his mother's drawing room.

'Give him his breakfast, Nessa, and then see that he plays in the garden.'

'I will,' Nessa replied, bobbing a little curtsey and taking the child out.

'He's a fine boy,' Lord Levisham said as he walked to the door.

'Yes, he is.' Eve's urge to protect her son was overwhelming. 'The Grange is Christopher's inheritance. I have to make sure his future is secured.'

'Which is the reason why you work so hard. And so you should. Thank you for this,' he said, indicating his shoulder. 'It's fortunate you were on hand. Who knows? Whoever it was that tried to kill me might have taken advantage of my weakened state and come back to finish me off.'

'Why would someone want you dead? An irate husband, perhaps? You do have a reputation of being something of a lothario, Lord Levisham,' she remarked, laughing lightly, a teasing light dancing in the depths of her soft brown eyes.

He cocked an eyebrow at her in mock offence, a smile twitching his lips. 'Are you saying that you are not surprised someone might want to shoot me, Mrs Lansbury?'

'Not really. Your reputation has preceded you. According to gossip, you are the sort of arrogant lord who would collect enemies with the same ease as one would collect snuff boxes. Not to mention the fact that you are a renowned rake who has seduced your way through England and the entire Peninsula. I wonder, your reputation being what it is, that some irate father or husband hasn't taken a pot shot at you already.'

Not in the least offended, Lord Levisham threw back his head and laughed loudly. 'I can see I shall have to watch my manners where you are concerned, Mrs Lansbury. Although, in my own defence, I must point out that my character has been somewhat maligned by those who have nothing better to do than spread tittle-tattle, for that's all it is. Do not believe all you hear.'

'I don't,' she replied, laughing softly. 'I'm sure there has been a certain amount of exaggeration. I shall reserve judgment.'

'Thank you. That is indeed generous of you.'

Eve followed him outside where Robert was holding his horse, having pacified it.

'You have been a very gracious hostess, Mrs Lansbury. Thank you.'

'I can be charming on occasion.'

He smiled. 'I suppose we all can. It shows our qualities as well as our faults. Although, you are not my idea of what a farmer's widow should look like.'

'Oh? And how would you define a farmer's widow, Lord Levisham?' A challenging light gleamed in her eyes.

'A middle-aged, fierce matron with white hair—'

'And a black cat and a broomstick, no doubt,' she quipped with a wry laugh. 'If things carry on as they have been doing for the past two years, you won't be far from the truth. When Matthew died, I had no idea how bad things were. I soon found out. As soon as everyone knew he had died, they were all tripping over each other to call in their debts. I paid them, relying on the harvest to cover the cost and see us through to the next year. But it didn't work out like that.'

'Are there no relatives you can turn to to relieve your hardships?'

'Matthew had no family—not that I know of. If he had, they would be distant relatives and not part of his life. I have family of my own, but I refuse to concern them with my troubles.'

Taking hold of the bridle, Lord Levisham turned to face her, his expression serious. 'Heed my words about Oscar Devlin. I did not speak lightly. I hope the harvest goes well.'

'As to that, we shall have to see. Every day I pray for a miracle—but why am I telling you, a stranger? Please go on your way and forget the Widow Lansbury.' She looked at him, seeing his raised eyebrows and how his silver-grey eyes looked into hers. His mouth had begun to curl, to lift in a smile of sardonic, knowing humour.

'If only it was that simple.' His white teeth gleamed, and his bold eyes laughed at her. 'It will be no easy matter forgetting you.'

She laughed. 'I'm sure you'll manage to do that.'

'While ever you are my neighbour, that will be difficult.'

'I'm not going anywhere. The administration of The Grange is my responsibility until Christopher is of an age to do it himself. There is no one else.'

'And if your son doesn't want to be a farmer, what then?'

'It will be up to him. He can sell The Grange to

someone else. It has to be his decision to make. In the meantime, I will continue to administer it to the best of my ability.'

'And, should you decide to marry again, what will you do?'

'That is something I shall have to consider very carefully.'

'You should marry a wealthy man. It would be the end to all your troubles.'

'And present me with new ones. I've been married. I didn't like it, not one bit. It will take someone very special to tempt me a second time.' She stepped back as he swung himself up into the saddle. 'Good day, Lord Levisham.'

He touched his tall hat, which Robert had retrieved. 'Good day, Mrs Lansbury.'

Eve stood and watched him ride away, standing in the warm glow of the sun. It wasn't the only reason she felt a warm glow as she continued to watch Lord Levisham's receding figure. When she'd stood close to him their gazes had met and lingered. Brief as such a moment of unspoken communication had been, it had been enough to cause her heart to flutter and heat to course through her body.

She had told him about her fears for the harvest and her commitment to The Grange. What she had not told him was of the sheer loneliness of being a woman trying to run a business against the opposition of her neighbours, or her bitterness at losing her husband to another woman—before he'd accidentally shot and killed himself.

She had met Matthew in London. He had escorted her to the theatre and soirees and, flattered by the attention he had showered on her, she had enjoyed being with him. Handsome, charming and well mannered, as an impressionable eighteen-year-old she had liked him and truly thought she could learn to love him—only to discover after the wedding that he had only married her for her generous dowry to shore up his own depleted finances.

After his death she had wondered how on earth she would cope without him, and the strain of having a six-month-old child to take care of had been so great that it was a miracle she'd managed to survive. But she had carried on, surprising herself. The agony she had felt upon discovering that he was in a relationship with another woman had shocked and hurt her deeply. When she had questioned him about his affair, he had turned on her, telling her just to be thankful that he had married her; to be grateful.

There was no help for it. She hadn't been able to undo her marriage, so she'd endured it. Feeling betrayed and degraded, it had been many months after his death before she'd been able to think of him in a cool-headed and unemotional way. It was her pride that kept her body and head up. It was her pride that was wrenched by his infidelities, not her heart.

She vowed that never again would she show fear or apprehension to any man, especially not one who would try to control and dominate her. Whatever feelings she'd had for Matthew had died along with him. They had both delighted in the birth of their son. Matthew had been so proud of him. Christopher was beautiful, perfect and healthy and with him hope had returned following Matthew's death.

Shoving the reminders of her past to the back of her mind, Eve continued to watch Lord Levisham disappear along the road that would take him to Netherthorpe, the grand country estate that had belonged to the Randall family for generations.

She was affected more than she could have imagined by the strange encounter with her illustrious neighbour. There was an aggressive confidence and strength of purpose about him, and he had the air of a clever man who succeeded in all he set out to achieve. Her instinct told her that he was a man with many shades to his nature, from the arrogant lift of his dark head and casual stance, a man with a sense of his own infallibility. Was what she had heard about him true? she wondered. Was he all that people said of him?

Secure in the knowledge that she would never know, on a sigh she went back inside to her study and opened the accounts ledger, flicking through the pages. The neat rows of figures looked exactly as they had the day before and the day before that. While Henry Doyle oversaw the farming side of things, Eve took care of the running of the house and did all the bookwork, keeping a tight rein on income and expenditure—the latter being greater than the former. This division of labour suited them both ideally, but Eve was not too proud to don her boots and work clothes and give a hand at busy times.

Sitting back in the chair, she thought back to how it had been on her marriage when Matthew had brought her to The Grange when, with the benefit of her dowry, everything that had been needed for their comfort had been in plentiful supply. They had entertained and been entertained by friends and neighbours. Now there was no time or money for fancy dinner parties. Then the stables had been filled with fine horses—the only horses that occupied the stables now were heavy, sturdy horses capable of working the land, and one for her to ride and pull the carriage.

Taking a key from her pocket, she placed it in the lock of a drawer in the desk and pulled it open. Taking out a small box, she opened it. On a bed of purple velvet lay a link of pearls. She fingered it lovingly. It had been her mother's, the only thing of value she'd possessed. It was with a heavy heart that she replaced it and locked the drawer. It would have to go. She would travel into Woodgreen tomorrow morning. There were pictures and other articles of value in the house she could sell, but those things belonged to Christopher, left to him by Matthew for his son's future.

Closing the heavy ledger, she left the study and marched into the hall, grabbing her hat and heading for the fields. The responsibility of the house, the land and those who depended on her was pushing her deeper into despair. But what was the use in worrying about it? What would be would be, so she had better press on and get on with saving this harvest. At least today the weather wasn't against her, which was a blessing.

\* \* \*

As Maxim left The Grange and its mistress standing on the steps as he rode away, he tried to define what had been so attractive about her. She certainly wasn't plain. She was tall and as slender as a greyhound. Her features were unusually striking—high cheekbones and eyes that reminded him of warm brown cognac, with dark lashes beneath the swooping arch of her eyebrows. Her real physical confidence was sensual and, despite her widowed state, there had been an assured, innocent vanity in her smile.

He was stunned by the experience he'd undergone. It wasn't just the widow's looks that had gripped him. She'd had an aura about her, some indefinable presence. He was no believer in fate, yet something had happened between them from the moment she had appeared in the woods. She'd felt it too. He'd seen it on her face.

He did wonder what her husband had done to her to deserve such bitterness. He couldn't remember a woman ever talking to him with such unaffected candour as she had. He liked the way she'd tilted her head to one side when she'd looked at him, and the way her shining hair, the colour of ripe corn, had been drawn from her face and fastened into a heavy chignon at the back of her head. He also liked the way she'd talked openly to him and the way there'd been something both innocent and knowing about her. He had never met anyone like her—but then, he hadn't been anywhere to meet anyone like her in a long time.

He thought of her son, a child with an attractive, curly-haired wildness about him. He had laughingly flung himself at his mother like a whirlwind as soon as he'd entered the room. Maxim had seen how she'd been with the boy. They'd shared a sense of belonging, an integral part of each other. They had something he didn't.

He smiled to himself, remembering it, but then a more pressing matter entered his thoughts and he became preoccupied with discovering the identity of whoever it was who had tried to end his life. Whoever was behind it, the incident could not be ignored. A cold, hard core of fury was growing inside him, shattering every other emotion he'd ever felt, leaving him incapable of feeling anything other than the need to find the person responsible.

## Chapter Two

On reaching Netherthorpe, Maxim was assailed by past memories of family and happy times.

The young groom who seemed to appear from nowhere tipped his cap and welcomed him home. 'Shall I take your horse, my lord?'

'Yes, thank you.' Maxim handed over the reins.

As his mount was led away, his gaze wandered to the house in which he had been born. Netherthorpe, a grand three-storey house built of mellow brick, had been built during the reign of Queen Elizabeth. That his brother would not be here to receive him was a deep sadness inside Maxim. He could not believe he would never see him again. He felt his throat tighten and a dull pain in his heart.

As brothers there had been many similarities between them except what they'd wanted from life. From the very beginning, Andrew—who had loved Netherthorpe with every breath he took—had been aware of the importance of the task that had been laid on his shoulders—a massive undertaking for anyone. And he had learned the ropes quietly, diligently and willingly.

Unlike Maxim, he'd been content and had asked for nothing more than to run the estate to the best of his ability. There had been no animosity or envy when Maxim, with the freedom to choose how he would live his life, had decided on a military career. Andrew had given him all his support and, on Maxim's return, he had watched him with quiet pride and admiration as he'd listened to the tales of his travels, his exploits and the friends he had made.

Maxim craved the closeness he'd had with Andrew. He needed his brother's common sense and insight to help him through the weeks and months ahead of him. It was necessary for him to quickly grasp the reins of the immense Randall estate. Andrew was a hard act to follow, and Maxim was determined that he would do his utmost to carry on Andrew's work. The years spent growing up here were memories to be treasured.

Before he reached the wide flight of steps up to the double doors, they were opened by Hoskins, Netherthorpe's long-serving butler.

'Welcome home, my lord. I didn't know what time to expect you.'

'Thank you, Hoskins.' Maxim was pleased to see this old retainer again, a man who had served the Randall family well over the years. Other than his light-brown hair having turned white since Maxim had last seen him, and a few more wrinkles on his thin face, he was little changed. 'I have to say, I didn't expect to be returning so soon. My brother's death was a shock to me, I don't mind telling you.'

'I imagine it was. Everyone was deeply affected by it. There was nothing anyone could have done.'

'No, so I understand from the letters I received from my solicitor—although I intend speaking to Dr Ennis, the physician who attended him at the scene. I was told it happened during a hunt.'

'Yes, that's right. Heavily attended it was, too. He'd ridden on ahead of the main body of the hunt and no one saw what happened until it was too late. Sir Edward was the first on the scene, but there was nothing he could do.'

'Whatever the truth of the matter, it was a tragedy.' Maxim walked towards the stairs. 'I decided to ride on ahead of my valet and baggage. They should arrive some time before dinner, I expect. Have some hot water sent up to my room, Hoskins, and then I'll seek my cousin. He's at home?'

'Yes, my lord, he's not far away. I'll have someone inform him that you are home.' Hoskins' gaze was drawn to Maxim's shoulder, his eyes widening with alarm on seeing the hole and dried blood. 'My lord! You are wounded. What on earth happened to you? Is it serious?'

'No. Someone took a shot at me when I was riding past The Grange. Fortunately, Mrs Lansbury was on hand to take charge of the situation. It's just a flesh wound—according to Mrs Lansbury, who was kind enough to dress it for me. As to who fired the shot, I'm afraid I have no idea.'

'Dear me! The perpetrator must be caught. In the meantime, shall I ask Mrs Peppard to take a look?'

'No, thank you, Hoskins,' Maxim said, striding across the hall to the stairs to go to his private apartment. 'Mrs Lansbury took care of it well enough. I need a bath—although I'll have to try not to disturb the dressing. Have some water sent up to my room— I'm covered in dust from the journey.'

'Everything has been prepared for you, my lord.'

'I'm sure it has. I'll see my steward in the morning. He can put me in the picture as to what's been happening on the estate of late and help me get into the swing of things.' His foot on the first stair, he hesitated and turned back to his butler. 'Mrs Lansbury is a widow, Hoskins. What did her husband die of?'

'Why, it was an accident, my lord. Shot himself while cleaning one of his pistols. Tragedy it was, at the time.'

'An accident, you said?'

'I'm afraid so. Fellow shot half his face away—not a pretty sight for anyone. His wife found him. Terrible it was for young Mrs Lansbury. Their son was just six months old at the time.'

Maxim digested this and nodded, his face grave. 'I see. Thank you, Hoskins.'

Later, bathed and in a change of clothes, Maxim went in search of his cousin, Edward. Andrew had possessed an intense dislike for Edward, a dislike he didn't bother to conceal. There were certain things about his cousin that irritated even Maxim, and he suspected he was more devious than he seemed. But he had always felt sorry for Edward, the only offspring of his father's twin brother, left without funds and with no choice but to reside with his maternal spinster Aunt Pauline in Hampstead. Being possessed of a fierceness to protect any member of his family, and to avoid any kind of scandal, Maxim had no reason to speak against his cousin and had always welcomed him at Netherthorpe.

He met with Edward in the library. It was the room Maxim loved best. Leather-bound books covered the walls and priceless artefacts stood on gleaming mahogany tables. A magnificent Rubens hung above the white marble fireplace. French doors opened onto a broad terrace and offered breath-taking views of the gardens and the deer park beyond.

Edward was lounging in a chair reading a newspaper, a large glass of brandy to hand. True to form, he didn't bother getting up, but watched his cousin closely as he strode into the room. Edward was a fair-haired, good-looking individual with snapping dark eyes and a taste for the flamboyant—lace cravats and spectacular vivid waistcoats being a speciality. The two greeted each other casually, Maxim's penetrating eyes levelled on Edward as he took a seat across from him.

'Good to see you back, cousin,' Edward said. 'I was about to depart for London until I got your letter informing me of the day of your arrival. Apart from the tragedy that befell Andrew, nothing has changed. In fact, things have been damnably dull of late, with no one to talk to but the servants.'

'Now I am home, Edward, feel free to depart for London whenever you wish. I was surprised when I received your letter informing me that you were at Netherthorpe when Andrew died.'

Edward shrugged. 'I came to beg a favour of him—and to give my favourite horse a gallop in the hunt.'

'Oh?'

'Things haven't been easy of late—living with Aunt Pauline. Knowing the Dower House was empty at Netherthorpe, I hoped he would rent it out to me.'

'And what did Andrew decide?'

'He didn't. Said he'd think about it.'

'What do you know of what happened to Andrew, Edward?'

'I explained everything in the letter I sent you. What happened was hardly surprising. Andrew was a bit wild on a horse—as well you know. He went at fences any sensible man would have second thoughts about.'

'That still doesn't explain what happened. Andrew was a superb horseman. It's hard to believe he died when his horse unseated him.'

'That's what we all thought, but it happened. He—he was seeing Lady Elena Devlin at the time. Did you know?'

Maxim stared at him. 'Sir Oscar Devlin's wife?' Edward nodded. 'But it wasn't like Andrew to take up with another man's wife—a neighbour, at that.'

Edward shrugged. 'No—but it's true. I tried persuading him to end the affair, but he was besotted with the woman.'

Maxim wondered if he would ever know the truth of it. What he did know was that, well into his thirties, Andrew had been feeling the pressure to marry and start a family of his own. If what Edward said was true, and Andrew had indeed been in a relationship with Elena Devlin, then he must have been smitten with her to delay finding a woman to grace Netherthorpe without the added complication of already having a husband.

'Whatever he was doing, Edward, was entirely his own affair. Andrew was a man of steadfast character and unimpeachable honour, and I would be grateful if you did not cast aspersions. I appreciate the fact that you were here to take over the running of the estate. I applaud your loyalty.'

'It was the least I could do.'

'Nevertheless, I am indeed grateful.' Maxim also realised that Edward was next in line to the title and the estate—unless he himself married and produced an heir.

During the early days back at Netherthorpe, Maxim gave himself up to adjusting to his new way of life and the day-to-day running of the estate. Bailiffs were called to give an account of their management, accounts gone into, acres of land ridden over, meetings held with his tenant farmers. At other times he restlessly wandered from room to room in his grand house, unable to escape the throbbing emptiness that was gnawing away at him with an ache that increased with each passing day.

He missed his military life and his fellow soldiers and, now that he was home, the absence of his brother cut through him like a knife. And there was also the added concern of this other matter—someone who meant to end his life. There had been no further attempts, but he did not rest easy.

Eve took the carriage into Woodgreen with the precious pearl necklace in her pocket. Fortunately, there were no other customers in the pawn broker's shop, but she knew she would have drawn attention to herself on entering it, and that it would be gossiped about in every establishment in Woodgreen. The shop was stashed with silverware, worn jewellery and all manner of treasures, most of the items waiting for their previous owners to buy them back. In most cases, this didn't happen.

The pawn broker inspected the necklace closely, judging the quality of the pearls. Eve watched him, hoping he would be generous, while knowing he wouldn't give her its value. Eventually, after much haggling, she accepted his price and shoved the money deep into her pocket, asking him to give her six months and she would come and buy it back. She left the shop, secure in the knowledge that she could at least afford to pay any workers who came looking for casual work.

Taking the reins of her carriage, she headed out of the small town, unaware of Lord Levisham. He had watched her go into the shop and had been tempted to speak to her but, noting the shop was a pawn broker's and having no wish to embarrass her, he'd held back. Not until she had driven away did he go inside.

* * *

The following morning Eve was out in the fields at first light to organise the day's work along with Henry. There were two other permanent workers, but more help was needed. A catastrophe occurred when one of the carts broke an axle and one of the horses went lame. Henry was in despair. Then the unexpected happened. Several canvas-covered carts pulled into the field filled to capacity with men and women, some with growing children and babes in arms. Eve stared, incredulous, as they climbed out carrying pitchforks, scythes and all manner of tools for working the fields. One of them approached, a big, burly man. He tugged his cap out of respect.

'Has Sir Oscar Devlin sent you?' Eve asked, unable to believe that he would do such a thing, for she couldn't begin to understand where they had come from if not from Sir Oscar.

'We were encamped at Netherthorpe ready to begin work with the harvest. We come every year. Lord Levisham sent us—he's got his quota of workers this year. He's heard of your bad luck and wishes to help, which is why he's sent us to work here while ever we are needed.'

Eve couldn't believe their good fortune. She didn't wish to feel beholden to Lord Levisham and she could not understand his motives for doing this. But the sight of the gypsies, the men and women who had come to help overwhelmed her with gratitude. Knowing that she had been presented with a chance to save the harvest before the weather broke, common sense prevailed over her pride.

'I see. That is indeed considerate of Lord Levisham, and I cannot pretend that you are not needed, so welcome to The Grange. You can get to work immediately. My foreman, Henry Doyle, will show you where to make up your camp and instruct you about the work.'

The days slipped by and the weather held. Eve was kept so busy that there were literally no moments to spare for anything that did not have to done at once. Nessa kept Christopher entertained for most of the time and sought her out whenever he became fractious and asked for her. Corn was scythed and stooked and, when dry, it was taken into the threshing sheds and flailed and bagged. What was left on the ground was to be picked up by the gleaners.

With everything safely gathered in and their work over, the workers were preparing to move on in the morning. Dusk had fallen and Nessa had taken a very tired Christopher to his bed. With a feeling of exhausted contentment, and dressed in one of her old cotton gowns, Eve sauntered towards a tree where she would sit and watch the merriment in the meadow next to the open field. Canvas-covered wagons and tents had been erected on the edge of the wood, and hobbled piebald horses grazed nearby. The trill of laughter could be heard above the thrum of a guitar. It was a scene of contentment and laughter as they ate the meat pies and cakes and drank their ale round the camp fire.

Eve sat down on the ground, her back resting against

the stout tree and her legs stretched out in front of her, listening to the songs and the sound of the guitar. Relieved that the harvest was secure, and reassured that Nessa would be putting Christopher to bed, she began to relax for the first time in weeks. Thinking how pleased Matthew would have been, recalling his smiling face, she felt a stab of guilt, but it soon passed.

Over the top of the hedgerows, she could see the tall chimneys and roof of The Grange. It was three miles from Netherthorpe and three miles from Woodgreen. The Grange was a beautiful old house, built of red brick and timber. With fifteen rooms over two floors, it had been the home of the Lansbury family since it had been built when Charles I was on the throne. Matthew had loved to entertain, and as hostess Eve had always been charming and polite, but she couldn't say that she'd enjoyed herself. Matthew had been loud and had always drunk far too much, which had made him bad-tempered. Not until his death had Eve discovered the truth of his finances. He had spent heavily, with nothing put away for the future.

With her hair loosely arranged in a heavy coil at the back, and her face tanned by the harvest sun, she breathed deeply, closing her eyes, closing her mind to thoughts of Matthew. Now was not the time to dwell on the past. The evening was warm and sultry, and insects flitted about in the air. The sun was setting in a cloudless sky and the trees cast long shadows across the stubble field. Over the borders the same scene would be enacted on other farms. She relished the ultimate peace of resting there—she wanted this peace, this absence of thought, to go on for ever.

It was into this scene that Lord Levisham arrived on his huge bay stallion. Tilting her head, Eve smiled up at him, too tired and content to greet him properly on her feet. He was carelessly dressed in a loose white shirt and leather waistcoat, and his dark hair tumbled untidily. His neck was tanned from the hours he had spent in sunnier climes.

Eve's stomach flipped over. He was far too handsome for her peace of mind. The curve of that chiselled mouth and the glitter in his eyes as they roamed appreciatively over her aroused curious sensations deep within her. Sensations she wanted desperately to deny. There was something thrilling and vastly appealing about him as he regarded her steadily. The fading light caressed his compelling features, making her breathlessly aware of the strength and rugged character inherent in his face.

As he dismounted, and not wanting to be found looking at him, she averted her gaze, but not before she had seen a world of feelings flash across his set face—surprise, disbelief, admiration—but only for an instant. He stood over her, his unfathomable eyes locking on hers.

'Do you mind?' he said, pointing at the ground.

'Not at all. You must excuse me. I'm far too exhausted to get up at present.'

'You're forgiven.' Sitting beside her, he drew up one knee, resting his arm on it.

Eve glanced at him, liking his relaxed, easy manner. 'I did not expect to see you here, Lord Levisham.'

'I wanted to make sure that all was well and that you had overcome your bad luck.'

'Yes, and I have you to thank for that. How kind of you to take time in your busy life to think of me. Thank you for sending the workers. I'm grateful.'

'Don't think of it. It was the least I could do when I became aware of your predicament.'

'We would have found it difficult trying to manage without them. It's their last night at The Grange. I shall miss them when they move on. For a short time, they have brought life and colour to The Grange, which has been sadly missing of late—especially now when they dance and sing and play the violin and guitar. One can almost imagine they are transported for a short while to the vibrancy of the north African countries or the like.'

'That is true. It's nothing like the English scenes we are used to.'

A young woman suddenly appeared from a group sitting around a fire. Pulling her shawl from her shoulders, she threw it on the ground, hoisting her flounced, vibrant crimson skirts above her slim ankles. In the soft light her face was serious, her eyes fixed on the man strumming the guitar. Her gleaming black hair was wound in a heavy coil at the nape of her neck and fixed with a tortoiseshell comb. Eve and Lord Levisham were transfixed as they watched her take a few tentative steps, her arms stretched above her head, stamping her sandalled feet in staccato movements. Bells attached to the belt at her waist gave out a gentle, tinkling sound.

Her back long and straight, she began to dance, so lost in the passion of the music that she seemed unaware of those who watched. She grasped her skirts and swirled them in a flurry of crimson, moving in an attitude that was both coarse and sensual, twirling wrists and swaying hips as the chords of the guitar strummed out. The woman's eyes kept straying to the musician. He could play the fiddle as well as the guitar and had everyone dancing and clapping to the rhythm.

Eve sighed, transfixed by the sight. 'She dances wonderfully,' she murmured. 'So light on her feet, so graceful, and completely carried away by the music.'

The dancer's fingers snapped out the rhythm of the music. They continued to watch, mesmerised, neither of them moving as the guitar built in intensity. The dance became wild and intensely passionate before ending in a ferment of clapping hands and shouts of more.

'Her name is Anya,' Eve said quietly, turning to look at her companion. 'She dances every night. I usually allow Christopher to watch with me and listen to the music, but we finished late, and he was dropping off to sleep.'

'Has the harvest gone well?'

'Well enough. The ideal weather we have been blessed with has allowed us to get on. Everyone has worked hard, and everything is gathered in. The workers will be moving on to pastures new in the morning.'

'I'm glad I was able to help. We have more workers than is necessary at Netherthorpe and, when the group turned up, naturally I thought of you.'

'How are you settling down at Netherthorpe? I imagine it's been a while since you were home.'

'Two years.'

'And, now you're no longer a commissioned officer having to take orders from your superiors, how do you think you will settle down to being a country gentleman? I don't suppose you've had time to reacquaint yourself with the people who live and work on the estate.'

'Not yet.'

'Well, like your ancestors, you must watch over them—and lead by example,' she told him with a forceful laugh.

His expression was one of mock horror. 'Mrs Lansbury! Are you telling me that I will have to reform?'

'Will that be so very difficult?'

His eyes twinkled at their shared humour. 'Impossible—but I value your advice.'

'I imagine you are actually extremely good at what you do. Are you going to stay at Netherthorpe—or do you intend living in London for most of the time?'

'As yet I don't know what I'm going to do. I expect I shall spend most of my time here, but I have to journey into London shortly to see my lawyer—so many things to sort out. It's hard to believe that twelve years ago I was a young man of eighteen, a soldier with a promising career, happy to go wherever I was sent. I did well, seeing service in America, and later in Spain, gaining promotion to captain and later to major. My hopes of continuing my military career were dashed when news reached me of the death of my brother.'

'I can understand that—and being so far away and fighting a war could not have been easy for you.'

'No, it wasn't. As next in line, that was the moment I became the Earl of Levisham, and I knew my life would never be the same. Andrew's death and my arrival has thrown Netherthorpe into confusion. I loathe the idea of the niche that is all carved out for me that I am expected to fill. I will do my best—as Andrew would have wished me to do. He had large boots to fill, and I will honour him by being the best Earl of Levisham I can be.'

'Were you close to your brother?'

He nodded. 'As close as brothers can be.'

Meeting his gaze, Eve saw the reflective, almost tender glimmer of light in his eyes.

'Andrew was born to the earldom. Our parents loved us equally, but because Andrew was the elder—the heir—he was singled out for special attention and made aware of his importance. As the second son, I could choose a career, which I did, secure in the knowledge that my brother wished me well. I'm beginning to realise the difficulties of managing such a large estate—with more land in the north of England and Scotland. Andrew did well—although it took its toll—and I got accolades of my own, which is made easy when there's a war on. I don't mind admitting it's going to take me a while to adjust to life as a country gentleman. I'm trained to lead men into battle, not manage an estate.'

The admission sounded pained, and Eve could sympathise. She didn't imagine soldiers of his rank— a major—would sit around with his fellow officers baring his soul. As they sat beneath the tree, Lord Levisham's lack of formality and his direct manner of speech made it easy for Eve to converse freely and honestly.

'I can see his death has hit you hard.'

He nodded. 'I was in the thick of it at the time. I couldn't believe it. I'm told he was unseated from his horse and hit his head—which I find hard to believe. Andrew was an expert horseman—none better.'

'Do you think there was something suspicious about his death?'

'I don't know. I hope not, although when I questioned the local physician who attended him—Dr Ennis; you must know him?—he did not think his death was consistent with a fall from his horse onto soft ground. His neck wasn't broken. There was a large open wound on the back of his head, as if he had been hit with a heavy object. He suspected it might be murder, but nothing could be proved. My own life has been threatened—as well you know—for whatever reason; I still have no idea. But, if whoever it was is intent on killing me, then perhaps the next time he attempts it he will succeed.'

'Please don't say that.'

He smiled a cynical smile, looking at her from beneath hooded lids. 'Why? Would you be sorry, Mrs Lansbury?'

Eve paled and averted her eyes. 'I hate the thought of anyone being murdered—being shot—no matter who it is. I have good reason. You must be on your guard.

Remember, there are more ways to kill a man than by shooting him.'

'I know that. Edward, my cousin, was at Nether-thorpe when the tragedy occurred. Edward, who was more than capable of running the estate in my absence, is the son of my father's twin brother—in fact, should I not produce an heir, he is next in line to inherit Nether-thorpe. His own father, who married the daughter of an impoverished country baronet, left him in dire straits. Left with no choice but to sell his home, he went to live with a maiden aunt in London.'

'I have seen him on occasion when out riding on his visits to Netherthorpe. Was he close to your brother?'

'No, they didn't get on. Andrew was a country man, well liked and respected by all who knew him. He was athletic and loved any kind of physical activity—especially hunting. He was more at home on a horse than on two legs, whereas Edward lives for pleasure. He is one of the most intelligent, erudite of the Corinthians, as well as being one of the most influential members of the *ton*. He has an acid wit that accepts no boundaries and is able to shred a reputation in minutes—when he chooses a human target, that is. Andrew thought him tiresome and idle and would lose patience with him—constantly reciting the old adage that one can choose one's friends, but one's relations are a different matter entirely.'

'Relations are more often than not close.'

'The proverbial blood being thicker than water—is that what you think?'

'No, not always. I am glad I am close to all my sisters.'

'Did you ever meet my brother?'

'When he was out and about his business—and we were introduced when my husband and I attended a social event in town. When I came to live at The Grange, and got to know my neighbours and the people of Woodgreen, it seemed to me that all of them rotated like planets around Netherthorpe. You were frequently talked about. Woodgreen is a small community and people like to pick at any interesting snippet of gossip.'

'And believe every rumour that comes their way— convinced that there is no smoke without fire. No one is ever quite what they seem, Mrs Lansbury—not even you. Edward is still at Netherthorpe, although he intends leaving me to it, now I'm home.'

Looking at him, with his arm draped imperturbably over his raised knee, his other leg stretched out in front of him and his eyes glowing in the evening twilight, Eve saw there was something undeniably engaging about him. He made her feel alert, alive and curiously stimulated.

'I'm sure you'll soon get used to it.'

He turned his head and looked at her. 'Like you did when your husband died?' When she didn't respond, his expression became grave. 'I heard he killed himself in an accident when he was cleaning his gun. I can't imagine how difficult that must have been for you.'

Eve tensed at the memory. With surprise, she was conscious that he was now studying her with a different interest. 'Yes, it was. But I had a child to raise—a child

who had known his father for just six months—and
life had to go on. An uneasy darkness hung over The
Grange for a long time afterwards. Matthew… He—
he was a difficult man. He was having an affair—an
affair of long standing, as I found out shortly after we
married. It was no secret.'

'Would you mind if I enquired as to the identity of
the lady in question?'

Eve turned her head and looked at him. 'Lady? She
was no lady,' she stated firmly. 'It was Sir Oscar's
wife—Elena.'

Lord Levisham's eyes narrowed. The woman must
be devoid of scruples to have jumped into bed with
his brother after Matthew Lansbury's demise—if Edward was to be believed. 'Good lord! That's a bit close
to home.'

'Close to home or not, it narrows down to the same
thing.'

'And Sir Oscar? Did he know of the affair?'

'Oh yes, but he turned a blind eye to it.'

'And is his wife still with him?'

'Of course. Lady Devlin is a wealthy woman in her
own right—far more so than her husband. She already
had a reputation before she married him. She was also
illegitimate, so she had to look outside her own class
for a husband. Sir Oscar is a greedy man. He will want
to hold on to what she brought to the marriage.'

'And Sir Oscar wants to get his hands on some of
your land. Will you sell, do you think, in the end?'

'The Grange has a lot in its favour. It's prime land,
for one thing, so, no, I won't be selling. Matthew's fa-

ther farmed The Grange and his father before him. It's Christopher's birth right. I owe it to him not to sell. I blame Matthew for leaving me with this mess. Adultery does not sit easy with me, Lord Levisham.'

'He hurt you. I can see that.'

The warm blood mounted in her face. 'It was more than that. I was both angry and hurt—and my pride took a battering. I don't think I would have known if I hadn't come across them one day while out riding. Oh, I'd heard rumours, but I didn't believe them—or didn't want to believe them. Lady Devlin didn't speak to me but the way she looked at me... No one has to be wise or old to understand when one is despised.' She smiled bitterly. 'She is everything I am not—rich and beautiful, and I don't cut such a fine figure in the drawing room.'

'Permit me to disagree. You are a beautiful young woman who is wasted here at The Grange. You'll give all your life to the place, and one day—perhaps when your son marries and brings his wife here—you'll wake up to find that life has gone sour and stale and you're too old to marry anyone else.'

Eve sighed, twining a piece of straw round her finger in quiet contemplation. Lord Levisham was right. Life in all its glorious richness was passing her by. The feeling that she'd been cast off into a life devoid of fun, that she was no longer worthy of anyone's love or attention, was painful and the unfairness bit into her anew. Was there to be no end to this soul-crushing austerity day after day, the constant grind to make enough money to keep a roof over their heads? All she wanted was a little extra to raise her spirits.

'Maybe. That seems to be my lot in life,' she uttered quietly. 'I have come so far since Matthew's death. I wondered at the time how on earth I would carry on—being a woman, there were those in the community who wanted me to fail. It was a struggle, but I ignored the prejudice toward my sex. I had the audacity to prove my abilities, despite ridicule, and battled people's opinion of feminine weakness.'

'And now?'

'Now I am just a widow, an independent woman of independent means—however small they may be.' She laughed and he laughed with her. In that moment, maybe for just that moment, she felt free of anxiety, the companionship between them warming her. 'I also have my son. He means everything to me. I will do my best for him—for his future.'

'Of course you will. I don't doubt that.'

Tilting her head, she looked at him. 'I think you are shocked that I speak of things so openly.'

'Not shocked at what your husband did, but I am surprised that you can speak of it to a complete stranger.'

'Where's the sense in hiding it? Everyone in Woodgreen knew it was going on.'

'You seem remarkably sure of yourself, Mrs Lansbury.'

She nodded. 'I am. I've learned to be. It is the only way I survive. I am the youngest of five sisters. All of them have done well for themselves and are happily married with a number of offspring. I thought it would be the same for me when I married Matthew. It wasn't. He was a gambler and a womaniser. He also enjoyed the tempo of the social scene in London. The style suited him.' She uttered the words without coyness.

'Is that where you met, in London?'

'Yes. I was living with my sister at the time in Kensington when I first saw him. He was in town to see his solicitor. I was introduced to him by my brother-in-law, who works for the government. I was taken aback when he proposed. I demurred at first, but my sisters told me not to look a gift horse in the mouth, telling me he was a good catch and that I could do worse. He was handsome and charming, and I was flattered by his attention. And so, tired of being passed back and forth among my sisters, I married him.'

'And how old were you when you married?'

'Eighteen.'

'A naïve and virginal eighteen,' Lord Levisham murmured softly, his eyes on her flushed face.

'Yes, I was. I think he thought of me as a child.'

'And you loved him, of course?'

Eve turned her head and looked at him sharply. She was very conscious of him studying her, deliberately and at some length, and her new consciousness of him made her avert her eyes. She was taken off-guard by the question, but it was asked politely and with a subtle interest, and she saw no reason not to appease his curiosity.

'Why "of course"?'

'Isn't passion supposed to be the characteristic of

eighteen-year-old women? Aren't all young ladies supposed to be in love at that age?'

'Passion, maybe. Clear thinking isn't.' She remembered how it had been as Matthew's wife. How in private he could be smug, condescending and annoying—and often cruel in his remarks to her. She would shrink before the anger she never failed to rouse in him when she'd begged him to curb his ways.

'No, I didn't love him in the romantic sense of the word—which I have since come to believe is for fools and dreamers. If I'd had any of that in my nature before I married Matthew, I'd had it knocked out of me by the time he died. Not physically,' she was quick to add. 'But there are other emotional and controlling ways.'

'I'm sorry to hear that. He wasn't worthy of you.'

She shrugged. 'Maybe not. Who's to say?'

Eve hadn't meant to give so much away, but there was an openness, a directness, about this man that made her want to tell him everything. Discussing her personal life wasn't something she did. It was a relief to let her guard down with this relative stranger. It had been a long time since she'd had anyone to confide in.

'Nothing stays the same as the beginning,' she went on. 'When everything is bright and wonderful, and everything seems possible. I try not to dwell on the past. It never does any good. Matthew was a good-looking man—charming, when the mood took him, which I didn't see very often. Sir Oscar must be thirty years his wife's senior without a romantic bone in his body. Little wonder Elena was attracted to Matthew—or he to her. Clearly, she could give him something I did not.

Elena is a beautiful woman. She only has to snap her fingers to have men at her feet.'

'I met her on a couple of occasions when I was at home, but the meetings were brief, with no time to form an opinion one way or another.'

'And now you have other things to occupy your mind other than Elena Devlin. I expect you'll find your life so very different from now on. I would like to say, at least you won't be getting shot at any more, but after what happened to you on your return I'm not so certain.'

'Don't worry. I'm a trained survivor. If I can survive the mayhem in Spain and Portugal, I can survive anything.'

Eve didn't doubt it. 'Do you know who it might have been?'

His jaw hardened. 'No. But I will find out. I have spent precious little time at Netherthorpe these past few years. Nearly everyone is a stranger to me, so I find it odd that my would-be assassin is trying to dispose of me here. I just wish I could think of a reason why someone is so desperate to have me dead.'

The look that appeared on his face gave Eve a chill, but it was briefly seen. 'Jealousy, hatred, greed... Someone from your military past, perhaps? Someone out for revenge?' she suggested.

'I have thought of that—gone over and over it in my mind. My military training taught me always to be prepared for the unexpected. I've learned to be careful of who I trust, for assassins come in many different guises. I admit, I've made enemies in the past, but I can't think of one who would want to kill me.'

'How is your wound, Lord Levisham?'

He turned to face her, a roguish smile curving his lips. 'Doing nicely. Would you care to take a look?'

'No. I'll take your word for it. Does it pain you?'

'No more than a slight discomfort.'

He cast an eye at her dress, that was tight-fitting at the bodice and emphasised the outline of her long legs beneath her skirts. His eyes paused for just a moment on the curve of her breasts. His gaze wasn't salacious, though. More that of a trainer appraising a new race-horse before buying.

'You did well with your ministering. Have you got any other hidden talents you would like to tell me about?'

'Not that I know of.'

Hearing hoof beats on the road that ran by the field, Eve looked towards the gate. Sir Oscar came into view, his wife Elena by his side. They paused, taking in the scene. Eve had not failed to notice that Sir Oscar rode by on occasion; in fact, wherever she looked he always seemed to be there. No doubt he was resentful to see the work progressing smoothly. Lord Levisham had shown his power when he had sent the gypsies to her, whereas Sir Oscar would have been glad if her harvest had been spoilt, believing it would have set her one step closer to selling him the land.

# *Chapter Three*

Unhurried, Eve got to her feet and walked towards them, her gaze sliding to Sir Oscar's wife dispassionately. Elena Devlin was the last person she wanted to see. Attired in a figure-hugging lapis-blue habit and matching hat with white feathers, set jauntily on her dark hair with curls dangling over her shoulder, Lady Devlin was glamorous, beautiful and cold as steel. What had Matthew once said of her? Vivacious, exciting and rare—like vintage champagne.

Eve could not agree. She was enveloped in a musk perfume—musky as a cat, Eve thought with distaste and a well of bitterness. Her features were delicately moulded, all perfectly proportioned. Her whole style was elegant, and Eve was miserably conscious of her own dowdy and dishevelled appearance: her callused hands, hair uncombed and the dust of the fields on her boots and the hem of her skirt.

There was not a man in Woodgreen whose eyes did not devour Lady Devlin when she rode through town—

she was their idea of paradise—nor a woman who didn't wish they could be like her. She had a talent for flouting rules—such as stealing another woman's husband.

Sir Oscar dismounted and stood holding the reins of his horse. His greedy eyes passed over the fields, missing nothing. Eve stiffened at his scrutiny. When his eyes finally rested on her, they narrowed as if in disapproval before he gave a curt nod. Eve did not avert her eyes.

'Sir Oscar!' she said, aware that from atop her horse Lady Devlin was surveying her with a critical eye and a smug smile on her carmine lips. 'Can I help you?'

'You've got the harvest in, I see. Have you considered my offer of buying the land?'

'There's no need. I'm not selling. I thought I'd made that perfectly clear.'

'I thought you might have changed your mind. You are struggling financially. I would make a fair offer to a bright young widow like yourself.'

'One which I would be forced to refuse.'

'The farm will go to rack and ruin run by a woman with no head for business—and for what? What I am prepared to pay will make you a wealthy woman of independent means.'

'You are wasting your time. I don't think you have heard me. The land is not for sale.' Sir Oscar really was a self-regarding, pompous man who was incapable of listening.

His eyes hardened. 'You will.'

'I will not. I am no fool, Sir Oscar.'

'I'm not saying that you are. But you have a lot to learn.'

Lord Levisham appeared from behind the tree, where he had been speaking to Henry. Having heard some of the conversation between Eve and Sir Oscar, he approached them. Sir Oscar was surprised to see him there.

'Ah, Lord Levisham! I heard you were back at Netherthorpe. Welcome home. What happened to your brother was a tragedy. Couldn't believe it when I heard—such a competent rider, especially on the hunting field. My condolences. Have you left the army?'

Lord Levisham nodded, his face impassive. 'I was left with no choice. Netherthorpe cannot run itself.'

'No, of course it can't. Have you met my wife, Lord Levisham? Elena.'

Lord Levisham's eyes flicked to the woman on the horse and he inclined his head. The expression on his face remained unchanged. 'I have—some time ago, when I was home on leave. Lady Devlin, my pleasure,' he said with polite formality. He fixed his eyes on Sir Oscar. 'Since you are here, Sir Oscar, I feel I must speak for Mrs Lansbury. I am far from happy in respect of your dealings with her.'

Sir Oscar started, clearly taken by surprise. His eyes narrowed as he prepared himself for an attack. 'And why is that? Not that it should concern you, Lord Levisham.'

'But it does—Mrs Lansbury being a widow and a neighbour. It saddens me to think a man of your standing would target a widow so persistently. I hope you can find it in you to put an end to the matter and that you will act honourably.'

Without raising his voice, Sir Oscar turned to leave. 'You insult me, Lord Levisham. It is clear to me and the whole of Woodgreen that she is struggling. I thought to alleviate some of her worries by offering to buy a small tract of land on which to build some houses for my workers. Mrs Lansbury knows nothing about matters of business. It is a trait unbecoming in a woman to meddle in such affairs. I merely made the offer to stop her getting into debt and disrepute.'

'I am sure Mrs Lansbury appreciates your concern, but does she have your word that it stops here?'

Mounting his horse, Sir Oscar looked down at them, Eve standing several paces behind Lord Levisham. 'I made Mrs Lansbury my final offer some weeks ago. I will not make another.' He looked at Eve. 'In the future, should you wish to sell, you know where I am. Oh,' he said as he was about to ride off. 'I noticed the fence is down in the bottom meadow. I suggest you get someone to fix it before your stock get onto my land. Any damage to my crops, you will pay for.'

Eve steeled herself. 'That fence was repaired last week and I have no stock in that field.'

He shrugged her off as he would a tiresome child. 'If you say so.'

As soon as he had ridden away, accompanied by his wife, Eve's resentment at Lord Levisham's arrogance and domineering manner to take it upon himself to speak for her came with a vengeance. Suddenly, what she had begun to feel for him was dangerous. She had sworn after Matthew's death never to let another man have power over her. Time and again throughout the years of those pain-filled days she reminded herself of the agony he had inflicted on her during their marriage, and she fiercely renewed her vow never to let it happen again—never to give her heart to any man who would try to control her.

Behind the pattern of her beautiful face, she was outraged. The red blushes on her cheeks had settled into a dark glow, the flush of sudden battle in her face.

'How dare you?' She flared up, having felt the shift of power move towards him.

'I'm sorry?' he said, though Eve got the impression her response was not the grateful one he was expecting.

'How dare you use your power to speak for me? I was married to a man who controlled my every move, and I will not tolerate anyone else doing that. I am capable of fighting my own battles. Whatever drove you to challenge Sir Oscar, please do not do so again. My affairs are my own and I am quite capable of dealing with difficult neighbours myself. Any problem I have with him, *I* will deal with. I do things my way and take my chances.'

Lord Levisham's face darkened with annoyance, and Eve could almost feel his struggle to hold his temper in check. 'In which case, I offer my sincere apologies.'

'Thank you. Now, I would offer you refreshment, but if you will excuse me I have things to do. Good day, Lord Levisham.'

Turning on her heel, she began to walk in the direction of the house. Lord Levisham followed, halting her by catching hold of her arm and speaking close to her ear from behind.

'Go if you must, but before you do, I will give you a warning. Just one,' he enunciated coldly. 'Call it advice, if you prefer.'

'If I wanted advice,' Eve retorted, spinning round, her eyes sparking with green fire, 'I would not come to you.'

'Perhaps not, but I will repeat what I said on our first meeting. Have a care in your dealings with Oscar Devlin. He is not to be trusted, and not for one minute do I believe he will give up trying to obtain the land—by fair means or foul.'

'Thank you for the advice,' she said coldly. 'But I am perfectly aware of the nature of the man.'

'Then be on your guard. I am truly sorry if I have offended you or hurt you in any way. It was not my intention.'

'You didn't hurt me. I am simply furious that you should have the audacity to speak for me. No one has the right to do that.'

'Wait.' He reached out and took her arm, halting her when she was about to walk away. He eyed her to gauge her response—the expressionless face, the distrustful eyes, the taut shoulders.

Eve glanced down at his hand, giving him the message that she was deeply offended to be touched. He uncurled his fingers. Lord Levisham's nearness threatened to destroy her confidence and composure, but only threatened. He was far too bold to allow even a small measure of comfort. With all her senses heightened sharply, a spark of self-preservation ignited within her. She stepped back, her retreat necessary to cool her burning cheeks and to ease the unruly pacing of her heart to some degree. She lifted her head imperiously, her eyes glinting as they glared into his.

'I don't want you to say anything else. I think we have both said far too much as it is. I don't want you to touch me. Now please go.'

He nodded slowly and stepped away from her. When he spoke, his tone was brusque. 'Should you need help in any way, you know where I am. Goodnight, Mrs Lansbury.'

Without another word, he mounted his horse and rode away without a backward glance.

Eve stood and watched him go with a feeling of regret that she didn't care for. Anger and humiliation had made her boil over, otherwise she would not have spoken so harshly. She felt a sudden stillness envelope her. When Levisham stood so close to her, she had been vividly aware of the heat of his body, the spicy scent of his cologne and his maleness, and had been overwhelmingly conscious of him.

It was a long time since she had felt so helpless, so vulnerable, and she was angry and resentful of the way Lord Levisham had taken charge of the situation with Sir Oscar. Even her marriage to Matthew had not created the furore inside her as did this strange relationship she had with Lord Levisham, although she had been young and innocent. She was irritated by the way in which he'd skilfully cut through her superior attitude.

She was about to return to the house when the head of the workers approached her.

'We are moving out in the morning, Mrs Lansbury. I want to thank you for giving us work. We'll be down this way next year.'

'Thank you, that is good to know. If you come to the house, I'll settle things with you.'

'No need, Mrs Lansbury. Lord Levisham has given us payment.'

Eve stared at him. 'Oh… I… I didn't… I see.'

If she had been angry before, now she was incandescent. How dared he take it upon himself to do this? How dared he? No one had insulted her as much as this and it was more than her pride could bear. Dazed and unable to form any coherent thought, she stalked to the house with her fists clenched, wanting nothing more than to confront that arrogant earl and vent her fury. At the full realisation of what he had done, renewed life began to surge through her. Her magnificent eyes shone with humiliation and wrath. She was appalled and outraged.

The unspeakable cad! Just when she was beginning to trust him, to respect him and believe he had been unfairly maligned, he had to go and do this. She didn't like his proprietorial manner, not one bit—it reminded her far too much of Matthew. She should have been wary of him. He was the type of person who thought he only had to beckon to a girl and she would come running.

And coming face to face with Elena Devlin had done nothing to improve her temper. The look she'd given Eve would have caused most people to turn away, but Eve had reacted with studied nonchalance, deliberately meeting her eyes. It had had the desire effect. Lady Devlin had been the first to look away. Although the brief encounter had left a bad taste in Eve's mouth, it did at least feel as though she'd won a small victory.

Eve entered the house and went into her office, glad to be alone. The cross words she had exchanged with Lord Levisham, and the anger they had stirred in her, had affected her more than she realised. It was a long time since anyone had tried to lord it over her, and Lord Levisham's attitude had reopened an old raw wound. Matthew had done that. He had tried to control her all the time, unable to accept that she had a mind of her own. But before that, when Lord Levisham had ridden into the field, there'd been no doubt that his presence had disturbed her.

She remembered the things she had said to him in that short time when they had sat on the ground leaning against the stout trunk of the same tree—close, but still strangers. She had listened to the things he had said, as though thinking out loud and not for anyone else's ears. Of how he had felt about his brother, his regret at leaving the army and the pressing sense of the future being shaped in a way he didn't want it shaped.

Yes, they had spoken openly, but would they be able to forgive each other for the things they had said, and the weaknesses they had confessed? Would they despise each other for that? They had both lost someone close, tragedies both of them, and the anguish was still with them. They were not friends—he was the Earl of Levisham and she the widow of a farmer—just two people who had met and talked too much. It would be better if they did not meet again but she would have to see him to repay the money he had given the workers.

Watching Eve Lansbury made Maxim reflect on his life before he'd joined the army, and on all the things he had missed. There had been pleasurable moments for him, both at home when he had been on leave and in Spain or wherever his military duties had taken him, but none of them had been of a serious nature.

This had been down to him. Because of his military duties, which had often been fraught with danger and had taken him away for many months at a time, he had purposely steered clear of becoming closely involved with any woman. But that didn't mean he'd given up the thrill of the chase, the excitement of seduction.

It had been six months since his last short affair—a Spanish lady called Gabriela, voluptuous and a willing partner in bed. She'd wept when he'd left her, but he'd had to move on. And, when the letter informing him of Andrew's death had arrived, he'd known the time had come for him to leave his rakish ways behind. His priority now was Netherthorpe and making sure it was run in a way that would have made Andrew proud—but he hadn't reckoned on Mrs Lansbury.

Ladies of her station in life had never entered his sphere, and the primal rush of attraction he felt for her surprised him. He could not dismiss her from his mind. Something about the bleakness in her eyes when

she had told him of her life married to Matthew Lansbury and her work had moved him. She was unlike
the women who floated around in his social world—
women of unbridled self-indulgence whose lives revolved around the latest fashions and expensive jewels;
women who had a raging ambition to marry a title or
a high-ranking officer.

He admired Eve Lansbury, who was fiercely struggling to hold on to her home, with a depth of feeling
that was new to him. Many women of her situation
would have given up before now, but Maxim knew she
would rather face a firing squad than betray the slightest hint of weakness. She was caring and capable, and
her capacity for loyalty was unquestionable, having
taken over the running of The Grange and doting on
her son. She would make any man a perfect wife, and
in an ideal world would be the sort of woman to marry
and settle down with—but not for him. It was not an
ideal world and the difference in their status made her
unsuitable to be the wife of an earl. But as a mistress?
Maybe. On their two previous encounters she had responded positively to him—he had not imagined that,
or that he was strongly attracted to her.

He smiled as his mind drifted back to how it had
felt to sit beside her in the lowering sun, the smell of
harvested corn heavy in the sultry air. The drab, un-
fashionable dress she had been wearing, which had
seen better days, was an insult to her femininity. Mentally he stripped her of the unflattering garment and
saw her draped in a fashionable gown with gems at
her throat—blood-red rubies against her soft flesh—

in the flimsiest lace negligee barely covering her luscious body. The image was enough to arouse his loins and he decided he would order a cool bath to ease the aching discomfort.

The entrancing image of her as she had attended his wound wouldn't leave his mind; and, as he had watched her expressions as she had chatted with him, he had become aware of an old tug deep in his gut. The idea of having possession of that fragile beauty woke the sleeping demons inside him. Not only did she make him blind to anything but the demands of his own body, she effortlessly aroused other more powerful emotions he had tried to set aside since Andrew's death.

She was a tempting-looking woman. So tempting, in fact, that he had a mind to see if she tasted as sweet as she appeared.

Eve was more in control of her emotions the following morning when she took the reins of her carriage and drove to Netherthorpe. But her mind still burned with the memory of what Lord Levisham had done and she wasn't ready to be forgiving. It was half an hour's drive to Netherthorpe. Never having been to the house before, she had no idea what to expect. Parkland with grazing deer seemed to go on for ever. She was relieved when she reached the high stone walls that surrounded the house and grounds. Massive wrought-iron gates stood open beneath a stone arch surmounted by the Randall family crest.

Passing through, she followed the winding drive flanked with trees. The calm of the morning held a kind of radiance that dazzled her. It was in this radiance that Netherthorpe came into view with its tall chimneys and crenelated roofs against the pale blue sky. It took her breath away, reminding her of something out of a fairy tale. Eventually the grounds opened out and she saw the well-designed gardens gently sloping away from broad terraces. In the centre was a large ornate fountain which sent water spuming into the air.

The house was old and imposing. Everything of the importance and majesty of England was there, taking pride of place in the surrounding rich and beautiful countryside like some grand old lady. Pulling the horse to a halt in front of the house, and trying not to let her nerves take over, she climbed out and headed for the door at the top of a short flight of wide stone steps. It was intimidating. Taking a deep breath, she took hold of the heavy brass ring and knocked on the door, which was opened almost at once by a male servant attired in black.

'May I help you?'

'Yes, thank you. I'm here to see Lord Levisham.'

'And may I ask who is calling?'

Eve could tell by his tone that he did not approve of her calling so early and without a proper invitation. In his world, the proper etiquette for visiting involved calling cards for invitations. 'Mrs Lansbury from The Grange.' She smiled tightly, not prepared to be fobbed off. 'Is Lord Levisham at home?' If the servant was surprised, he hid it well. There was no more emotion in the lined face than was permitted in a well-trained servant.

'Of course. I should have recognised you. Please come inside while I ask if he's available.'

'Please don't bother. I'll announce myself.' Hearing voices coming from one of the rooms leading off from the hall, she headed towards it, ignoring the servant's startled expression and objections. She couldn't help but take in her surroundings as she crossed the hall. The height and deep shadow made it cool, almost like a church. At any other time, she would have paused to take a better look and admire, but her mind was on other things.

Opening the door to what she presumed must be Lord Levisham's study, she marched inside. Lord Levisham was seated at his desk along with another gentleman she recognised as his cousin. Of slender athletic build, good-looking and fair haired, his manner was so indolent that he gave the impression of being half-asleep. She met his gaze and felt a prickling on the back of her neck that warned her not to trust him. He was fastidiously tailored in turquoise satin, his neck cloth tied into perfect folds.

Lord Levisham looked up. His eyes snapped to attention, his expression instantly alert. For a moment he found himself speechless. Only when Eve descended on him was he jostled back to reality. Pushing back his chair, he stood up.

'Mrs Lansbury! What brings you to Netherthorpe so early? What a delightful surprise.'

'Is it? I doubt you will feel that way when I leave. This is not a social call.'

His cousin peeled himself out of his chair and

stretched languidly, his smile and manner deceptively mild. 'I think I'd better leave you to it.'

Eve looked at him. He spoke in a slow, deep voice, essentially undramatic, conveying the perfect measure of its owner's self-control. They had never met but she felt an instant dislike. He had about him an air of corruption and a ruthlessness that made her uneasy. It was nothing she could put her finger on. Being alone and observing people in the quiet of The Grange gave her an instinct for it. He appeared respectable, but there was something there nonetheless. He was looking at her from beneath his hooded lids. There was something in his eyes that she felt she did not want to understand or even know about. Something crouched and waiting. His manner gave him away as the type who regards himself superior to other people.

Like Lord Levisham, he wore the look of the well-bred of generations and possessed the complex traits that thrived in the families of those who were born to govern. But there was a fastidious air of supercilious taciturnity about this man that his cousin did not possess. She saw his eyes pass over her and his lips curl with distaste, which she ignored. His hooded eyes were half-closed, reminding her of a lizard.

'Please don't leave on my behalf,' she retorted sharply, feeling that prickle of discomfort again. 'What I have to say to Lord Levisham will not take long.'

He hesitated and then sat back down, deciding to stay where he was.

Lord Levisham walked round the desk to stand before her, a roguish smile sweeping across his handsome face. There was a kindling of fire in the depths of his eyes that touched her like a hot brand and kindled fresh ire. How dared he look at her like that after what he had done?

'You've saved me the trouble of coming to see you—to apologise for any offence I may have caused you yesterday.'

Eve regarded him through narrowed eyes. 'You were going to come to me?'

He grinned, clearly hoping to placate her. 'May I offer you refreshment?'

'No, thank you. I told you, this is not a social call.'

He nodded, perching his hips against his desk and folding his arms across his chest, his manner as languid and irritating as his cousin's. 'Then what can I do for you? You look upset about something.'

'Upset?' She flared. Slowly she moved towards him. Planting her small feet firmly in front of him, she faced him squarely. 'Yes, I am upset, but I am also furious.'

'Still? I was hoping you would have got over it by now.'

'I am sorry to disappoint you, but I am still furious.'

He was so close she could smell his shaving lotion and the masculine scent of him. 'You did something to which I would never have agreed had I been consulted from the outset. I have come to return the money you paid the workers. You had no business doing that. None whatsoever,' she said, loathing the fact that she couldn't take her eyes off his mouth and the waves of heat that washed over her at every word he uttered. Even though she told herself she loathed those penetrating eyes that told her he knew everything about her, because she had stupidly used him as a confidant, she couldn't stop her own eyes from staring into their silver brightness.

'I was trying to help.'

'Then please don't. I will be the judge of what is best for me. I don't want your money,' she snapped, placing a heavy purse on the desk—money she had found hard to find at such short notice. 'How dare you feel sorry for me? I am no simpering English miss, afraid to stand up for herself. I will not be pitied. I told you, I speak for myself and pay my dues without interference from anyone. That includes you, Lord Levisham.'

'I'm sorry if I've offended you. Call it payment for what you did for me. You probably saved my life.'

'As an experienced tried and tested military man many times over, I am quite sure you are capable of doing that yourself. I do not want payment for what I did. You insult me, Lord Levisham. You are arrogant and egotistical, and completely ignorant in your dealings with others, so kindly do me the favour of minding your own business in the future.'

Calmly he said, 'I thought you'd be pleased.'

'Pleased? You unspeakable cad,' she flung back. 'I am far from it. I find the idea of being indebted to you distinctly distasteful.'

He cocked a sleek black eyebrow. 'Beggars can't be choosers.'

'You're right, they can't, but I am no beggar. I will not be obligated to you.'

'Damn it, Mrs Lansbury,' Lord Levisham said, unable to repress his annoyance over her argumentative attitude. 'I don't want you to feel obligated to me.'

'I don't. I don't owe you anything and I will take nothing from you.'

Shoving a heavy lock of hair back from his forehead, Lord Levisham sighed heavily. 'You are a stubborn woman, Mrs Lansbury.'

'You have no idea just how stubborn I can be. So far you have only scratched the surface.'

'Are you always so unreasonable?'

'You are the one being unreasonable. Now, if you will excuse me, I will go. I have work to do.'

'Just a moment, if you please. There is something I wish you to have.'

'Oh? And what might that be?'

Walking round the desk, he opened a drawer and removed a box, a box she recognised immediately. The last time she had seen it it had been in the pawn shop in Woodgreen. Incensed by this new offence, she stared at it without attempting to take it. Then, feeling her fury rising to fresh heights, she looked at him.

'How could you? Just when I thought you couldn't do anything else to humiliate me, you have to do this. How dare you interfere in things that do not concern you? How dare you? I am not even going to begin asking you how you knew… How you…'

Picking up the box, she backed away. 'If you are expecting me to thank you for this then you are mistaken. You should not have done it. How dare you act in such a high-handed fashion? To take so much for granted… The worst part of all this is that I am still beholden to you. Be assured that I will lose no time in seeing that you are repaid.'

With her head held high, she strode to the door and left. Striding past the astonished butler, she let herself out of the house and went to her waiting carriage. Her mind was in turmoil as she reflected on her highly charged encounter with Lord Levisham. Normally in control of her emotions, she was simmering, seething with anger. She found his interference into her life insulting and unacceptable, and she sincerely hoped she would not have the misfortune to come into contact with him again. Climbing onto the carriage, she was about to drive away when Lord Levisham came striding towards her.

'Mrs Lansbury, please wait,' he said as she was about to drive off.

She looked down at him coldly. 'I think everything has been said, Lord Levisham. I've no need of a knight in shining armour.'

'I apologise if I have offended you—'

'You've already said that,' she snapped. 'I am offended, and who can blame me?'

'I don't. I can only apologise.'

Eve glared at him, evincing not the slightest desire to forgive him. 'There you go again. You really must stop repeating yourself. It becomes tedious. I must go. I have things to do.'

His face tightened, his lips compressed. He lifted one eyebrow ironically. 'You know, you really should do something about that temper of yours. You're lit up like a firework that's about to explode at any minute.'

'Explode? Believe me, Lord Levisham, you wouldn't want to see my temper explode.'

'Pardon me for trying to advise you on your faults.'

'Faults? Why, you unspeakable, insufferable… And I don't suppose you have any *faults* yourself, have you, Lord Levisham?'

'On the contrary. I would be the first to admit that I have many. I am far from perfect.' He smiled, his teeth flashing white. 'Now, have you finished berating me and being rude to me, or are you to continue giving me a dressing down?'

She looked at him with icy equanimity. 'I was not aware that I was giving you a dressing down or being rude. That was not my intention. You and I have met on two occasions, Lord Levisham, and already you presume too much.'

'Out of concern and because I wanted to repay your kindness.'

She gave him a baleful look. 'Then I hope you are satisfied.' She had no idea how his mood lifted at the sight she made sitting there with all her outrage wrapped around her.

Suppressing a dangerous urge to widen his grin, he said, 'Satisfied? I am not satisfied—and I will save your blushes by keeping to myself what would make me satisfied.'

Reading what was in his eyes, Eve looked away and, to her eternal mortification, heat flooded her body. 'Damn you, Lord Levisham! I am certain that I have never disliked any man as much as I dislike you at this moment…' Or felt so wonderfully alive with anyone else, she thought.

The man was incredible! One minute he was taking liberties by paying her workers and buying the necklace she had pawned—which she found offensive and unacceptable—and the next he was treating her reaction and their altercation lightly, as though it was of no importance. She became uncertain, and was beginning to feel foolish and bad tempered, but she was still angry and would not let him off the hook lightly. If she were to forgive him this, there was no telling what he would do next.

'You should not have got back my necklace—which I intended retrieving at a later date—and, when anyone works for me, *I* pay their wages, not you. Nor should you have taken the liberty of speaking for me to Sir Oscar and that—that woman.'

'That woman is his wife.'

'His adulterous wife,' Eve added contemptuously.

He nodded. 'As you say.'

'Yes, I do say. Where my husband was concerned, I believe she used him to relieve her boredom.' Her eyes settled on Lord Levisham. 'Whereas your brother was a different matter entirely. I am sure your cousin will have told you of their closeness, how quickly she made herself available to him when my husband died.'

'I am aware of that,' he replied coldly.

'Of course you are.' She saw his face harden, though he didn't react in any other way. Her gaze swept over the magnificent house behind him. 'Netherthorpe is by far the finest estate for miles. Elena Devlin seems to make a habit of collecting men—and your cousin is no exception, by the way, just in case he has omitted that piece of information. She changes her lovers with the seasons. Where will it end, I wonder? Have a care, Lord Levisham. She might already have you in her sights for her next victim. It's possible that neither you nor your cousin will remain unscathed in your dealings with Elena Devlin.'

Seeing his jaw clench, she smiled. 'Oh, I'm sorry. It would appear you didn't know about your cousin.' She sighed mockingly. 'Dear me! I really shouldn't have let my tongue run away with me, but it was common gossip when your brother died how quickly she latched onto your cousin.'

'No, you shouldn't,' he replied tightly.

'It's just another of my faults, Lord Levisham. Like you, I have several. On a different note—which I advise you to consider very seriously—I advise you to have a care. Your brother also died in unfortunate circumstances, so perhaps you should look closer to home for your answer as to who is trying to kill you.'

'What are you saying?'

'One of the motives for someone trying to kill you could be for personal gain. I understand that your cousin Edward is next in line to inherit.'

His eyes narrowed. 'May I ask what you are getting at?'

'I know he is your cousin and you are close, so you won't like what I'm going to suggest.' She knew the risk she was taking, but somehow she found the courage to say, 'People in this close-knit parish like to talk and his reckless behaviour on the hunting field and exploits with the ladies hereabouts has not gone unnoticed. From what I know of him, he's as clever as two wily foxes, and I would find it hard to trust him.' She spoke in all honesty, not having liked the way he had stared at her throughout with the calculating glare of a manipulator.

'That's mad. You can't seriously think that Edward…'

They looked at each other for several seconds, Maxim in particular knowing that men were capable of almost anything when a juicy carrot was dangled before them. His expression hardened, clearly not wanting to believe what she was suggesting. 'You shouldn't listen to gossip, Mrs Lansbury. Nothing good comes of it.'

'Maybe not, but I believe that old adage "there's no smoke without fire". Is it possible that it was your cousin who was trying to kill you that day? After all, he has much to gain.'

The muscles in his cheeks tensed and flexed as he met her eyes. 'No, I do not think that.' His tone was casual, but there was steel behind it.

'Nevertheless, it's a possibility.'

'No one who knows Edward would think that.'

'Perhaps you do not know him well enough.'

Anger darkened Lord Levisham's eyes. 'I believe I do. Take it from me, it's not Edward.'

'Maybe you're right. I hope for your sake you are, but I think you should keep a close eye on him all the same.' With a shake of the reins, she urged her horse on. 'Good day, Lord Levisham.'

'Wait.'

She halted the horse and looked back. Slowly he walked towards the carriage, resting his hand on the edge of the seat and looking up at her.

'A word of advice before you go, Mrs Lansbury.'

'And what might that be, Lord Levisham?'

'Don't let what has happened to you—what you do in the future—define you. Anger is a bad counsellor.'

'How is it anything to do with you what I do?'

'It isn't.' From beneath half-closed lids, his eyes held hers. A ghost of a smile touched his lips. 'A pity,' he murmured. 'You and I could be—friends.'

She looked at him coldly. 'You are mistaken. You are who you are, Lord Levisham—the Earl of Levisham. We are neighbours. You and I can never be friends. What you did when you took it upon yourself to pay the workers and buy back the necklace I took to the pawn broker was wrong. Why did you do it?'

'Because you are alone and friendless, a prey to all dangers and all snares. I was sincere. I beg you to believe that.'

'Whether I do or not is immaterial. And you were mistaken. I am neither alone nor friendless, and as far as I know I am not in danger. I am not interested in your warnings. Although, supposing I am in danger, why are you so anxious to save me?'

'Perhaps because I have never been able to bear to see a beautiful woman destroyed—or maybe because you were there when I was shot. I want to give you back the equivalent of what you did for me that day.'

'You have understood nothing and learned nothing, even now,' she uttered scathingly. 'Like most men, you think that women should bow to your wishes and merely thank you politely. I am sorry to disappoint you. I am my own mistress. I will not be controlled—not by you, not by anyone. I make my own rules. They have served me well since my husband died. They will do so in the future. Good day, Lord Levisham.'

As she travelled back to The Grange, she was determined to put Lord Levisham out of her mind. He was a man she was better off not thinking about. There was a purely sensual, physical attraction between them that neither of them could deny, which was the best reason in the world for them to stay away from each other, and she would never have to see him again. For some reason, that thought did not give her as much pleasure as it should have and she frowned, wondering why she should feel this way when he was the most provoking, infuriating man she had ever met. She couldn't trust with her emotions a man who had the reputation of a rake.

To her alarm and shame, she was conscious that underneath all her anger was a growing excitement— that, in a peculiar way she could not explain, she had actually enjoyed the confrontation between them. Appalled by that admission, she told herself it was mere anger making her heart do strange things, but with a sinking feeling in her stomach she realised that she was lying to herself.

# *Chapter Four*

Maxim watched her drive away. She sat erect and did not once look back. It was as if a rod had been thrust into her back. She had entered the house like a whirlwind and like a whirlwind had exited. He could not believe she had been and gone. There was no accounting for women when they took offence. He had intended to pay her a visit to break the ice. It had just got a hell of a lot thicker, and all because he'd had the audacity to retrieve her necklace from the pawn shop and pre-pay the workers—this chivalrous attempt of his to ease her burden had made her furious. She had confronted him as a coldly outraged, beautiful virago he didn't recognise.

There was an edge to her that was cutting, but beneath her glaring eyes and acrimonious tongue he sensed the warmth and passion in her, the longing to be free, to be wild and to do as she liked when she felt like doing it. In all fairness, he could not blame her for that. In fact, God help anyone trying to tame her—if such a thing were possible, which he doubted—and to break that spirit of hers. Her husband, the man who should have been her life's companion, had obviously treated her very badly, but he had not broken her.

Striding back to the house, he turned his thoughts to what she had told him. Edward had told him that his brother had been seeing Elena Devlin, but that Edward was also in a relationship with her was news to him.

The fact that Mrs Lansbury had suggested his cousin might have shot him gave him food for thought. It had simply never occurred to him, and his mind shied away from the thought—a man he'd known all of his life. But, for all that, he had no illusions about Edward. He was wilful, and often vicious in his opinion of others, but Maxim had not thought him capable of carrying out the murder of Andrew and making an attempt on his own life. Mrs Lansbury was no fool. She had made it obvious that she didn't like Edward, that she was suspicious of him.

Maxim cautioned himself not to jump in with both feet when confronting Edward. But the feeling of suspicion had infected him, and it shocked him to experience this doubt. He would keep his thoughts to himself, but he would watch his cousin carefully. Unconsciously he massaged his wounded shoulder, which ached when he was tense. On entering the study, he let his eyes settle on his cousin's face. He felt like a hound that had scented the fox. The smell was still weak, but it was definitely there.

'Well, I never!' Edward exclaimed, emitting a low whistle when Maxim walked back into the room and poured himself a drink. 'Who would have thought it? You've certainly managed to get on the wrong side of your neighbour, Maxim—and you've not been home two minutes. You must have had something to talk to her about. You were gone a while.'

'You'd be amazed what we talked about, Edward. What happened to Andrew was mentioned. Everything that happened that day he died remains unclear.'

'There was nothing suspicious about it, Maxim. His horse's girth snapped and he was thrown. That's all there was to it.'

Maxim listened with growing disquiet as Edward's account of what had happened spun out. He was relishing how he had taken control of the tragedy in a rather conceited way, portraying himself a hero, the man who had saved the day rather than a man Mrs Lansbury believed should be held under suspicion of murder.

'There is more to it, Edward. I won't let the matter rest until I know the truth.'

Edward pursed his lips, as if coping with a sour taste in his mouth. 'I can't see why on earth you're still questioning it, Maxim. It was an accident. The whole thing looked pretty cut and dried to me.' He shifted uncomfortably in the chair.

'It's a question of why a man with Andrew's ability on a horse should fall off and kill himself. As far as I'm concerned, there is more to it.'

Edward looked shaken by Maxim's vehemence. Discussing Andrew's death was plainly unacceptable to Edward. He rubbed his temples, trying to hide his unease at his cousin's persistence to get at the truth.

'Look, Maxim, it was a bad time for all of us who were there that day.'

'But they weren't there, Edward, were they? Only you saw what actually happened—only you to give an account.'

'I hope you don't think I had anything to do with it. Dear God in heaven! As if I would.'

Maxim looked at him directly. 'Did you?'

Edward's eyes bulged and his body exploded into life. He shot to his feet, his elbow overturning the glass on the table, puddling the brandy on the polished surface. 'I say, Maxim, I take exception to that—that you would think I am capable of doing Andrew harm. What in God's name are you talking about?' His eyes darkened with suspicion. 'Ah, don't tell me. Did Mrs Lansbury put that thought into your head—that I killed Andrew?'

'She—did query the possibility.'

'Then she had no right, and I hope you told her not to air her suspicions to all and sundry. To conjecture is all well and good, but to spread malicious gossip— that is quite another matter. Andrew took a tumble from his horse and broke his neck. Ask Dr Ennis, if you don't believe me.'

'I have. His neck wasn't broken. It was a severe blow to the back of his head that killed him after he fell from his horse—which, I might add, was caused by the girth being cut. It didn't simply snap, apparently.'

'What? And you think I would do that?'

'In truth, Edward, I don't know what to think. According to Dr Ennis, you were the only one there to see what happened.'

Edward's face had flushed in a dark rage. The sinews of his neck stood out like cords. 'If you would take the trouble to make further enquiries, you will find several others were present when he was thrown from his horse.'

'They were too far away to see what actually happened, apparently.'

'But close enough to witness if someone hit him over the head. In any case, why would I do such a thing? For what reason? No doubt Mrs Lansbury has pointed out that I have the most to gain from his death.' Maxim's eyes darkened and he looked away. 'She did, didn't she? I might have known. No doubt she also accused me of trying to shoot you.' He took Maxim's silence for assent. 'Ah—so she did. I might have known it.'

Maxim stared at him hard. Edward thrust his hands into his pockets, his body rigid. His voice was a low growl of anger when he fought for control.

'Someone did. I cannot ignore it, Edward.'

Edward poured himself a brandy, seeming to deflate as he sat down with one leg hitched over the other. 'I can see why I am the obvious suspect—in both cases—but I swear to you, Maxim, I am completely innocent. You must believe that.'

Maxim sat opposite him. The hurt on Edward's face and in his eyes seemed genuine. The strength, anger and suspicion that had brought him to confront Edward suddenly seemed to desert him. He wished he'd never entered into this conversation. He didn't want to make a scene, nor did he want to be at odds with Edward over this. However, he would make a point of keeping an eye on him in the future.

'Yes, of course I do, Edward. I'm sorry if I've given offence—although, since returning to Netherthorpe, it's all I seem to do. First Mrs Lansbury and now you.'

Edward smiled, suddenly more like his old jovial self. 'Apology accepted. Both you and Andrew have been like brothers to me. I have nothing but the deepest affection for you. I would no more think of harming you than I would my own mother—God bless her. Was anything else said that might blacken my name?'

Elena Devlin sprang to mind but, sensing another conversation coming that he did not want to have, Maxim shook his head. Until he had more information about what had happened to Andrew, he could think of nothing to say to Edward that would not give away his feelings.

With that, Edward began to brighten up. 'Let's forget all about it. But what a woman! Beautiful and impressive as a tropical storm. Mrs Lansbury certainly had her dander up. It would seem that her husband's treatment of her and his subsequent death has robbed her of all pleasure. Beneath those rags—'

'Come now, Edward, you exaggerate,' Maxim was quick to say, more affected by Mrs Lansbury's visit and her suggestion that it might be Edward who was trying to kill him than he cared to consider just then. 'In my opinion Mrs Lansbury looked perfectly presentable—if a trifle irate,' he added, although he had already decided that Eve Lansbury belonged in beautiful gowns and glittering jewels. Better by far than the sombre grey dress she must have worn day in and day out.

'No, well, I suspect they hide a multitude of delicious curves. She's a firework. Something tells me she will not be an easy conquest and certainly not a woman who is easy to forget.'

'I have no intention of conquering Mrs Lansbury. She is my neighbour—a very charming neighbour, I grant you, if a trifle angry. There has been a misunderstanding about a transaction between us. Nothing more that.'

'Then why did your eyes light up the minute she entered the room?' Edward said, helping himself to a pinch of snuff. 'I trust you will enlighten me as to what your true thoughts are concerning your charming neighbour. Damned engrossed you were.'

'My thoughts are my own affair, Edward—though favourable,' Maxim added, with a cynical curl to his lips and an appreciative gleam in his eye as he sat at his desk and took a deep swallow of brandy.

'With a look like that, would I be right in assuming you have singled her out to become better acquainted? Can't say that I blame you and, if you are contemplating making her one of your amusing bed warmers, then you are going to be disappointed. There are certain things you should know about that adorable widow—since you've been pursuing those damned Frenchies in the Peninsular for the past few years.'

'Go on,' Maxim urged, lifting his arrogant brows

and waiting, his look both suspicious and intrigued. His curiosity was piqued.

Edward went on to regale Maxim with Eve Lansbury's attributes and shortcomings, much to Maxim's irritation. If Edward were to be believed, according to Lady Elena Devlin—who'd had a long-standing affair with him—the widow's husband had informed her that his wife was as cold as an iceberg and set with wilful thorns.

'As a result, she has been dubbed the Ice Maiden of Woodgreen. And the unkind—though some would say appropriate—sobriquet has stuck. It's unfortunate, since the widow has spirit. She should prove highly entertaining in a chase, which makes her a challenge to the likes of me.'

'I can see that, but she's a beautiful woman whose experience as a wife has been to be treated mercilessly by a man who was in love with another woman. Do you not think the lady had good reason to be cold to her husband?'

'Since when has anything like that mattered to you and I, Maxim? Mrs Lansbury sometimes travels to stay with her sister in Kensington—although it is a rare thing to see Mrs Lansbury out in society. Her sister takes an understanding view of the matter—some might think it admirable. Personally, I consider it a damn waste of both time and a beautiful woman.'

Maxim considered what Edward had said about Eve Lansbury with renewed interest. 'She has a sister in Kensington, you say?'

'Yes—her husband, Sir John Portman, is a member of the government. Mrs Lansbury's sister—one of four, I believe—took her and her brother under her wing when their parents died. Then she married Matthew Lansbury, who ended up accidentally shooting himself. Where the delectable widow is concerned, well, it's hard to believe that any man's hands have ever touched that deliciously soft skin of hers.'

'She has a three-year-old son, Edward, so she is not a young virgin looking for her first romance.' Though Maxim would dearly like to silence Edward, what he was saying about his charming neighbour was mostly true.

'Since her husband died, all she cares about is that wretched farm and that son of hers. Any man who is foolish enough to show an interest in her I imagine she will send packing.'

'Including you, Edward, which is why you are so ready to point out her faults to me.'

Edward lifted his arrogant brows. 'Including me— if I were to try, that is, which I won't, since her rejection would do my reputation no good at all. Although you could prove to be a different matter. With your breeding—not to mention your wealth—your potent attraction for the opposite sex has always been a topic of much scintillating feminine gossip. You do seem to have an extraordinary effect on them. But, if what has just happened between the two of you is anything to go by, then I very much doubt even you will melt that particular iceberg.'

Mild cynicism marred the lean handsomeness of Maxim's features as he refused to be drawn on what his thoughts might be concerning the young woman who had probably saved his life.

'Are you insinuating that I've lost my touch, Edward?'

'Wouldn't dream of it, old boy,' Edward said, sauntering to the window and looking out, his gaze fastening on the tall chimneys of the Dower House beyond the park. 'It's a shame to allow the Dower House to remain empty, Maxim.'

'I hadn't given it much thought. We don't have a dowager to put in there at present.' Maxim eyed his cousin suspiciously. 'Are you still living with Aunt Pauline, Edward?'

At that moment a quick change came over Edward's face. His eyes darkened and an odd smile touched his mouth. 'Unfortunately, yes. She takes care of me, panders to all my needs,' he said with the smugness of a man for whom being served by others was important.

'I know what you want me to say, Edward—that you can have the Dower House. Andrew must have had good reason to want to keep it empty, so I shall respect his decision. The answer is no.' Maxim had no objection to Edward coming to Netherthorpe as a guest, but to have him living permanently on his doorstep was definitely not to be considered.

Edward sighed. 'I thought it might be—but I would like to make a wager.' He grinned broadly, rather like a child contemplating his favourite toy. 'You know how I love a wager.'

Apart from one sleek dark brow cocked in question, Maxim's features remained impassive. 'A wager? I'm listening.'

'A wager that if you fail to seduce the delectable Mrs Lansbury before Christmas…'

'And why should I want to seduce her?'

'To prove that you can—that you haven't lost your touch.'

The challenge was thrown lightly, and Maxim teetered on the brink of accepting when caution reared its head. Seducing any woman who was reluctant to be seduced was not his thing. But the lovely Eve Lansbury had captured his attention and he found the challenge was intriguing. Besides, her parting words, that they would never be anything more than neighbours, was a challenge in itself. If his conscience pricked him at all at the calculating way he was considering the wager, he ignored it.

She was the most fascinating, beguiling creature he had come across in a long time and, for his sins, she fascinated him. The memory of her fury would not leave him, and her angry words and cold manner didn't make her any less desirable to him. In fact, he found that her very dislike of him aroused the hunter in him. It was difficult for him to set aside thoughts of her. He was a man who must win, whatever the odds stacked against him. Whenever he set his mind on having something, he was not easily dissuaded.

'And if I don't?'

'Then you will allow me to take up residence in the Dower House—and good riddance to Aunt Pauline.'

'I think Aunt Pauline will say good riddance to you,

Edward. And what is in it for me—besides the lovely Mrs Lansbury?'

'My favourite horse, if you succeed. I know how much you admire the stallion—you can't help being drawn to him. Cost me a pretty penny, I can tell you, and I shall be reluctant to part with him, but that's all part of the game.''

Maxim rose to the challenge with a confident smile. Edward was right. It was a damned fine horse. 'That's unfortunate for you. If there is one thing I dislike, it's seeing my opponent lose.'

'My thoughts exactly. Think on it, Maxim. To seduce a woman famous for her strict morals… Not a virgin, unfortunately, but she might as well be. So—a wager it is, then. No need to put it in writing. A gentleman's agreement will do.'

Pouring them both a brandy, Maxim resumed his seat behind his desk. Suddenly Eve Lansbury had become an exciting enigma, a mystery which had multiplied tenfold. Since her husband had died, gentlemen had hesitated to go near her, to take liberties with her. Suddenly she had become a challenge he could not resist.

The trouble was, he conceded, if he did succeed in getting her into his bed, he would be unable to let her go.

Eve's four sisters were all married and scattered in different parts of the country. Marian, the eldest, had done well for herself, better than any of her sisters. Their father—who had died of a seizure ten years earlier, two years after his beloved wife—had made his living as a merchant in the cotton trade in Lancashire. He'd been able to provide generous dowries for all his daughters, along with a commission for Robert in the army. Marian's husband held a responsible position in the government. He was fond of Robert and had paved the way for his entry into the Royal Artillery.

Eve and Christopher travelled to London with Robert, who was to go to Woolwich to begin his career shortly. It would be nice to escape from The Grange for a breathing space she had begun to feel she sorely needed. The visit also coincided with Marian and her husband John's twentieth wedding anniversary, and Marian insisted on Eve being present to take part in the celebrations, which were to be held at the Portmans' spacious house in Kensington.

As a rule, Eve preferred to keep a close eye on things at The Grange and not to have to endure the pitiful looks of her sisters and their spouses she always got on her visits. But the busy time was over, and she knew she could leave things in Henry's capable hands, so she had no excuse for not going.

On their arrival at the house, under Nessa's supervision, Christopher was immediately gathered up by the servants and whisked away to be admired and fussed over, to his obvious delight.

'I'm glad you're here, Eve.' Marian hugged her affectionately. 'A break from that place you try to run single-handedly will do you the world of good.'

Eve settled on one of the comfortable sofas and, relaxing into the cushions, sipped her tea appreciatively.

'It will, Marian—although I had to come and see Robert settled at Woolwich. He's terribly excited about beginning his career.'

'I know, although I suspect you are going to miss him.'

Eve nodded. 'Yes, I'm afraid I will—and Christopher. We've both become used to having him around.' She smiled, reaching out and giving Marian's hand a fond squeeze. 'Don't look so worried, Marian. I know how concerned you are for me, but you needn't be.'

Marian's face had more wrinkles now and her hair was streaked with grey. She pursed her lips. 'Of course I'm concerned about you. You look tired, Eve, and thinner than when I last saw you. That farm of yours takes too much out of you.'

'It's work, Marian, and it has to be done.'

'And just look at your hands,' Marian said, taking hold of Eve's hands and examining the calluses. 'They are not the hands of a lady.'

'There's no shame in that.'

'Of course there isn't. But you must have time for yourself.'

'I will, now that the busy time is over. I have a good foreman in Henry. I know I can rely on him to get things done. It's been nice having Robert to keep me company and shoulder some of the work. Worry not, Marian, and please don't fuss. I promise that, when things pick up, I will become more retiring. I will visit you all the time and we will take tea with your friends, visit all the best places and stroll in the park beneath our parasols.' She laughed. 'In other words, dear sister, I will become respectable.'

'And pigs might fly.'

Eve laughed, but on a more serious note, how she wished she could spend more time in London with Marian. Her sisters would never know the loneliness, the frustrations and the despair she kept hidden from them. Despite this, she had grown fond of The Grange, and looked on it as home, but life there was so small, so insulated from what went on in the world outside.

'Why not?' she replied. 'There's a first time for everything.'

'To make life easier for yourself, you could sell off some of the land to Sir Oscar Devlin—he's been hankering after it for long enough. You could invest the money you make from that elsewhere.'

Eve stared at her. 'Are you being serious? I cannot sell off the land. It's Christopher's inheritance. There were a few conditions attached to Matthew's will, one of them being that I cannot give away any money or property hereafter. The second that if I should remarry, The Grange remains Christopher's. Unfortunately, he made no mention of what I should do in years of hardship.'

'And if anything should happen to Christopher?'

'Only then will it come to me. The Grange was everything to Matthew. He left it in my keeping in good faith, that I would take care of it until our son is of an age to take over. No one knew that things would turn out like they have. Things might have been different had he lived.'

'Yes, well, we'll never know, will we?' They sat for a moment in companionable silence as they sipped their tea, and after a moment Marian said, 'Has the new Earl of Levisham returned to Netherthorpe yet? What a terrible tragedy it was when his brother died. I believe the new earl is a military man. He'll more than likely find running an estate the size of Netherthorpe difficult after spending most of his adult life fighting the French.'

'Yes, I expect he will,' Eve replied. 'As a matter of fact, we have met. Someone tried to shoot him, would you believe?' She gave Marian a brief account of what had happened, leaving out the lengths he had gone to to interfere in her life. As she spoke of him and remembered her dealings with him, she drew a long breath, striving to get control of her emotions.

'I would dearly like you to find someone special, Eve—someone to love, who will whisk you away from that farm of yours.'

'It isn't mine, Marian. Until Christopher is man enough to take over the reins, then that is where I must remain.'

Marian sighed, knowing there was nothing she could do to persuade her sister away from The Grange. 'Then you must make a point of coming to London more often. You are always welcome here.'

The whole family was together for the first time in years. Eve's other sisters and their spouses with their children of various ages and sizes arrived. The house came alive with laughter and music. Eve took comfort in the presence of her sisters—Marian, Mary, Judith and Sarah. They were all so excited to be together again.

When they gathered for pre-dinner drinks the night before the anniversary celebrations, John announced that there would be an extra guest. Sarah, a proficient pianist, was at the fortepiano trying out some music from sheets belonging to Marian.

'And who is that?' Marian asked distractedly, trying to listen to what her other two sisters were discussing.

From where he sat holding court with his four brothers-in-law, all imbibing his finest brandy and cigars, John said casually, 'Maxim Randall, the Earl of Levisham.'

Eve's eyes flew open, and she almost dropped the sherry John had just handed to her. 'Lord Levisham? He—he is coming here? But…but I don't understand. Do you know him?'

'No—at least, not until today. I was introduced to him at my club. He's recently back from Spain, where he's been fighting the French with Wellington. Fine fellow. When I realised he came from Woodgreen, Eve, I thought it only polite that I invite him to the celebrations. I thought he might refuse, but when I mentioned your name—that you are my dear wife's sister—he accepted the invitation.'

Yes, Eve thought, feeling as if a great weight had been dropped on her, and taking a larger sip of her sherry than intended, he would.

Having come to the end of a piece, Sarah swivelled round to look directly at her younger sister. 'The Earl of Levisham? Goodness! He sounds very grand. Have the two of you met, Eve?'

'Yes,' Eve mumbled, having no wish to get into a conversation about her illustrious and infuriating neighbour. 'A couple of times.' A quiet came over the room as everyone looked at each other, eyebrows raised, waiting for Eve to elaborate. Instead, she got to her feet, smoothing down her skirts. 'If you don't mind, I'll go and look in on Christopher. What with all this excitement and being engulfed with so many cousins, Nessa might be having trouble settling him down.'

'There's no need,' Sarah was quick to say, wanting to hear what Eve had to say about Lord Levisham. 'Christopher was fast asleep when I went to check on Celia.'

Celia was Sarah's daughter and closer to Christopher's age than any of his cousins. Already they had formed a close bond. Eve gave Sarah a tight smile. 'I'd still like to check on him.'

She quickly made her exit, breathing a sigh of relief that she'd managed to escape their questions. Thrown into a turmoil of agitation, and wishing to be alone, she went to her room. Though she hadn't seen or heard from Lord Levisham since their angry altercation at Netherthorpe, she had reacted to John's news that he was to attend the next day's celebrations far too quickly for comfort.

He was popular and handsome, and those who didn't know any better might even think she was lucky that he had singled her out. She'd done her best to make it crystal-clear that she did not welcome his attention, but it would seem he hadn't understood. The past weighed heavy on her, and she knew how Marian worried about her. Eve would like to show her that she was capable of attracting a man if she put her mind to it. But that was pathetic. She would do better to show her that she was comfortable in her own skin.

Everyone was in high spirits when the day of the party arrived. At the appointed hour the house steadily began to fill with guests. The atmosphere became joyous as people greeted each other. Footmen moved among them, offering refreshment. Voices were harmonious, with laughter rising above the conversation. The hall and downstairs reception rooms to be used during the evening were decked with flowers and the dining room gleamed with brightness—of silver, crystal and pristine white table cloths.

Eve, who felt uneasy about the evening, was relieved that a large number of guests were present. Hopefully, with so many people milling about, she would escape having to converse with him…but somehow she doubted it.

Since his arrival in London and conscious that someone was out to kill him—the reason why still eluded him—Maxim had had no interest in partaking in society events until he encountered Sir John Portman at his club. On being introduced by an acquaintance of his, Sir John was most interested when he learned Lord Levisham was from Woodgreen and a close neighbour of his sister-in-law at The Grange.

By the end of a pleasant evening, and several glasses of liquor, Sir John issued him with an invitation to the party they were holding for their wedding anniversary. With no wish to turn down an invitation to an event where he would be sure to become reacquainted with the delightful Mrs Lansbury, he accepted.

The angry words they had exchanged had continued to burn inside Maxim since their parting at Netherthorpe. The thought of her would not leave him—like an itch he must scratch. Thinking of her, he was torn between torment and tenderness. When his hurt and anger had diminished enough and he was able to think more rationally, he reconsidered what had transpired between them. Remembering her reaction, when he had thought he was helping her, he ached with remorse. It mattered to him what happened to the beautiful, intelligent young widow who was rare and unspoiled, a woman who had succeeded in touching his heart—which was something all the other women had failed to do.

The wager he had made with Edward against his better judgement concerned him, and his conscience that he'd thought long since dead began to resurrect itself. Realising the enormity of what he'd done, he'd already begun to regret the wager the day after he'd agreed to it. How could he have agreed to seduce and dishonour a woman he found so full of goodness, who was trusting and candid with a combination of wisdom and naivety, and undeniably lovely? Eve Lansbury was above a mere dalliance. His mind spun in an inescapable vortex of guilt and self-hate. May God forgive him.

It was madness, and he hated himself with a virulence that nearly knocked the breath out of him.

For the first time in a long time, he had met a woman without guile. Her lovely face passed before his mind's eye, a face of much seriousness, with a ripe, opulent beauty that made his heart beat faster. Never in his wildest dreams had he imagined anyone like Eve Lansbury. What a lovely woman she was. She was artlessly sophisticated. For some peculiar reason that was quite beyond him, it mattered to him what she thought of him. He felt a great warmth and tenderness for this damaged woman. He knew what his immediate interest in her was, but the future was another matter for him.

It surprised him how desperate he was to make amends. Since meeting her he'd been like a peach split open, the soft heart of him all exposed. Several days after their parting, he had ridden to The Grange to apologise for his unmannerly treatment of her, only to be told she had left to stay with relatives for an indefinite period.

Returning to Netherthorpe, he had decided not to pursue Eve Lansbury with the intention of seducing her. She would be in no danger from him. To hell with Edward and his wager, he had thought as he'd urged his horse on. It was off. Edward could live in the Dower House.

He was determined to endear himself to Eve Lansbury by being charm personified, if necessary, even if it meant subduing all his natural instincts. So two reasons had brought him to town. One was to see his solicitor and several business associates, and the other was to seek out Eve Lansbury. And where that lady was concerned there remained tension inside him. This chance must not be squandered.

Arriving at Portman House in Kensington, he was greeted warmly by Sir John and Lady Portman. A large assortment of guests milled about, drinking champagne as they wandered into the room where dancing was in progress. When he enquired after her sister, Lady Portman told him that she would join them presently when she had settled young Christopher down for the night.

There were at least a hundred guests socialising in the parlours and huge drawing room, where the furniture had been removed and the carpet drawn back for the dancing. The strum of the musicians' instruments could be heard above the chatter of the guests. The night was warm and tall French windows were open onto the terrace and the lantern-lit garden beyond.

Mingling with the guests, elegant, wealthy, friends and acquaintances of his host, the ladies with glittering jewels draped round slender necks and dangling from earlobes, Maxim took a glass from the salver of a circulating servant. Of course, by now everyone knew who he was and were impatient to be introduced. His arrival among them had caused quite a stir. It wasn't often that a man with so colourful a background appeared among them and, if the reaction of the guests was an indication, he was as popular as he had ever been. He moved among them with confident ease and assurance. He conversed politely, seeming to give them his full attention, but the major part of it was concen-

trated on the door as he waited for the sister-in-law of
Sir John Portman to make an appearance.

Sauntering towards the French windows, he stepped
into the shadows on the terrace. With one shoulder non-
chalantly propped against a pillar, from his vantage
point he idly watched the crowd through the French
window as he waited.

And then, as if he were seeing a dream, there she
was. Everyone paused in their conversations and
glanced her way. His gaze was drawn to her. Pleasure
lit his eyes, followed by pure masculine admiration
as his gaze drifted over her. The effect of seeing her
again surprised him.

She was unaware of his presence, and he watched
her stop to converse with some guests. He was momen-
tarily dazzled by her. Was this the young woman he had
met at The Grange, the young woman who had faced
up to him with so much anger because he had dared to
go above her head and pay her workers' wages?

Instead of wearing an unflattering dress, the young
woman now wore an empire-style gown of sapphire
blue, with a scooped neckline accentuating her firm
breasts. He was content to watch as, with regal poise,
this proud, striking young woman, with large luminous
eyes beneath thick, dark lashes and exotically winged
brows, moved serenely from group to group, untouched
by the noise and bustle all around her.

Observing her with the impartiality of a connoisseur, looking for flaws that others would miss, he
found only perfection as she passed before his gaze
with an elegance that drew the eye. Her back was

straight, her head tilted proudly. Her colouring was more vivid in this glamorous setting, Maxim thought. Her hair was the same vibrant golden-brown, glistening with innumerable shades beneath the light of the chandeliers. A single string of pearls lay against her throat in perfect complement to the gown. Her smile was dazzling and she seemed to bestow it on every one of those present—and, did he imagine it, or did everyone resume talking with more animation than before? He smiled. Eve Lansbury could lift the mood of a room simply by walking into it.

Maxim's whole sum and substance became concentrated on the slender young woman as she drifted about like a butterfly. She had an individuality that had drawn him towards her from the start, an individuality that had nothing to do with her beauty or her creamy complexion. She also possessed a subdued strength and subtleness that gave her an easy, almost naïve elegance she was totally unaware of. There was nothing demure about her. Where other young ladies would keep their eyes cast modestly down, Eve Lansbury showed no such restraint, which had much to do with the independent life she led and the fact that she was a widow and a mother.

On reflection, he thought he was right—she belonged in beautiful gowns, he decided. They suited her far better than the sombre clothes she wore at The Grange. He continued to stand in the shadows, admiring the alluringly beautiful woman, and far more intrigued by the indefinable presence that made her stand out so clearly from the rest. And then, as if she sensed his presence, she glanced towards the French doors and began making her way towards him.

## Chapter Five

Eve arrived downstairs after making sure Christopher was settled for the night, and after greeting several of the guests already assembled her gaze sought out Robert. Her tall, handsome young brother, attired in his fine evening dress, had stepped out onto the terrace and was now in conversation with Lord Levisham, hanging onto his every word as he was regaled by his exploits in Spain. As usual that particular gentleman's appearance set off uncomfortable feelings—a mixture of irritation mingled with an odd sort of longing and anger, and the disconcerting ability to be natural.

From the moment she'd known he was to be present she had been unable to think of anything else. She was conscious of a knot forming in the pit of her stomach. In a moment she would have to face him again and the prospect filled her with a volatile mixture of emotion, excitement and dread. There was comfort to be gained from the knowledge that she was dressed in attractive attire and she wondered what he would think. Angry with herself for caring even fleetingly, she lifted her head imperiously.

Robert's face was a little flushed with the effects of the wine and the exertions of dancing with a pretty young woman, whose smiles had been for him only. Like all her sisters, Eve was proud of her brother, their parents' last child. They wished him well in his chosen career, yet they all shared an agony of apprehension that he would have to go to war.

Eve stood and watched them. The young woman who had been the focus of his attention earlier ventured outside to claim him and they disappeared to enjoy another dance together. Taking a deep breath, Eve stepped onto the terrace. Her eyes riveted on Lord Levisham, fastidiously tailored in black evening attire. He was just as supremely powerful and splendidly and unbearably handsome as she remembered. She watched as a slow, lazy smile crept across his face as she started towards him.

'Good evening, Lord Levisham,' she said coolly. 'Forgive me if I appear surprised. I didn't expect to see you here this evening—although, come to think of it, my brother-in-law did mention that he'd encountered you at his club.' The roguish smile he gave her made her heart somersault.

'A pleasant surprise, I hope.'

'That remains to be seen. I am merely surprised, that is all.'

'You look ravishing, by the way. The dress you are wearing is far more flattering than the dresses you wore on our previous encounters.'

Resentment hardened her expression as she smoothed the silk of her gown. It was a gown she seldom wore—a vivid sapphire-blue, delicately embroidered in the same colour thread. She'd had it since she'd been married to Matthew but had never had occasion to wear it since. 'The dress I am wearing tonight would not be suitable for the work I do at The Grange. What are you doing here?' she asked, her look deliberately cold and ungracious. 'I had no idea you were acquainted with my brother-in-law.'

'I'm not. I have business with my solicitor so I had to come to town. I made your brother-in-law's acquaintance at his club, of which we are both members. When he knew that you and I are neighbours, he kindly invited me.'

'And of course you accepted.'

'Naturally. I couldn't turn down an opportunity to see you again.' He spoke with slow deliberation and the corners of his lips twitched with amusement. His eyes gleamed at hers as he added softly, 'It is my first society event since returning from Spain. I am happy to report it far exceeds my expectations and I am glad I came.'

Eve turned aside, tossing him a cool glance askance. 'There are several attractive ladies present for you to ogle, Lord Levisham.'

'It might look like that, but in truth I was watching just one.'

'My sister has set a room aside for gaming. It's attracted quite a few gentlemen. You might find it more enjoyable than making polite conversation with the ladies.'

'Not at all. I enjoy talking to you. Would you honour me with the next dance? Or the one after that? Or book a dance in advance at the next event you attend?' He smiled. 'I know I must be coming across as desperate, but too bad. I don't want this ill feeling between us to continue.'

She shrugged. 'Thank you, but I don't care to dance—and I don't think I shall be attending any more social functions while I am in London. You'd better ask someone else.'

'I am asking you. Had I wanted to dance with someone else, I would have asked them. How about the next time you are in town?' He smiled ruefully but she didn't respond in kind. Her expression was unfathomable but, when she finally spoke, there was no room for misunderstanding.

'When Robert is settled at Greenwich, I intend returning to The Grange.'

'And to your work.'

'Of course. It is what I do.'

'Of course it is, but the awful consequences of your husband's death do not have to last a lifetime. Anyway, I just wanted to apologise. How you live your life is entirely up to you.'

'Up to me?' She gave him a weary look and there was a slight droop to her shoulders. 'It's not the life I would have chosen, if that's what you think.'

'No, I realise that.'

'It's obvious you don't have children, otherwise you

would know that one's whole world revolves around them, that nothing else matters. You give them life and it's your responsibility to take care of them until they are old enough to take care of themselves.'

'When I am fortunate to have offspring of my own then I imagine I will be the same.' He sighed, moving closer. 'I put it badly. I'm not always good with words—too long in the company of soldiers, talking to men all day. I don't want to spar with you,' he said with quiet sincerity. 'That's the last thing I want to do. I should not have taken it upon myself to retrieve your necklace and pay the workers. Assume I meant well, even if it didn't seem like it at the time.'

'Yes, I see. You should know by now that I make my own rules, Lord Levisham.'

'I realise that, but the thought of you striving to fetch in the harvest made me anxious in a way I can't explain. All I knew at the time was that I wanted to help in some way.'

'I'm touched and grateful, but you should not have paid them.'

'No, I shouldn't. I did not express myself in the way I would have liked to. I already know you are an exceptionally able and independent woman in an age when the status of a woman counts for very little.'

Tilting her head sideways, Eve gave him a hard look. 'I suspect you share the failing of most men and suffer from the masculine delusion that women do not have heads for business. That they should be guided by the superior knowledge of men and have no opinion of their own.'

He laughed. 'Heaven forbid I should think that and, if I did, I would not dare say so to you. I have never met a female who would want to do what you do, but I do like a woman who is not afraid to speak her mind.'

'Good.'

He gazed at her for a long moment, his devilish, sensual mouth turning upward in the faintest of cynical smiles. 'You are an extremely forward, quite outrageous and outspoken young woman, Mrs Lansbury.'

'If you got to know me, you would have to become used to my manner and the way in which I deal with people.' She met his gaze candidly. 'Do you not approve of me, Lord Levisham—of what I do?'

'It is not for me to approve or disapprove of what you do.'

'Nevertheless, you are quick to voice your opinion.'

'That is my nature and my right. I have already decided that you are a hard-working and very unconventional young woman.'

'I am concerned with none of that. I do detest all the restrictions of the social system that enslaves women.'

'And I imagine you would like to redress the wrongs of our misguided society. Are you so uninhibited by the prejudice of class that you would break the mould of convention that has encased women for centuries?'

'I despise convention—as you will have gathered. I live very much as I please, but without causing offence to those I love and those who love me.'

'And, to add to all that, you rarely dance.' His gaze captured hers. 'Will you step out of your self-imposed restrictions and do me the honour of dancing with me?'

Eve stared at him. Those glowing eyes burned into hers, suffusing her with a growing aura of warmth. 'I told you. I do not care to dance.'

'That's a pity. After all, this is a social occasion and that is what people do at social occasions—they dance. You do dance?'

Her smile was feral. 'Of course I do. I prefer not to.'

'You distress me, Mrs Lansbury.' His mouth twisted in a lightly mocking grin. 'You give me no grounds to hope for better things.'

'At last you have something right.'

He laughed briefly. 'You seem to take special delight in taunting me. But I am not to be deterred. There isn't a woman alive who doesn't like to dance—and I do not believe you are any different.' His mouth curved in a faint, cynical smile. 'Why are you so stubborn? When you came out here, willing to risk yourself alone in my company, you have to expect certain consequences.'

'Do I? Such as?'

'I think it is time I adopted a different approach through the thick mire of our disagreement. It's time I tried a little persuasion of a different kind.' His eyes pinned hers and held them.

'Persuasion? What kind of persuasion?'

Maxim noted the pulse beating in the long curve of her throat before his gaze settled on her lips. 'A kiss?'

She drew a long, steadying breath and slowly expelled it. She hesitated before answering, her magnificent eyes searching his deeply. 'Are you being serious? You presume too much on the strength of a slight acquaintance.'

He gave her a rather tight smile. 'You forget the time we spent together sharing confidences, Mrs Lansbury, when we sat beneath a tree and were content in each other's company.'

'No,' she said softly, remembering how happy she had been for the time they had sat beneath that tree. 'I am willing to consider putting the disagreement behind us, but I do not trust my heart and mind to withstand the barrage of your kind of persuasion. Anything of a more intimate nature is out of the question.'

His expression was one of mock-disappointment. 'I should have known that kind of teasing wouldn't go down well, especially since our relationship has yet to recover its former warmth. Nevertheless, do I detect in the softening of your behaviour some glimmer of hope for a much more pleasurable understanding between us in the future?'

'It is possible.'

He smiled at her, but his smile wasn't returned. Before he could flounder any deeper into the mire, she turned away and looked inside the room at the people dancing.

'You can have that dance now, if the offer still stands.'

'But I thought you said…'

'I've changed my mind.'

Maxim was more than happy to oblige. What was more, the dazzling, captivating smile she suddenly favoured him with was worth any amount of trouble he'd taken to come to London.

\* \* \*

The musicians were playing a waltz. No one could fail to notice when Lord Levisham led Eve onto the dance floor and drew her into his arms. He was totally unaware of himself or the effect he might produce on those gathered in the room. Eve had the thought that he was like a large, predatory hawk in the midst of a gathering of tame, colourful peacocks. They parted for him as if he were royalty. There was something in his mien that made people give him space.

He slid his hand about Eve's slender waist and, capturing her hand and drawing her close, swung her into the dance. The unbelievable pleasure of his touch, of being in his arms, took her completely by surprise. But, as light as his grip was, she felt the steel beneath.

He was a superb dancer and moved with a lithe, athletic grace. He whirled her around and she seemed to soar with the melody, marking their progress with an effortless glide over the floor. She gazed at him admiringly, liking the way his superbly tailored black coat clung to his splendid shoulders. His face had lost some of the tan he had acquired in Spain, but it was still darker than that of any other man present and, against his gleaming black hair, his pristine white shirt and neck cloth stood out in sharp contrast.

A disturbing awareness of his closeness—of the warmth of his hand at her waist, the strength of his fingers holding hers—intruded into her thoughts. Everything was forgotten as she was whirled around in time to the music by a man who danced with the elegance and easy grace of someone well trained. There was a quiet sense of power in his movements. Trying to concentrate on her steps, Eve glanced at him. His face was expressionless, but there was something in his eyes, and to her horror she felt herself blush as if she were a young debutante at her first dance.

Lord Levisham bent his head, giving the impression to the matrons and dowagers clustering the edges of the dance floor that he was paying her an intimate compliment. Eve noted with a great deal of irritation that each one of her sisters' eyes were bright with interest behind the cover of their fans. She was all too conscious of Lord Levisham's dark, enigmatic presence as he held her in his arms, and of the fact that the eyes of all the gathering must be fixed on them at that moment.

'We have an audience,' Lord Levisham murmured as he whirled her past a group of ladies.

'They are my sisters,' Eve explained crossly. 'I'm used to stares and whispers. I can well imagine the questions that will come later.'

Lord Levisham laughed softly. 'Then give them something to talk about and hold up your head. Look into my eyes as if you like me and smile.' He arched a sardonic brow, perfectly composed, aware of the interest they were attracting. 'You may even flirt with me a little, if you so wish.'

Eve looked at him, utterly confused by his appearance at the celebrations and not knowing what he wanted of her. Had he come because he was sorry for what he'd done and hoped to make amends? Unable to understand him, she searched his sultry eyes, resenting his easy arrogance at assuming that she would be ready to fall at his feet as if nothing untoward had happened between them. Not at any price would she consent to be treated so.

'And if I don't?' she said stiffly in response to his remark, rebellion stirring in the depths of her dark eyes.

'Pretend.' His firm arm tightened about her waist, forcing her into an awareness of his lithe body of which Eve was aware, knowing he was perfectly alive to the effect it was having on her when he held her in his arms.

'I can't pretend.'

'I'm sure you can if you try. I watched you earlier when you greeted the guests. Look at me like those doting swains were looking at you when you spoke to them. Or have you used up all your smiles on them?'

'Of course not, but at least they were civil, their remarks flattering.'

'Every man resorts to flattery when there's something they want from a beautiful woman. Don't be deceived when they shower you with pretty compliments and speeches. They're all after only one thing.'

'The gentlemen you speak of are Marian and John's guests. They are polite and charming.'

'And no doubt they told you that you are the most beautiful woman here tonight.'

Eve noticed an irritating spark of mischief dancing in his eyes, and she sensed he was playing with her. 'I beg you not to mock me, Lord Levisham.'

The mischief disappeared from his eyes and his expression above the snowy whiteness of his neck cloth became serious.

'Mock you? You are mistaken if you think that. I would neither mock nor offend someone I hold in such high regard as yourself. You, Mrs Lansbury, are so much at variance and a complete contradiction in terms of appearance. Not only are you beautiful, but you also have a spirit I admire. You have a strong, wilful determination which belies your outward appearance.'

'My word. I did not expect that.'

'No? Then allow me to finish. I admire you greatly. I admire your forthright character and strength of mind. If you had been born a man, without the restrictions imposed on your sex, I believe you would achieve anything you so desired.'

Eve was filled with astonishment—he never failed to surprise her. She stared at him, her eyes wide in her flushed face, more than a little surprised by what he had said. In the depths of his eyes, which rested upon her as boldly as ever, Eve saw something relentless and challenging. She looked away, trying to clear her mind of the warm, intoxicating haze his nearness inspired.

'You—you have to be jesting,' she murmured.

'I am not jesting. I never jest about serious matters. Whenever we meet, you always succeed in getting on the wrong side of my character. No woman has ever done that. As a man you would make a formidable adversary. A man would be proud to do battle with such a worthy opponent.'

As he continued to whirl her around in the dance, Eve was at a complete loss for words. She told herself that, despite the changes in his character she had discovered, he was still arrogant and conceited, the kind of man she disliked most. Yet he was unlike any man she had ever known, and she found herself drawn to him against her will. He had succeeded in making a definite impression on her which was both stimulating and exciting.

But she should be warned. She already suspected he was a man adept at getting what he wanted, that he was a man of power, and she sensed an element of danger in becoming too well-acquainted with him.

His lips curved in a smile, his eyes capturing hers. 'So, if those gentlemen told you that you are the most beautiful woman here tonight, then I have to say that I agree with them—but don't let the compliment go to your head.'

She laughed softly, unable to remain cross with him. 'I won't.'

He held her gaze without blinking. The admiration in his eyes was unmistakable. She was flattered and alarmed by her response to him, by the dangerous stirring in her blood. Was she seeing a different side to him? He was surprising her all the time. A large part of his charm lay in the way he gave her his undivided attention, his air of distraction suddenly gone. No doubt he was like that with all the women.

'So there is hope that you will forgive me?' He smiled ruefully.

It wouldn't take an awful lot of trying, not that it was impossible. His eyebrows rose and he looked at her in speculation. The truth was that it was hard to go on being angry with someone when they were holding you in their arms. It was much easier when you were alone, brooding on your grievances. Looking into his eyes, she thought what a curious and fascinating man he was. There were so many conflicting sides to his nature that astonished her. It was clear to her now that she had been quite wrong in her earlier assertions and was mature enough to admit it.

'I might be persuaded. We shall have to see. Although, it seems I owe you an apology. I had no right to judge you. I am sorry if I offended you.'

His gaze settled on her upturned face. 'And I too am sorry.'

'You are forgiven.'

'You must believe that it wasn't deliberate. It was never my intention to cause you distress. I never for one second thought you would take offence.'

Eve met his gaze, hearing his sincerity. Her expression became less stiff. She observed him for several seconds in silence. 'I believe you, Lord Levisham. Consider it forgotten.'

'Maxim.'

She stared at him. 'Pardon?'

'I would like you to call me Maxim.'

'I do not think that would be appropriate—in fact, it would be highly irregular—but "Lord Levisham" is such a mouthful.'

'There you are, then. You have my permission to call me Maxim.'

'That is generous of you.'

He grinned down at her. 'I have my good points.'

'If you say so,' she said, laughing softly. 'Why, even scoundrels must have their good points.'

'Then have I managed to vindicate myself to you—just a little?'

'A little, despite your previous transgressions.'

'I do my best.'

'It wasn't your fault. You thought you were trying to help and perhaps my reaction was extreme.'

'I am sure you had good reason—although, having experienced the volatile nature of your temper and the quickness of your tongue at first hand, I shall take more care in the future.'

'I did you an injustice. I'm sorry.'

'And will you call me Maxim?'

'Since I am the unconventional type, very well—Maxim.'

'Thank you. Are you going to grant me permission in turn to use your Christian name?'

'I have a feeling that if I don't you will use it anyway.'

'I take it that's a yes?'

She nodded. 'Very well.'

Eve was intensely aware of her gloved hand in his, of the closeness of their bodies as they danced on the now crowded floor beneath the glare of hundreds of candles. It was sensual, and she found herself wondering what it would be like for Lord Levisham to make love to her. Heat flooded her body, and it was suddenly difficult to breathe. She tried to concentrate on the dance, but it only made her more aware of him, the natural movement of his body as she followed his lead.

The waltz reached its conclusion and Maxim led her off the dance floor. Eve was aware of something new between them—an accord, an understanding. She was also aware of the intrigue swirling about them. They separated when John came to whisk Lord Levisham away to introduce him to some of his friends, and Eve circulated among the guests.

The evening was turning out to be a splendid affair, which was all down to Marian. The tables in the large dining room groaned beneath the weight of all manner of delicious dishes on white damask table cloths edged with the finest Honiton lace, silver cutlery and white crockery with a narrow margin of gold, the best and most expensive English china. Colourful flowers that decorated the room and the tables added a light and graceful effect.

A large part of Eve's time was occupied talking to the guests, but she was aware of Maxim throughout. Later, tired of making small talk, Eve's eyes sought out Maxim of their own volition. When she couldn't find him, disappointment washed over her...but then he was there, standing close behind her. She instantly felt his presence as if it were a tangible force. She even recognised the elusive sharp scent of his cologne. Her heart gave a leap and missed a beat. His breath, when he spoke, was warm on the back of her neck.

'Can I get you something to drink? Champagne... lemonade?'

'Oh, champagne, I think. With all my sisters' children claiming my attention and being drawn into their frantic games, I'm awash with lemonade.'

'Then champagne it is.'

Sarah immediately pounced on her, impatient to know all there was to know about Eve's relationship with the most illustrious guest present.

'What a dark horse you are, Eve. Earlier you would have us believe you only had a passing acquaintance with Lord Levisham and yet you have been within each other's sights all evening. It has been noted.'

'Really, Sarah, I don't know what you're talking about.'

'Come, now, you're not so innocent you cannot tell when a gentleman is interested in you. He's charming and devilishly handsome. It's clear you are the reason he is here tonight. One only has to observe the two of you together to see he is quite taken with you. He's certainly handsome.' She sighed almost dreamily. 'I do so like handsome men.'

'I know. That's why you married Charles,' Eve commented teasingly.

'Oh, no,' Sarah said, chuckling softly as she glanced across the room to where her husband was in conversation with Marian. 'Charles is sensible, reliable and conscientious, but also sensitive, gentle and idealistic. *That* is why I married him.'

'I agree; Charles is all those things. He is a paragon among men.'

'Yes, he is, and reasonably handsome—but not quite in Lord Levisham's class. He will have an unenviable task on his hands, taking over from his brother.'

'Indeed he will.'

'And then there is his military background. It all adds to his mystery and charm, I suppose.'

Eve glanced at her. 'Does it?'

'Mmm, I think so. Lord Levisham does have a certain reputation with the ladies—so I've heard. Unless being a soldier has changed him. The ladies used to positively pander to him, and no one dared give him the cut. Of course, the aristocratic mamas on the look out for suitable husbands for their darling daughters considered him highly suitable, and on the times he came home on leave tried to lure him into their clutches, but he always declined their invitations. Have a care, Eve. He must be thirty or older—I don't know. And, now he's home for good, he might decide it's about time he settled down and filled his noble house with his offspring.'

'I do realise that, and I'm not about to make a fool of myself, Sarah.'

'Of course not. But, after what you suffered when you were married to Matthew, you will be careful, will you not, Eve?'

Eve sighed, seeing Lord Levisham making his way back to her carrying two glasses of champagne. Like all her sisters, Sarah, only two years older than Eve, loved her dearly and was speaking out of concern. But why must she be so obtuse? After all, being an older sister, she must realise that with Eve having been through a bitter marriage, and experiences at the hands of her husband no woman should have to endure, it had made a woman of her. She did not welcome bitter reminders of her past.

'Please don't worry about me, Sarah. I'm no longer a vulnerable child in need of protection. I may not be as worldly wise as you or any of my dear sisters, but I am not stupid.'

'I can't help it, Eve. I hate to think of you all alone at The Grange. I will try and visit you more. I promise.'

Deeply touched, Eve hugged her. They had always been close as children and then into their youth—brushing each other's hair, praying together, sleeping in the same room and whispering secrets in the darkness, always aware that one day they would be torn apart by marriage.

'I wish you would, Sarah, but I am well aware of the realities of life. You have nothing to worry about where Lord Levisham is concerned.'

'Well, I'm sure you know what you're doing—and there's nothing stuffy or conventional about him. You know, I'm only speaking to you about this for your own good, don't you, Eve? We only want your happiness, as our dear mother would have wanted if she had lived. Just imagine, Eve,' she whispered as Lord Levisham came within earshot. 'If anything should come of your relationship, you could be rich and a countess! How I would envy you.'

Eve laughed at her sister's exuberance. 'Stop it, Sarah. You let your imagination run away with you. Nothing like that will happen. Be assured of it.'

Sarah hovered by Eve's side until she had been introduced to Lord Levisham then gave herself up to her husband's demands that she dance with him. Eve watched them go before giving her attention to Maxim.

'Shall we step outside to drink our champagne?' he suggested. 'It is quieter out there. And perhaps a walk through the garden—now we have declared a truce. Agreed?'

She looked at him a long moment and indecision flashed across her face She glanced at the assembled company, considering the propriety of taking a stroll in the garden alone with him. His eyes were gently enquiring, and Eve was intrigued by this confounding man. Never had she met a man who perplexed her more. He smiled and she felt her own mouth begin to follow, feeling her antipathy towards him melting all the time. Her indecision turned to resolution. The arrogance she had come to know so well was gone. However, suspecting this to be only a temporary state of affairs, she was determined to make the most of it.

'Yes—yes, of course,' she replied. 'It is agreed.' With so many guests milling around, she was feeling the heat of the house.

It was not without a certain pleasure that Eve accompanied Maxim onto the terrace. They stood at the stone balustrade, looking out over the lantern-lit garden. The air was soft and languid, the sweet scent of roses and honeysuckle hung heavily. Myriad stars shimmered in the dark-blue velvet sky. The moon was a pale silver orb in the east.

'Have you learned anything about the person who tried to shoot you?' Eve asked.

Placing his glass on a wrought-iron table, Maxim leaned lazily against the balustrade and looked at her.

'No, nothing. I'm still as bemused about what happened as I was then.'

'But, you are careful.'

'Of course.'

'And did you leave your cousin at Netherthorpe?'

'No. Edward is here in London. I've thought about what you said about him being behind it but, having known him all his life, I have no reason to believe he would do me harm.'

'I sincerely hope you are right. It is not for me to speculate.'

'I do not suspect my cousin of being behind it— the reason is too obvious—but I will be keeping my eye on him. I do not fear Edward, nor will I hesitate to distance myself from him if he makes a nuisance of himself.'

'I saw you speaking to Robert earlier. No doubt he was sounding you out about the military.'

'He was. He's a fine young man—he'll make a good soldier.'

'I'm sure he will. Robert has qualities and failings necessary to make an excellent soldier. He's clever, resourceful, cunning and not averse to taking the occasional risk if he believes the situation is worth it.'

Maxim grinned. 'And clearly has a sister who adores him.'

She laughed. 'That too.'

He saw the consternation in her eyes. 'You are concerned about him.'

'I shall miss him. He's been a tower of strength to me these past months. Robert is the youngest of us all. Of course I am concerned—even though he is now a grown man, old enough to decide for himself what he wants to do with his life, and soldiering is all he's always wanted. I'm worried he might be sent to the Peninsular.'

'I can understand your concern. Try not to worry too much. By the time he's done his training, the war in the Peninsula might be over.'

'I sincerely hope so. But there will always be another war somewhere to fight.'

Maxim smiled. 'If only the world were a different place—everyone perfect—everything would be much simpler. I think, Eve, that you need cheering up. I am going to suggest taking you for a ride in my carriage if you are agreeable.'

Her eyebrows rose with surprise. 'That is extraordinarily considerate of you. What—now?'

'Tomorrow. Would that suit?'

'I—I thank you for your kind invitation, but—I—I—'

'I do want you to come—the reason for my invitation being that it would give me the chance of proving to you that I have some redeeming qualities.'

There was no mistaking that he was in earnest. Eve felt a stirring of warmth in her heart and, not for the first time, a dawning of respect. He was making it extremely difficult for her to refuse his invitation. 'You don't have to prove anything to me.'

'But I believe I do.'

'Why should you? Why should you feel it necessary to have such sentiments?'

'I realise now that my manner must have seemed impertinent and presumptuous to you and, having a tendency to do things without restraint, I hope that eventually you might view my character in a more amiable light.'

'You don't have to do that.' She looked at him steadily. 'I do not understand you. You are quite surprising.'

'If you knew me better, you would know I am full of odd surprises,' he said, his gaze caressing her face and settling on her moist mouth. 'I am paving the way with good intentions for the future. You see, leaving the army and taking up my new position at Netherthorpe, my life and associates are going to be somewhat different from what they have been.'

Eve was silent, declining to ask if she could be named among his new associates. It was not without a certain wild pleasure that she hoped she would be, although she would not allow herself to think of him in any light other than as an acquaintance—pleasant or otherwise remained to be seen.

'Then I wish you well. As for myself, everything will continue as it has before.'

Maxim arched a sleek black brow quizzically. 'Taking care of everyone at The Grange has left you little time for enjoyment—and romance.'

His voice was low and seductive, yet not without a hint of teasing. His eyes were persuasive and compelling, and he was standing close, so close that Eve's eyes were drawn to his; insects played lazily around them both.

'Romance!' She smiled a slow, teasing smile, while giving him a sidelong glance from beneath her lashes. His tone was light, teasing almost, and she was surprised to discover that she did not mind that she was flattered by it. In fact, the gentle, flirtatious play with words was quite new to her. She found herself warming to the attentions of a man again, a handsome man with wickedly dancing eyes, and she wanted to savour all the delights she had denied herself for so long.

She could understand her physical attraction to him. What she could not understand, and what worried her, was this strange, magnetic emotional pull she felt towards him. There were times he spoke to her in that deep, compelling voice of his, or looked at her with those silver-grey eyes, when she almost felt as if he were quietly reaching out to her and inexorably drawing her closer and closer to him.

'I don't remember saying anything about romance.'

'No—but you must have encountered such a weakening state of affairs, surely?'

She sighed, letting her gaze drift over the garden. She'd known nothing of love. Her sisters had spoken of the sweet torment she would feel in her marriage bed. She had allowed herself to dream and to wonder what it would be like to be married to Matthew, how he would kiss her and tell her how she set his senses alight. After all, Matthew had been a handsome man with his broad shoulders and curling brown hair.

She'd soon discovered marriage was nothing like her sisters had told it would be. It had only taken the one night in her husband's bed for her to know that marriage wasn't what she had expected or wanted, and the sting of disappointment had been deep. Matthew was difficult. He would lie and dissemble. She'd been married just two months when she'd known she was to bear his child.

'No,' she said at length in answer to his question. 'At least, not that I've noticed. But you must have encountered it yourself to describe its effects. And if, as you say, it has such a debilitating effect on one, then I must strive to remain in control of my emotions at all times and keep my eyes wide open.'

He suppressed a smile. 'That is exactly the answer I would expect of a woman who is always forthright.'

'Does it offend you? Would you prefer it if I were all simpers and smiles?'

'Heaven forbid,' he said, moving closer to her. 'Now *that* is not in your nature. But I would very much like to kiss you, Eve—and I am sure you will not be disappointed.'

## Chapter Six

Eve didn't look away. She couldn't. All her senses were afire. His eyes held hers like a magnet, warm and liquid with desire. She saw what was in them and felt afraid and excited at the same time. A whirlpool of emotions rose and fell between them. Everything that surrounded them seemed to fade until she was only aware of his eyes. He was standing very close, looking down at her penetratingly.

The silence stretched between them, lengthening and becoming dangerous, but Eve could not move. Feeling herself to be in the grip of some powerful emotion, she did not want to move—even though it was an emotion that threatened to destroy her sensibilities and overwhelm her. Never had she been as aware of another human being as she was of Maxim Randall at that moment.

The moment was one which saw a heightening of both their senses. Maxim placed his hands on her upper arms and pulled her close, his hands gentle, controlled yet unyielding. His eyes darkened and his gaze dropped to her lips, moist and slightly parted. His closeness made Eve feel too vulnerable, but she was unable to move away. She caught her breath, able to feel the heat emanating from his body, to feel the power within him and the warmth of his breath on her upturned face.

'Then what are you waiting for?' she said softly, placing the palms of her hands on his chest.

When he lowered his head, she lost sight of his eyes and fixed her own on his lips. They brushed hers gently, testing their resilience, then, with the confidence that there would be a welcome, he covered her lips assuredly. The kiss almost sent her to her knees. Sensations she had never imagined overwhelmed her. The feel of him, the smell of him, sank into her bones. His lips began to move on hers, kissing her thoroughly and possessively, exploring every tender contour. She found herself imprisoned in a grip of steel, pressed against his hard, muscular length, her breasts coming to rest on his chest. Alternate waves seemed to run through her body, but there was also another, far more disturbing sensation.

Having been married to Matthew, Eve was not ignorant of the intimacies between a man and a woman, but she was totally innocent about the sort of warmth, the passion, Maxim was skilfully arousing in her, warmth that poured through her veins with a shattering explosion of delight. It was a kiss like nothing she could have imagined, a kiss of exquisite restraint.

Unable to think of anything but the exciting urgency of his mouth and warmth of his breath, Eve felt herself falling slowly into a dizzying abyss of sensuality. His hands glided restlessly, possessively, up and down her spine and the nape of her neck, pressing her tightly to his hardened body.

The kiss ended and he drew back a little without releasing her. 'Well, I am surprised. You are delectable, Mrs Lansbury—delectable and quite wonderful—and I want more of you.'

Before she could protest, he lowered his mouth to hers once more, taking her lips with gentle expertise that made her gasp. Stunned into silent quiescence, at first she froze at the initial shock of the renewed contact, then a sense of wonder stirred within her subconscious mind, rousing her to a dazzling awareness of what he was doing to her. The assault on her senses was immediate and immense as she caught the clean, masculine scent of him, the feel of him, the taste of him. Often she had dreamed of such a kiss, but the experience of it made those insubstantial dreams seem like shadows.

Divested of the anger that had fortified her before Maxim's appearance tonight, her body relaxed. Sliding her hands up over his chest to his shoulders, feeling his body's heat and vibrancy through his clothes, she unwittingly moulded her melting body to his. He kissed her long and lingeringly, a compelling kiss, his lips moving back and forth, exploring with slow, searching intensity, gentling imperceptibly. And beneath the demanding persuasion was an insistence that she kiss him back that was almost beyond denial, and a promise that if she yielded it would become something quite different. His kiss became more demanding, ardent and persuasive, a slow, erotic seduction. It was tender, wanting, his tongue sliding across her lips until she became lost in a wild and beautiful madness with blood beating in her throat and temples that wiped out all reason and will.

Any warning that her mind issued was stifled by the blood pounding in her ears and the shocking pleasure of being held in the arms of the man whom she had decided she would not allow to breach her self-control. His arm tightened, forcing her closer, while a large masculine hand curved round her nape, long fingers caressing soothing her flesh.

When he finally released her mouth, he lightly traced the curve of her lower lip with his forefinger. Each of them was aware of a new intensity of feeling between them, a new excitement. They stared at each other for a second of suspended time, which might as well have been an hour or two. Eve had a strange sensation of falling. She tried to think rational thoughts, but her body was alive to his presence. She looked up at him, at the dark, questioning eyes. She could not move. She heard her own voice come out of the darkness.

'Well,' he said, his warm breath caressing her lips. 'I am surprised, Mrs Lansbury. It is clear to me that you like being kissed. I suppose I should apologise for having allowed myself to get carried away—but that would be hypocritical, for I enjoyed kissing you.' When she didn't reply immediately, he grinned and murmured, 'Surely I cannot have rendered you speechless?'

'It certainly took my breath and, yes, I liked it very well,' she confessed, still drifting between total peace and a strange, delirious joy. At the same time a feeling of disquiet was creeping into her as her mind came from the nether regions of the universe to where it had fled. 'It's been a long time since I kissed anyone.'

'Then it was surely good, for being out of practice.'

'We—we had best go back inside,' she said, desperately looking for conversation, knowing they were both gripped by something they could not control.

'Do I see in your warming behaviour, in your response to my kiss, some glimmer of hope for a much more pleasurable understanding between us in the future? And do not deny what you feel, because I will not believe you.'

'I can't deny it,' she murmured, basking in the warmth of his smouldering gaze and the lazy smile that curved the firm, sensual mouth that had gently, then fiercely, explored hers. 'But it is too soon—too difficult and too complicated.'

'It doesn't have to be.' Tipping her chin up, he looked deeply into her eyes and said quietly, 'What do you think of my method of persuasion?'

Eve drew a long, steadying breath and slowly expelled it. She hesitated before answering, her magnificent eyes searching deeply into his. 'In truth, I do not trust my heart and mind to withstand the barrage of your persuasion.' Her feelings were nebulous, chaotic, yet one stood out clearly among all the others—desire. She had not wanted him to stop kissing her, and she was impatient for him to repeat the act. Something had happened to her while she had been in his arms, something quite splendid, daunting and exciting. For a moment she had forgotten everything in acute pleasure such as she had never experienced before.

They stood facing each other and, when she took a step away from him, he smiled. 'It's no use trying to pretend this does not exist.'

'What?'

'This—between us—you and me. It's there—has been from the beginning. You did not resist me when I kissed you, and you did kiss me back—quite passionately, I might add. Don't try to deny it.'

'I won't—I couldn't if I tried—but I have a feeling that by doing so I did not see the folly of it.'

'As to that, only time will tell.' Maxim glanced further along the terrace as couples began to drift out of the house. 'I'm happy to know we are in accord, but we'll have to discontinue our amorous interlude—unless you wish for an audience.'

'No, not in the least. I think I should go back inside. My sisters are likely to come looking for me. Should they find me out here alone with you, they will give me no peace.'

'So, you will come with me tomorrow?'

'Not tomorrow. Since the weather looks set to hold, Marian is arranging a picnic for us all in the park. It's a rarity for all the family to be together at one time and there will be plenty of room for the children to work off some of their energy. Marian is determined to make it a memorable occasion. Join us if you like. You will be most welcome, if you can bear to be in such close proximity to a hoard of noisy children tearing about.'

'Thank you,' he replied, smiling softly into his eyes. 'I might do that.'

Eve was content to stroll slowly back to the house close by his side, as if the kiss that had held them entranced in a spell had actually transformed them into lovers.

The rest of the evening passed in a kind of haze as Eve danced more than once with Maxim. She gazed at his handsome face as he whirled her around the floor, marvelling at how this man could cause such a tempest of feeling in her.

When Maxim had left and the guests began to drift away, Marian took Eve aside. 'Lord Levisham seems to have taken a liking to you, Eve.'

'We were just talking, that's all.'

'When you weren't dancing together, he was watching you a good deal. I noticed you spent a good deal of time together. You danced with no one else during the entire evening, and when not dancing you were on the terrace. You must have found a great deal to talk about.'

'Yes, we…we did.'

'Then I would say you have an admirer.'

Discomfited, Eve laughed nervously and turned away. 'You are mistaken, Marian. Lord Levisham is a neighbour—which is the only thing we have in common.'

Marian gave her a penetrating, knowing look that said she did not believe her, but said nothing else. Under her scrutiny, Eve felt so transparent, her face grew warm. Making her excuses, she slipped away, making her way to Christopher's room to check on him before she went to bed.

Alone at last, now that she was away from Maxim and the delicious afterglow of their kiss had diminished, she told herself she would have to take a grip on herself—try to think about this new turn in their relationship and what it would mean to both their futures. What was it about him that both incited such passion, angered her and left her feeling so exposed? His strength of character was intoxicating. She was filled with too many conflicting feelings about him.

Deep inside she was afraid—afraid of the power he was capable of wielding over her emotions. He roused such wanton feeling in her, she could scarcely believe it of herself. These thoughts caused her to think about her life, and her eyes darkened with despair as she contemplated a future in which she would be just as she was now. Surely there had to be more to life than this?

And yet she feared any deeper feelings that might develop for Maxim Randall. They were already too volatile, and she feared losing control. Yes, they might have shared a kiss, but in reality there could never be anything between them other than neighbourly friendliness. Anything else would be too hard, too complicated. They inhabited different worlds. Neither could cross to the other's and there was no middle ground.

But, for this short time, she felt the light from her past was fading, that a door to her future was opening and a new light, even brighter, was shining through.

As Maxim left the party, his thoughts were fully occupied with the woman he had just kissed and who had returned his kiss so passionately. He had admired her freshness, her spirit. She was everything he had known she would be, and much more. He was astounded to discover he wanted her with a fierceness that took his breath away. He was a man not unaccustomed to the attractions of a beautiful woman, having admired and loved many in a casual way. And, because of his looks and his wealth, he had never had to work very hard at getting them to part with their favours.

But he had never been impressed with emotions of the heart. Romantic love was something he was unaccustomed to, for he had never met a woman who had impressed him with her intellect, wit and dignity. A woman who possessed an equal agility of mind to his own, enough to make him want to spend the rest of his life with her. But that was before he had met Eve.

For the first time in his life he found himself responding to a woman's intelligent individuality, making him both captivated and intrigued—although she had made it quite plain that there were certain unfavourable aspects to his character that did not endear him to her in the slightest.

However, he did not believe this for one moment, and felt that her almost prim exterior hid a woman of passion. She drew him like a magnet. He wanted her, despite the cool reserve she always adopted whenever they were together, which he suspected was her way of fending off predatory males.

He meant to capture her, to turn this calm, proper young woman into a tantalising creature of desire who, when aroused, would breathe a sensuality she was not even aware of. And meant to take her to the very heights of passion.

The morning after the party, with a whole day stretching ahead of them, and still celebrating the fact that they were all together as a family, Marian instructed cook to pack some food into baskets. The early-autumn weather was cool, but not too cool that they couldn't enjoy themselves in the park. They settled themselves away from the crowds of people who poured into Hyde Park to enjoy the last of the autumn weather before the climate change of winter.

The usual cavalcade of handsome equipages that congregated daily in the afternoon paraded through, along with gentlemen mounted on fine thoroughbred horses, colourful and elaborately clad dandies and women in the best society, the carriage company some of the most celebrated beauties in London.

The sun was pleasantly warm. Christopher was in his element among so many cousins of various ages, who tickled and teased him constantly. Eve was amazed that he didn't tire of so much attention but he revelled in it.

Rugs and table cloths were laid on the grass and baskets unpacked. This was all so new and exciting for Christopher, who had never experienced anything like it. The occasion was quickly taking on a party atmosphere. He insisted on helping to unpack the food from the baskets.

'Are you enjoying yourself, Christopher?' Marian

asked, handing the child a pile of napkins to place on the cloths, smiling as he did so with serious concentration. This done, he looked up at her and nodded his head, his curls bouncing and his eyes alive with excitement.

'This is what your cousin Amanda does when she gives a tea party for her dolls,' she told him as Christopher helped himself to an iced cake and began to shove it into his mouth.

Eve smiled at him, bending down and straightening his coat. 'I don't know what I'm going to do with him when we have to leave London. He's got so used to you all.'

Marian smiled at the little boy. 'Then you will have to come back soon. You have a beautiful son, Eve,' she said with undisguised admiration. 'It seems so long since my three were toddlers.' Her eyes rested lovingly on her many nephews and nieces. 'Just look at them all—as boisterous and audacious as a barrow-load of monkeys. Our parents would have been so proud.'

Coming upon the family scene, it was the woman swathed in a delightful light-green dress with a wide sash of a deeper shade of green on whom Maxim's attention was focused. He looked at the sunlight glinting on the golden strands of her glorious wealth of hair that was twisted and secured in a heavy knot at her nape. Her attention was on the children, a serene smile on her face as her eyes settled on her son.

It was a happy family scene with everyone enjoying themselves. He thought how demure and yet bold

Eve looked. A little away from the rest, with her back against the trunk of a stout tree, she sat in the same pose as she had when he had come upon her watching the workers after the harvest at The Grange.

The children were in high spirits. The younger children played on the grass, tumbling and fighting in one long burst of energy, running about trying to catch one another, shrieking with laughter. Maxim could see it was a bit too much for Christopher, the youngest of them all. He found it hard to keep up with them but, determined not to be left behind, he persevered. Some of Eve's nieces and nephews, who considered themselves too old now for childish games, had formed a group away from the rest and chatted among themselves.

Maxim's deep, masculine voice in greeting caused Eve to look up. Her heart gave a traitorous leap at the sight of his darkly handsome face. His crooked smile and the sparkle in his translucent eyes almost sapped her strength. She dropped her lashes in sudden confusion as his voice wound around her senses like a coil of dark silk. When she had got out of bed that morning, the kiss they had shared had been uppermost in her mind in the cold light of day.

A slow smile of admiration swept across his face as he beheld the vision of her. His eyes unabashedly displayed his approval as his gaze ranged over the full length of her. Waving a greeting to the happy group, Maxim sat on the grass beside her. 'I think we've been here before,' he murmured.

She looked at him, returning his smile, thinking

how attractive he looked in his black breeches and dark-green coat revealing an ivory-embroidered silk waistcoat. 'I believe we have, although the scene is somewhat different. We have children to watch instead of the dancer and musicians. I really did not expect you to come today. I didn't think being with a large brood of excitable children would appeal to you.'

'Why not? I happen to like children very much—especially a little boy with curly hair,' he said as young Christopher, seeing his mother talking to a complete stranger, came to investigate. 'He's a lovely boy.'

'Yes, he is. I adore him. He's such a happy, bright child, and charged with energy. I can't think what I would do without him.'

'You look lovely, by the way. Such a rosy colour in your cheeks. Is that due to the London air or to the re-union with your sisters?'

'Probably a bit of both. I'm not used to having all this time on my hands and so much relaxation.'

Getting to his feet, Maxim held out his hand to her. 'Let's take a walk.' He glanced at her sisters and their respective husbands, their nurses and nannies, and nodded to them pleasantly. 'I will feel less conspicuous—if you understand what I mean.'

Eve took his hand and he pulled her to her feet. 'I do, and I quite agree. A walk would be very pleasant.'

They set off at a leisurely pace, heading away from the curious eyes of Eve's family. Not to be left behind, and wanting to spend more time with the kind stranger, Christopher toddled after them.

They walked in silence for a while, content to be

in each other's company. The impulses that attracted them to each other, binding them together, were growing stronger. They were surrounded by people but felt alone in each other's company, the place beneath the trees shutting out the rest of the world.

Eve enjoyed being with Maxim. She'd enjoyed their kiss the night before and she could not ignore the passion he had stirred in her. This, and her wayward thoughts, shocked her. She wanted more. She wanted him in her bed. She wanted him every way a woman might want a man. But it couldn't be. She must hold back her attraction. No good could come of a liaison with her illustrious neighbour, the Earl of Levisham.

'I envy you your family,' Maxim remarked quietly, glancing back at the happy group. 'Marian appears to keep you all in control.'

Eve laughed. 'Ever since our parents died, Marian has danced attention on our needs and wants, thinking of us before herself, always hanging on to the reins holding us together. She's been the rallying point of the family for a long time.'

They continued to talk of inconsequential things—the weather, the park and Robert's departure for Woolwich the next day. The conversation led to Maxim's family, and Edward's maternal Aunt Pauline whom he had yet to visit.

'I recall you telling me Edward lives with her.'

'Yes, yes he does.'

'And is your cousin an only child?'

He nodded. 'His mother died when he was small and his father, my own father's twin brother, died when he was ten years old and left him with nothing but bitter memories. He was a rogue with a list of transgressions as long as your arm—so long and so abhorrent to those with any kind of moral standards, he would make the Devil himself blush.

'I recall how exasperated and angry my own father would get when he heard of his transgressions. Edward's father was like an explosive force, leaping and dancing through life, quarrelling, drinking, gambling with reckless extravagance over the wildest reaches of London and the Continent, seducing women he had no right to until he was shot through the heart by an outraged husband.'

Eve stared at him, appalled. 'But that is terrible.'

'Yes, it was—ghastly beyond belief. I remember how deeply my father was affected by it. He was his brother after all—the two of them had been close once. He had a cruel streak—didn't care that he hurt people, or how many, as long as he got his way.'

Eve thought she had never heard such desolation, nor felt it. It was a story of pain and humiliation so great that she felt pity for all those who had been affected by it begin to melt her heart. 'And Edward? I sincerely hope he doesn't take after his father.'

'They are alike in some ways. I have tried to ignore what people say about him. As a boy and then a youth, he spent a good deal of his time at Netherthorpe. Unfortunately, Andrew had misgivings about him and often went out of his way to avoid him, whereas I felt sorry for him. I even tried persuading father to let him come and live at Netherthorpe—which infuriated

Andrew. Father wouldn't hear of it and dismissed my suggestion. Edward's father had caused him so much grief and he was convinced Edward was a chip off the old block. So he went to live with Aunt Pauline here in London, coming to Netherthorpe for holidays.'

'Was he resentful of you and your brother—because you had so much and he so little?'

He nodded. 'Maybe—but as I was growing up, and with my sights fixed on a military career, I'm ashamed to say I never gave much thought to Edward and what he might be going through.'

Walking along beside him, Eve saw his lean, hard face bore a world of untold suffering as he spoke about his family. 'And now? Are you any closer to Edward now you are home?'

His eyes darkened with sadness for a moment, and then he shook his head. 'I would like to say yes, but I don't think so. I am aware as never before that he has some of his father's less noble characteristics, except that Edward is clearer of head and not given to his father's blustering and rages. Aunt Pauline is fond of him, and has done her best, but she is concerned about his outlandish behaviour and the endless series of scandals that seem to follow him through life.'

Eve stopped walking. He paused in front of her, looking down into her face upturned to him. 'Maxim, I have asked you this question once before... No doubt you will say it doesn't concern me, and you would be right, but there are times when I don't behave or express myself as a lady is supposed to.'

'Feel free to express yourself in any way you like

when you are with me,' Maxim said, his sensuous lips curving in a slow smile.

'I can be frightfully blunt,' Eve muttered softly, looking up into his dark face, which was relaxed into a noble, masculine beauty that drew her gaze like a magnet.

'So can I,' he replied. 'Now, what is the question you wanted to ask me?'

'Now you've had time to reflect on what happened to you when you were shot, do you really think Edward had nothing to do with your brother's death?'

Maxim became thoughtful, his eyes going beyond her. After a moment, he said, 'In all honesty, I don't know.'

There was a world of feelings in those words that struck deep into Eve's heart. She began to understand how difficult it had been for him to live with what had happened to his brother. He knew she sympathised and understood the horror and the torment he had endured. It had been so hard for him to tell her these things about Edward's father and the loss of his brother. She felt that, where Edward was concerned, he was having to face his demons—that Edward might have had more to do with his brother's death than he had been comfortable with considering.

'You told me your brother wasn't close to Edward, that they were never friends. Did Edward feel the same about Andrew?'

'As to that, I cannot say. After so many years have passed since we were boys, I don't know.'

'And no one has tried to take your life since that day you came home?'

'No. But that doesn't mean to say they won't try again.' With his hands locked behind his back, he began to walk on. She fell into step beside him. 'When I was in Spain, I always intended coming back at some point. But, while ever Edward was treating Netherthorpe as his home and Andrew was in no hurry to ask him to leave—which was odd, considering he could never wait to be rid of him as a youth—I was content to leave things as they were until news reached me of Andrew's death.

'When I arrived home, Edward gave me tremendous support. That was when I knew I had to stay and make the best of things, to live out my life at Netherthorpe. I can't wipe away the hurt of Andrew's death, but life goes on. I have to bury the past. I have already begun the long climb to settle in the place that is rightfully mine. I am duty bound to those who depend on me. I am single-mindedly committed to that.'

She smiled at him. 'It's a challenge, Maxim, a challenge I am certain you will win.'

He looked sideways at her. 'Like you did when your husband died, leaving you with a mountain of work and decisions to make.'

'Yes, I suppose so.'

'Are your sisters aware of how hard you work?'

'Not really. They would have to experience what I do themselves to know how difficult it can be. I try not to dwell on it when I'm with them. The times we are all together are few and far between. I refuse to be miserable. I practise detachment. I learned to laugh off their concerns.'

'What you really mean is that you've become a virtuoso of deceit.'

'Yes, I suppose I have. The last thing I want is for them to feel sorry for me. I couldn't bear that.'

'Now that I can understand, but I find it odd that you are considerate to their feelings when you will not permit them the same consideration for you. In fact, I do believe you are becoming soft.'

Eve's lips curved in a smile. 'Do you know, Lord Levisham, I do believe I am.' Tilting her head to one side, she eyed him quizzically.

'What?' Maxim asked, suddenly wary of her. 'What's going through that busy head of yours now, Mrs Lansbury?'

'I am wondering if this quiet, almost retiring man walking beside me really can be the arrogant rake I heard about before he took up residence on his country estate.'

'Retiring?' His chuckle sounded low and deep. 'Heaven forbid! Are you trying to ruin my image? How have I allowed you to imagine I am any less dangerous than society has painted me? On a more serious note,' he said, 'I did a lot of growing up in the army. Military life teaches you things you can't possibly learn in ordinary life. And now I've returned to Netherthorpe to settle down and take an interest in the estate—and maybe find myself a wife.'

There was a sudden sparkle in his eyes that Eve prudently ignored. 'Then I am sure you will enjoy being pursued by women who fancy the title of Lady Levisham, the wife of an earl, and have a respect for your beautiful house. I imagine the pursuit will be hot and strong. But what kind of marriage will it be, I wonder? I suspect that you would not allow marriage to impair your freedom. Will you pay attention to your wife, do what you call your duty and then be off to London to take your pleasure with your mistress? Should you have one, that is.'

'That depends on the woman I choose to wed. There isn't a scoundrel alive who can't be tamed by the right woman, and I firmly believe that one should constantly strive to improve oneself.' He raised one sleek, well-defined eyebrow, watching, waiting for her reaction. A faint half-smile now played on his lips, as if he knew exactly what was going on in her mind.

Eve laughed softly. 'I have a distinct feeling you are trying to proposition me, Lord Levisham,' she quipped, watching Christopher as he went on ahead, his curly head bobbing as he ran.

'Now there's a thought. I may have been painted a rake in the past, but I am a fairly honest person. Shall I convince you of my merits?'

'You've already tried that,' she said, reminding him of his assault on her lips the night before. 'I should have slapped your face for your impudence.'

'Now why would you want to do that? As I recall, you enjoyed kissing me just as much as I enjoyed kissing you.'

'Nevertheless, marriage *à la mode* would not be for me.' Eve looked at him and felt a curious warmth for the man whose profligate reputation had given her every reason to dislike him. She considered it rather odd that she didn't. A woman was always flattered to learn a man was attracted to her—as remarkable as it might be. She sensed Maxim was completely sincere, and she wasn't at all displeased.

Maxim paused and turned to look at her. A slow, roguish grin moved across his features. 'Then I feel I shall have to persuade you—and enjoy doing so.'

'Oh—is that so? Then I think you will have to put it on hold because my son is pulling on my skirts.' She smiled fondly down at her son's upturned face. 'There, young man,' she said, brushing his curls back from his forehead, thinking he looked quite worn out but happy. 'I think we had better get you back to the others.'

Without more ado, Maxim scooped the child up and swung him up onto his shoulders. Christopher squealed with delight, thinking it great fun. Burying his short fingers into Maxim's thick hair, he beamed down at his mother with his big, dark eyes and a smile stretching from ear to ear.

'It's good to see him so happy,' she said. 'You have a way with him. Now, I think we should be heading back to the others before they send out a search party. When will you be returning to Netherthorpe? I'm sure you must have plenty to do.'

'Nothing that can't wait—and not nearly as interesting as the company I am keeping in London.'

Meeting his gaze, Eve saw the reflective, almost tender glimmer of a warm light in his eyes. 'You didn't have anything to eat before we set off for our walk. You must. My sisters will insist.'

'Even though I am not hungry?'

She laughed. 'They won't believe you. I thought I should warn you.'

'When we both return to Woodgreen, why don't we have an outdoor *tête à tête* of our own? You and I— and Christopher, of course. It would be interesting to get to know each other better.'

'It would be quite impossible to do that.'

'Whenever I hear that word, I am always challenged to disprove it.'

'Then you will have to wait until next summer— when the sun is shining.'

'When are you to return to Surrey?'

'In a few days. I don't like being away from home too long, but Sarah is in no hurry to leave, so I thought I would stay a while longer. And you? When will you return to Netherthorpe?'

'My business in London is not yet finished. I might be here for another couple of weeks. I thought I might go to the theatre tomorrow night. I would be honoured if you would accompany me.'

'Oh—I—I don't know,' Eve floundered, taken by surprise. 'Just the two of us?'

'Yes. Why not? Look, I promise not to ravish you,' he said with half-closed eyes and a broad smile. 'Although, I must say, a fine-looking young woman like you…'

'Now you're making fun of me.'

'Why would you say that? I don't think I've ever seen more soulful eyes.'

Eve was torn between knowing she should refuse and accepting. In the end, she decided she would accept. What harm could there be? 'I can't remember the last time I went to the theatre.'

'Well, there you are, then. It's high time you did before you have to return to The Grange. What do you say? Will you come?'

'Yes—yes, I would like that.'

'Good. Then that's settled.'

They were approaching the others, who were sitting around on rugs. All heads seemed to turn at once to look at them as they approached. Eve gave Maxim an 'I told you so' smile when they immediately began to ply him with nourishment. He politely obliged, sitting on the grass and joining in the lively conversation. As they talked, Eve was vaguely aware of Maxim's appreciative gaze on her animated face as she handed Christopher a cup of lemonade.

Eventually, the excitement of the day catching up with him, the child's eyes began to close. Eve scooped him up and he twined his legs around her waist and buried his head in her shoulder. She cradled his head with her hand, rubbed his curly hair and clasped him tight as if she would crush him to her. He yawned and rubbed his eyes with his small fists.

'He's missed his afternoon nap. I gave Nessa the day off, so I'll have to take him back to the house. With all this excitement, he'll soon go to sleep.'

As if that was the cue for them all to return to the

house, everyone began to pack things away. When Maxim had gone, Eve could not get him out of her thoughts. It made her forget the loneliness of her life at The Grange. Then she began to consider that, and to wonder at the differences between them and what it would mean to their relationship, which was just beginning to flower into something deeper.

She thought she knew what it was leading up to. The kiss had been a prelude to what he hoped would come later—not that she would go along with anything like that, but it was there all the same.

## Chapter Seven

Eve looked at her sisters' faces, filled with curiosity. She must have shown signs of the elation Maxim's company always seemed to inspire in her.

'Well, you could have knocked me down with a feather when he turned up. I knew it, Eve,' Sarah said. 'He has a special interest in you. I just know it.'

'I'm afraid you might be right, Sarah. He's invited me to go to the theatre tomorrow night.'

Incredulous, Judith—Eve's senior by ten years, and more strait-laced than any of her sisters—stopped what she was doing. 'And?'

'And what, Judith?'

'Surely you are not going to accept the invitation?'

'Why shouldn't I? It will be fun. I'm looking forward to it.'

'And will there be just the two of you?' Sarah asked, as incredulous as Judith.

'I believe so, Sarah,' she said, rolling her eyes with frustration. 'Lord Levisham has merely invited me to the theatre, so don't go making more of it than that. I am not about to do something that will put me outside the pale of society and bring disgrace and shame to my family.'

'And you are on first-name terms, I noted,' Judith remarked.

'Why yes, Judith. But you must believe me when I say that my familiar use of Lord Levisham's first name—and he of mine—does not denote any further degree of familiarity.'

'Would you not consider taking me along?' Sarah said teasingly. 'You could always pass me off as your chaperone.'

Eve laughed lightly. 'Thank you, Sarah, but I don't need a chaperone any more. I'm a twenty-three-year-old widow with a three-year-old child. The restrictions that apply to unmarried young ladies no longer apply to me. In fact, the freedom to do just as I like is a relief, and I intend to enjoy myself before I have to return to Surrey.'

'And you really don't need a chaperone?' Sarah pressed with mock disappointment. 'I rather fancy a night out at the theatre.'

Eve laughed. 'No, Sarah. I really can take care of myself. And don't worry. I promise to act with the utmost discretion.'

Having spent a long day with his solicitor, discussing his inheritance and the many business ventures in shipping, coal mining and others, Maxim returned to his house in Mayfair. It had been bought by his grandfather and furnished with care some years ago. His grandfather had chosen the furnishings carefully, taking consideration with each and every article. Maxim was much like him. It was how he lived his life, preferring to acquire all of his possessions himself.

His mind fully occupied with the evening ahead, and the lovely Eve Lansbury, he entered his room, loosening his cravat. He paused, slowly making his way inside. Something was different. He sensed it. He could feel eyes staring, an almost physical sensation. A candle flame in the wall sconce wavered slightly. The doors to the balcony were slightly ajar. Out of the corner of his eye he saw the curtain begin to slide back slowly. Moving towards it, his hand went to the inside of his jacket, his fingers closing on the hilt of the small pistol he had taken to carrying since he'd been shot. His eyes on the French window, he saw a dark form move, merging into the shadows beyond.

Stealthily moving closer, he saw a man on the balcony covered in a long black cloak. The man raised his arm, a pistol pointing directly at Maxim. With reflexes that had been honed to perfection in Spain, where he had dealt with men seeking to kill him on a regular basis, Maxim was prepared with his own gun. His hand holding the weapon never wavered. His finger was on the trigger.

Both guns fired together, as if the split-second timing had been rehearsed. The would-be assassin's bullet went wide, hitting the wall behind Maxim, splintering the gilt frame of a painting. Maxim's bullet hit his assailant in the shoulder, sending him reeling back onto the balcony and careering over the edge, down to the garden below. Had there not been a crenelated stone wall, he might have lived, but his head made hard contact as he fell.

The door was flung open and Lambert, the butler, burst in, followed by a footman.

'My Lord—what on earth has happened?'

Maxim strode out onto the balcony and looked down. The would-be assassin was spread-eagled on the ground, a pool of blood spreading about his shattered head. Maxim hurriedly made his way down and saw the man was dead. He didn't recognise him. No doubt he was a man someone had hired to kill him. But why?

Lambert came up behind him. 'Is this person known to you, my lord?'

'No. I've never seen him before. How did he get into the house?'

'I've really no idea—not through the front door. He must have come in by the garden. Would you like me to take care of it?'

Maxim nodded. 'Thank you, Lambert. Report it to the constables and inform them I will be available tomorrow to speak to them.'

His mood on returning to his room to dress for the evening turned bleak. He pondered the silent admission that he was helpless before whoever it was trying to kill him, that he knew neither where to find him nor how to stop him trying again. As the dreadful incident went round and round in his head, he reached the depressing conclusion that his pursuit of whoever the person was trying to kill him had hit a stone wall yet again.

By the time he arrived at Kensington to escort Eve to the theatre, he'd put it to the back of his mind, but it was not forgotten.

Earlier in the day Eve accompanied Marian, John and Sarah to Woolwich with Robert. Parting with her brother was an emotional moment for Eve, but not so for Robert, who was looking forward to starting his new career.

That evening for the theatre she dressed in a gown of yellow muslin trimmed with gold embroidery, which set off the warm colour of her skin and golden-brown hair to admiration. Casting a critical eye at her reflection in the long pier mirror, she accepted the fan and reticule the maid gave her. Picking up her skirts, trying to calm her rioting nerves, she went to see if Maxim had arrived. He was already in the hall when she appeared at the top of the stairs.

The stunned admiration on his face when he saw her bolstered her faltering confidence. Having recovered her composure, she fixed her eyes on his chiselled features. His tall, lean form was breathtakingly decked out in clothes for the theatre. A small frisson of excitement passed through her, especially when those eyes locked on to her own and moved with exacting slowness over every part of her.

'Eve. You look—you look radiant.'

The familiar voice struck straight at Eve's heart as she watched him walk to the bottom of the stairs and hold out his hand. She felt it fill and almost burst with the joy of seeing him. She fought to calm her rioting nerves and maintain her equilibrium.

Resplendent in a claret coat, his lustrous black hair brushed neatly back and secured at his nape, he looked unbearably handsome. She placed her hand in his and he led her across the hall to where Marian was waiting with her silk wrap.

'Permit me,' he said, taking the wrap from Marian and drawing it round Eve's shoulders before whisking her away. He handed her into the carriage and climbed in after her.

Meeting his gaze, Eve saw the reflective, almost tender, glimmer of a warm light in his eyes.

'How was your journey to Woolwich today?' he asked.

'Well enough. I was sorry to see Robert go. I'm going to miss him.'

'And how was he when you left him? Do you think he'll settle down to military life?'

'Yes—at least, I hope so. Robert is patriotic, with a tremendous regard for loyalty and honour. He has the makings of a good soldier.' Eve looked across at her companion. He had a strained look about him, as if something troubled him. 'Is everything all right, Maxim? I—I can't help noticing that you look concerned about something. Has something happened?'

'You might say that. It would seem I am still in danger from whoever it was who tried to shoot me. I'm annoyed that the man died before I could question him.'

Eve stared at him in horror, meeting his unwavering gaze. 'He is dead? Are you saying that whoever it was has tried again? Goodness me! What on earth happened—and when?'

'Earlier this evening,' he replied, his face grim. 'I returned home to find a man lurking on the balcony. He took a shot at me—as you see, he missed. I had my pistol and returned fire.' He smiled wryly. 'My military training taught me to always be prepared for the unexpected.'

'Yes, but not in your own home.'

'Unfortunately, he fell off the balcony and was killed when he fell onto a wall below.'

Eve was incredulous. 'Were you unable to question him?'

He went on to recount what had happened and she listened in horror. 'Who was it? Did you recognise him?'

'No. He must have been hired by someone else to execute the deed.'

'So, whoever wants you dead is still out there.'

'It would appear so. I just wish I could think of a reason for someone to want me dead.'

'Maybe whoever it is who is trying to kill you will give up now.'

'I don't think so. There was no identification on the assailant. It will take some time—if ever—for the authorities to find out who he was. I cannot imagine why anyone would want to harm me, but I am not naïve enough to brush aside such obvious attempts at murder. However, after saying that, I have no doubt that the person who wants me dead will soon hire someone else when he fails to get results. I will have to meet with the constables tomorrow to offer some kind of explanation for this evening's debacle.'

Reaching the theatre in Covent Garden, they entered and made their way to their box. But, knowing about the second attack on Maxim's life, Eve's evening was already marred. When he had told her, she had known a tightening of fear so strong it seemed to take the breath from her body. For a moment she was held in a space of frozen time, unable to drag her eyes from the ones that commanded her attention. Noting her silence as she sat and looked down at the stage, Maxim reached out and placed his hand over hers.

'Don't concern yourself, Eve. I want you to enjoy the evening.'

Swallowing her fear and striving to be composed, she whispered, 'I will, but I feel whoever tried to kill you is still a threat. You will keep your pistol at the ready, won't you?'

Meeting her gaze, Maxim could see her concern for him in her eyes. His smile was gentle, his eyes warm, before his smile became roguish. 'Are you trying to protect me, Mrs Lansbury?'

She gave him a wobbly smile. 'You seem to need it from time to time. Please take care.'

'I intend to. Now, enough talk of assassins. Sit back and relax, and ignore all those who will stare and comment on the impropriety of being at the theatre alone with me.'

She laughed. 'I've told you, I do not allow convention to dictate my every move.'

'Unlike your protective sisters.'

Eve sighed and nodded. 'I come from a conventional family who believe in all the important things such as honour and integrity, doing the right thing and behaving in a proper manner.'

He arched a sleek black brow quizzically. 'And truth?'

'But of course. There has to be truth.'

'Then why don't you tell them of your difficulties in your everyday life and let them help you?' he murmured, reaching out his hand and gently touching the side of her jaw with the backs of his fingers.

'Because I don't want them to worry about me,' she replied, feeling her flesh burn beneath his touch. She stared at him, aware of how close he was to her. She could feel her body beginning to tremble, and the infuriating thing was that he was perfectly well aware of the effect he was having on her.

'Nevertheless, I believe they would want to know so that they can help you. As your neighbour, you can rely on me to keep an eye on you.' Taking her hand, he raised it to his lips.

'I have managed perfectly well until now. Why would you think I would need your help? I have given you no reason to suppose I would.'

A lazy grin swept over his handsome face and the force of that white smile did treacherous things to her heart rate.

'Admit it, Eve. Admit that you are here with me because you want to be. Because you find yourself irresistibly drawn to me—as I am to you. Is that not so?'

Eve looked at him, despite her desire not to, not for the

first time finding herself at a loss to understand him. For a moment his gaze held hers with penetrating intensity. The clear grey eyes were as enigmatic as they were silently challenging, and unexpectedly she felt an answering thrill of excitement. The darkening in Maxim's eyes warned her he was aware of that response.

Waiting for the play to begin, Eve looked around at the glittering mob of fashionable theatre-goers. The theatre was not so much a place to see a play as a place to see and be seen by others. The auditorium was filled with conversation, laughter and people moving about to pay courtesy calls on their friends, who received visitors in their boxes with all the dignity and grace as if they had been at home. It wasn't long before Eve and Maxim became the focal point of attention.

'We would appear to have drawn attention to ourselves,' Maxim remarked.

'So it would appear.' Feeling the heat of the theatre on her face, Eve flicked open her fan and worked it vigorously. 'It is you they recognise. They're probably surprised to see you back in circulation.'

'I believe it is you they are looking at. No doubt they are curious as to your identity.'

'Because I am with you. Any woman in your company would be bound to draw attention.'

'Do you mind?'

'Not in the least. Do you?'

Maxim chuckled. 'Not at all—as long as they don't turn it into a scandal.'

'Why would they? We are doing nothing wrong.'

'No, I agree. But mark my words, Eve. By tomorrow morning you and I will be the subject of gossip at many a breakfast table in London.'

'And where, pray, am I at fault in appearing in public escorted by a gentleman?'

'There is no fault, Eve—at least, that is how I see it. But others may be more judgemental.'

'I don't care. Let them. Anyway, it won't concern me,' she said, peering over the edge of the box to observe the occupants in other boxes. 'I will soon be on my way back to Surrey, so I'm afraid you will have to weather the storm alone—which shouldn't be too difficult when one considers your profligate past. You must have created numerous scandals.'

'Well, thank you for that, Mrs Lansbury. But a scandal can work two ways.'

'It can? How?'

'People don't forget, so you will be bound to me irrevocably, with no possibility of escaping me.'

Underlying the lightness of his words there was a faint suggestion that he would not be averse to making a scandal with her. Her fan shut with a click. 'So,' she said slowly, 'That appeals to you, does it, Lord Levisham? You find my company so pleasant that you would like to keep me tied to you in any way you have a mind—your prisoner for ever?'

Maxim looked at her from beneath hooded eyes, a slow smile curving his lips, a smile she could not help comparing with that of a wolf. But his voice when he answered was as smooth as silk. 'And what a delectable prisoner you would make. There is nothing that appeals to me more than to have you at my beck and call for ever and a day.'

Concealing a smile behind her fan, Eve turned her attention to the stage. 'Hold that thought, Maxim, for that is all it will be. I am beginning to realise that, as a friend, you are too dangerous by far.'

'You mistake me, Eve. I am not just your friend. I'd like to think I am more than that. I like being with you. I like your company. And do not rejoice in your return to Surrey without me. I shall return to Netherthorpe before too long. Here,' he said, handing her a lorgnette. 'These should prove useful if you want to spy on our neighbours.'

Eve took it, a frisson of pleasure coursing through her as their fingers touched. She enjoyed the casual banter between them when they were alone. In fact, everything to do with Maxim, everything that came from him or related to him, had become infinitely precious. Looking at him, she was conscious of a deep feeling of happiness. She felt light-hearted and joyous. She wasn't in love with him. Of course she wasn't. She had far too much sense to allow herself to love a rogue like him.

No, she wasn't in love with him, but she was attracted to him, strongly attracted, and she told herself that was only natural. Maxim Randall was a fascinating man, and she was only human. He was a seductive man that made you think of highly improper things. There couldn't be many women who could resist a man who looked like him. Everything around him seemed to disappear in that moment—the theatre, the glittering crowd of people, the artificiality of it all. It was as if he had the power of making any setting his own.

She wielded the lorgnette with interest. Her gaze was idly drawn to a gentleman across from them on the tier below. He was with two other gentlemen. She was about to look away when the gentleman rose along with the others to acknowledge a woman who had just entered their box.

Bending forward in her seat better to see, Eve's eyes became riveted on the scene when she recognised Edward Randall as one of the gentlemen occupying the box. The woman was Elena Devlin, looking more beautiful and vivacious than Eve had ever seen her, in a coral silk and silver lace gown. Her hair gleamed and her red lips were parted in a wide smile of sensuality.

Eve saw Edward introduce her to his friends and watched as Lady Devlin's fingers wrapped themselves with possessive familiarity around his arm when she leaned closer and spoke to him. Unable to tear her eyes away, Eve watched as Lady Devlin threw back her head and laughed uproariously at something one of the gentlemen said to her. She took a seat close to Edward.

It seemed as if Eve could not tear her eyes from the box where the two sat.

'Do you see anything of interest?' Maxim asked, having noticed her interest in something. 'Anyone you know?'

'Yes,' she murmured. 'As a matter of fact I do. Your cousin Edward, for one. He is here along with Elena Devlin. Who would have thought it? To brazenly flaunt herself with a man other than her husband… Why am I not surprised?'

As if sensing the lorgnette trained on her, Lady Devlin turned her head and looked up and across, a smug smile playing on her lips when her gaze fastened on Eve. Eve immediately lowered the lorgnette and drew back into the comparative shadow of the box, feeling like a child being caught out in some misdemeanour.

'What is it?' Maxim enquired.

'She saw me staring at her.'

Maxim laughed and gave a cursory glance in Edward's direction. 'It serves you right for being too inquisitive. Now, face the stage. The play is about to begin.'


Returning to his box during the interval, Maxim was surprised when he saw Edward heading towards him. His face was lethargic and flushed with liquor. He caught Maxim's eyes fastened on him. Was it Maxim's imagination or did his expression harden for a moment before he collected himself and a somewhat false smile stretched his lips?

'Why, good evening, Maxim.'

Maxim eyed him suspiciously. If Edward was behind the attempts on his life then, having no idea that his earlier attempt had failed, of course he would be surprised to see him. 'You appear surprised to see me, Edward.'

'Do I? That's because I am.'

'I was wondering when I would run into you. You

look as if you've been celebrating something or other. Your face is almost the same colour as your waistcoat.'

Edward looked down at his flamboyant scarlet and gold waistcoat with pride, puffing out his chest. 'It is rather splendid, isn't it?'

'It certainly catches the eye,' Maxim remarked dryly. 'Still, as long as the lady accompanying you to-night likes it, then I suppose that's fine.'

'Lady? Why, yes. Lady Devlin. She happens to be in London just now.'

'Without her husband?'

Edward shrugged his elegantly clad shoulders. 'Of course. We became acquainted when I resided at Netherthorpe. She's a fine-looking woman, don't you think?'

'A woman who thinks nothing of taking another woman's husband,' Maxim made a point of reminding him dryly.

Reproach flashed in Edward's eyes. 'I don't have a wife, Maxim, so that does not apply. What Lady Devlin chooses to do with her life is her affair.'

'Her husband might disagree with you. I've been meaning to call on your Aunt Pauline,' Maxim said, keen to move the conversation away from the controversial Elena Devlin. 'Is she well?'

'Very. I don't know how she'll feel when I tell her I'm to move out—when you lose your wager,' Edward remarked with a sly look at his cousin. 'Although you do appear to be making some headway with the delightful widow. Is that the delectable Eve Lansbury I have seen in your box? I must say, she's lost no time in putting your disagreement behind her. Perhaps I should put it down to your powers of persuasion. You always did know how to seduce the ladies, Maxim.'

Maxim looked at him coldly. 'The Dower House is yours, Edward.'

Edward was incredulous, and then a slow, disbelieving smile broke across his face. 'But the wager? Good Lord! Have I heard right? Have you lost your reason?'

'I have never been more serious in my life.'

'I see. Would you like to explain yourself? What has brought about this change of heart? Have you no longer any wish to seduce the widow? How can you fold as easily as that?'

'I can and I have. The wager is off, Edward. You can take up residence in the Dower House whenever you wish.'

'Then you're the most peculiar player I've ever had the pleasure of opposing,' Edward remarked. 'I enjoy a challenge and the pleasure is somewhat muted by the wager's outcome.'

'Then I am sorry to disappoint you. I have developed a regard for Mrs Lansbury. I will not dishonour her.'

Edward laughed. 'Don't tell me Cupid has smitten you, cousin. But have a care. You might turn out to have competition—and small wonder. Mrs Lansbury is quite out of the ordinary. She positively shines tonight.' Helping himself to a pinch of snuff, he lifted his arrogant brows.

'I have no intention of reneging on our wager. You can take up residence in the house if you wish.' Maxim took note of Edward's frown. No doubt he sensed something crucial was going on that he knew nothing about.

The play finished and Maxim escorted Eve out of the theatre to await their carriage. Gentlemen in expensive frock coats idled about, chatting with attractive young women, laughing and vying with each other to get closest to the ladies, as young men did. Their voices were filled with seductive promise, low and flirtatious, careful not to be heard by chaperones who had unwittingly left their precious charges unattended.

They went on to partake of a light supper at a nearby tavern favoured by theatre-goers. Lamplight lit the walls of the room, softening the well-worn tables and faces of some of the clientele. Relieved to be out of the cloying atmosphere of the theatre, Eve sipped wine as she waited to be served, enjoying the laughter and banter going on around her, feeling more alive and relaxed than she had in a long time.

'Thank you, Maxim,' she said, looking across at her companion, meeting his gaze directly. 'I can't remember when I enjoyed myself more.'

He smiled lazily, lifting his glass in a toast. 'Here's to many more such evenings, Eve. You enjoyed the play?'

'Very much—as much as I intend to enjoy this delicious meal,' she said, moving her reticule from the table to make room for the dishes a pretty serving girl had brought.

They shared an exquisite meal of turtle soup and

stuffed partridge, delicious vegetables and fresh fruit, washed down with more red wine.

They were on the point of leaving and had just got up from their table when Edward appeared, accompanied by a raucous group of friends. Lady Devlin was among them. On seeing Maxim, Edward waved the others on to their table—Lady Devlin clung to his side. Maxim acknowledged them. Eve, however, gritted her teeth and shut her eyes, praying with all her might that anger should not get the better of her will.

'Maxim, you have met Lady Devlin?'

'I have had that pleasure,' he replied, coldly polite.

There was an interlude of bowing and curtseying, Lady Devlin favouring Maxim with a smile so dazzling that it did not fail to contain a strong element of flirtatiousness. His hard, direct gaze told Eve their encounter gave him as little pleasure as it did her. With tremendous will, she stood beside Maxim and faced Edward Randall and Lady Devlin, hating every moment she had to breathe the same air as this woman, who had been Matthew's mistress for the entire time Eve had been married to him. But she would not be brow beaten. She had her pride.

Edward took Lady Devlin's hand and drew her to face Eve. 'I believe the two of you are already acquainted,' he said.

Eve's eyes were cold as they met Edward Randall's. She saw mischief dancing in their depths. He knew perfectly well what he was doing, what Elena Devlin had been to her husband. She shifted her gaze to the woman whose hand he held. 'Lady Devlin,' she responded.

Lady Devlin nodded briefly. 'Did you enjoy the play?'

Determined not to partake in any kind of light banter, Eve looked at her coldly. 'Yes, I did.' Elena Devlin was behaving as if the encounter was the most natural thing in the world. Looking at her with sardonic amusement, she said, 'What have you done with your husband, Lady Devlin?'

Lady Devlin shrugged. 'I left him in Surrey. It's more than I can allow for him to accompany me to town. He lives for his work and pleasure has no part of it.'

'Why? Does he cramp your style, Lady Devlin?'

She smiled sourly. 'You might say that. He also has a tendency to nod off when he attends the theatre—which is more than I can bear.'

Eve could read no expression in Lady Devlin's attractive features, and as she regarded her closely she felt her thoughts probed by careful fingers. She suppressed a shudder. Tall and slender, her nose aquiline and her hair perfectly coiffed, Lady Devlin was quite beautiful. As beautiful as a statue was beautiful—remote and cold. Her eyes were equally as cold, and her lips showed a bitter twist. There was an indefinable poise about her, a certainty, and she had power. One thing Eve ascertained when she met her cold eyes—the woman didn't like Eve any more than Eve liked her.

Sensing her discomfort, Maxim placed his hand beneath her elbow. 'You must excuse us,' he said. 'Our carriage is waiting. We were just leaving.'

'I will not detain you. Although,' Edward said, stepping forward to waylay them, 'We're to have supper. I see you have eaten, but perhaps you would care to join us for a drink?'

As Eve shot Edward a disbelieving look, his eyes gleamed their challenge, daring her to accept. The thought of sitting down to dine with Elena Devlin was anathema to her.

'I don't think so.' As Edward waited expectantly for some plausible excuse, Eve said, 'It's been an enjoyable evening. It would be a shame to spoil it by staying any longer.'

In spite of all her resolution to remain composed and in control, it was all Eve could do not to fling herself on this woman. How she longed to slap the smile from those lips and deeply hurt that proud and vicious heart. Averting her face, she turned her back altogether.

Eve's tone, her very posture, was cool and aloof. Maxim peered at her as they left the tavern, trying to read her expression. He wasn't sure what he expected. An acknowledgement of what had just passed, he supposed. His gaze went to Edward, who was standing several paces away.

Somehow Eve managed to make it to the carriage. She paused for a moment before placing her foot on the step, took a deep breath and wondered why on earth she'd allowed that woman to get under her skin. She took another deep breath and allowed Maxim to hand her up into the carriage, taking yet another deep breath to stop the trembling inside, and didn't look back as the driver whipped up the horses and the carriage sped away from the theatre.

Maxim was watching her with concern. 'I'm sorry, Eve. That wasn't very pleasant. Knowing the situation between the two of you, Edward should not have forced the issue.'

'No, he shouldn't, but he knew exactly what he was doing. I know he is your cousin, Maxim, but in my opinion he is cunning and ruthless and not to be trusted.'

'I take it you don't like him?'

She sighed, shaking her head. 'No, not one bit.' Looking across at him, at the worried lines creasing his brow, and remembering that whoever was trying to kill him had tried again, she was filled with concern. 'I'm sorry, Maxim. It doesn't matter one way or another what my opinions are concerning your cousin. You are the one who has to deal with him. It must be so difficult for you, having to take up this new life that has been thrust on you while someone is trying to kill you. You must miss your military life.'

'Yes, I suppose I do. It was my life for such a long time. What about you? What do you have in mind for the future?'

'Do I have to have something in mind? I shall carry on doing what I'm doing—which must appear to be a terribly boring existence to someone like you. I suppose I shall wait to see what happens.'

'You don't have to do that. You could call on ambition and prod fate.'

'I can't say that I've ever done any prodding. Have you?'

'All the time. If I see something I want, I go all out to get it.'

'It's all that military training—your ambition and lust for power over whoever you happened to be fighting at the time.'

'Not entirely. It's in my nature—at least, that's what my mother used to tell me.'

Eve laughed. 'Your mother loved you and she would have allowed you to indulge your whims. I think what you mean is that you are both pushy and forceful.'

He looked at her and smiled. 'You are different when you laugh. You should laugh more often. You look quite stern when in repose.'

'Really? I didn't know that.'

'Perhaps it's only when you are with me.'

'I can't think why.'

'Maybe because you disapprove of me.'

'And why would I do that?'

'For several reasons.'

'Tell me.'

'I don't think I will. To do so would be to increase your disapproval.'

'If you are referring to the rumours I heard of your ill repute, or the blunders you made at the beginning, then I have told you that you are forgiven. Otherwise any disapproval you believe I might harbour against you is all in your imagination.'

'So you don't disapprove of me.' He sighed, making himself more comfortable and smiling across at her. 'It's amazing how two people can get to know each other on a journey.'

'Maxim, we have been to the theatre. Why should being in a carriage do that any more than anywhere else?'

He grinned. 'Because we happen to be alone—in a more intimate atmosphere. It does help.'

'Does it?'

'Absolutely. I feel it—and I think you must.'

'I suppose I do—although I haven't really thought about it until you mentioned it.'

'I find I have a natural interest in you, and I think our past encounters—some good, some not so good, I am sorry to say—makes a special bond between us. Don't disappoint me by saying you do not feel it.'

'Of course. We are friends, Maxim—friends who happen to be close neighbours also.'

'And our encounters have taught me a good deal about you. I am eager to learn more.'

'There is not much more to know about me.'

'I know you enjoy the theatre.'

'I do, very much. Tonight brought light relief to my humdrum life. Thank you for asking me, Maxim.'

'You're welcome. How does your son like London? I expect he finds the bustle of town so much more exciting than rural life.'

Eve laughed. 'He certainly does. I was so looking forward to showing him the sights, but he's a little young to appreciate them properly. All he wants to

do is play with his cousins.' She gave a wistful sigh.
'I don't suppose I can blame him. He's on his own at
The Grange for most of the time. There's such a vari-
ety of things to amuse him here, with attention showered on him from all and sundry, that all he wants to
do is wallow in it.'

'Then, with her son otherwise engaged, it would be
my pleasure to entertain his mother. If you are willing,
and it will not shock your sisters too much, I would like
to show you the sights of London—a trip on the river
perhaps, and to Hampstead Heath. Another visit to the
theatre, even. The prospects are endless.'

'Thank you, Maxim. I would like that.'

'Then that's settled.'

## *Chapter Eight*

Eve was light of heart and happy during the days that followed. She knew she was becoming more and more attracted to Maxim and she told herself she need have no fear. She was no innocent, and she would always remember the sort of man she was dealing with—a man of the world with a reputation as a philanderer, perhaps looking for amusement while he was in London. She was determined not to forget that and pride herself on her common sense.

But during the days that followed she was able to set that aside. He seemed to go out of his way to please her, making the days a wonderful medley of shifting emotions, days when she could be happy and carefree. She gave herself up to the sheer enjoyment presented to her and looked forward to their outings. They visited the pleasure gardens and took a trip on the river, and it was on their visits to the galleries that she saw a different, more serious side to him, discovering he was something of a connoisseur of art and that his knowledge of England's history was profound. Their discussions were highly enjoyable, often heated, sometimes critical of the other's opinions.

Her sisters quietly watched these expeditions with interest and were curious as to where these outings were leading, but Eve assured them they had no need to fear. They were happy days and she savoured them to the full. But these halcyon days were coming to an end and the time was coming when she would have to return to Surrey.

At the end of two weeks, she had an uneasy feeling that she was becoming Maxim's victim. She had lost sight of that fact in her joy of being with him. From the moment she had met him she had been telling herself she was drawn to this man because of his compelling good looks and his powerful animal magnetism. She had almost convinced herself that it was so, that the strange hold he had over her was merely his ability to awaken an intense sexual hunger within her. But that was just the tip of the iceberg, because what she felt for Maxim Randall went way beyond anything physical. It was something deeper, something dangerously enduring, which had been weaving its spell to bind them inexorably together.

They were in the carriage on yet another visit to the theatre. Unable to resist her, Maxim had drawn her to his side and, taking her in his arms, kissed her soundly. He broke the kiss but kept his arms around her. She relaxed against him. Touching her face, he bent his head to rest his forehead close to hers. 'You see?' he said, his breathing ragged as he looked into her eyes, 'How much power you have when you choose to wield it?'

Eve did see that she, who had convinced herself she had no influence over anything in her life, felt as captivating and alluring as the most beautiful woman on earth. A joy she had never felt before blossomed inside her.

'Thank you,' she said, 'For making the kiss so enjoyable. I feel I must tell you that you have a strange effect on me, Maxim Randall. When you took it upon yourself to interfere in my life, I was determined to dislike you. I tried, but for the short time we have been together I have seen a different man to the one I had painted in my mind, a man who melted my self-engendered resistance. I resented that. I wanted to dislike you, but that didn't work either. And, now you have kissed me again, I no longer know what to think.'

He gazed down at her seriously. 'High praise indeed. It would seem you are confused about me, Eve. I can see your dilemma.'

'Can you?' She believed he could. Maxim Randall had a razor-sharp perception of her deepest fears. 'I have been so unsure of myself. Because of who you are and your somewhat dubious reputation I didn't want to like you, but when you came to London and sought me out—I unwittingly made more problems for myself that I bargained for.'

'And that scares you?'

'Yes, if you must know. Yes, it does.'

Maxim was both touched and faintly amused by her confession. 'Do you fear me, Eve?'

'No, not you,' she said quietly, feeling his eyes on her, causing the colour in her cheeks to deepen. 'It's what you might do to me that I'm afraid of.'

Raising his hand, he touched her cheek with the backs of his fingers. A wonderful languor began to swell inside her, spreading through her with a glorious warm sensation. It didn't seem possible that the feelings she had for Maxim were growing out of all proportion. No matter how hard she tried to fight them, they grew stronger and stronger the more they were together until there was nothing but this joyous moment dominating her every waking moment. He let his hand drop. Eve looked into his eyes. They were narrowed and intent, glowing with need, with warmth.

'I should have known what would happen when I sought you out here in London. You are not a woman a man can ignore. I want you, Eve. I've had many women—I cannot deny that, or that I enjoyed each one—but none of them meant anything to me. They were a diversion. Would that you were a diversion too.'

Eve gazed at him. 'I might well have been that for this short time, but I shall have to go home soon.'

'Are you telling me you are getting homesick?'

'No, not really, but I have been away too long as it is. Besides, I have taken up too much of your time.'

'The time has not been wasted, Eve. Quite the opposite.'

'I have enjoyed our outings. These past days have been most agreeable. I hope they have been for you too.'

His answer was to lean towards her and kiss her

softly. His touch sent a delightful shiver of pleasure inside her. Their lips touched once and then twice, and then she tasted the tip of his tongue, tasting of heat and wicked temptations. Eve responded by parting her lips softly under his and welcoming his kiss, tangling her fingers in his thick, dark hair, savouring the feel of his hands as they moulded and teased her breasts that ached to be free of the restricting gown.

'Don't go yet,' he murmured, his lips close to hers, his breath warm on her flesh. 'I think you know well enough to deduce certain things about the way matters are between us. I would like us to get to know each other better.'

Eve knew what he was asking of her, and she was ashamed that it presented some temptation. Why had she let it go so far? Why had she allowed her emotions to become involved? He had not suggested an affair—which would be exciting and torrid—or marriage, and at this present time she wanted neither. She wanted freedom now—to throw caution to the wind, no encumbrances. Her aching body wanted more from him.

And why not? she asked herself. There was a part of her that understood the danger of giving herself to this man. Not so much the loss of her innocence, since she had lost it already. That did not concern her, but the knowledge that Maxim Randall could steal her heart did.

The voice, however, was easily drowned beneath the sensual flood of pleasure that raced through her body at his closeness. Her arms lifted and circled his neck. She felt as if she had been waging a war against fate since the day she had met him. In this moment she did not want to fight against destiny. She wanted to lower the ruthless barriers she had erected around herself since her marriage to Matthew, and for a short while, just be a happy, carefree young woman who desired a man. She wanted Maxim Randall, and damn the consequences.

Maxim raised his head after yet another kiss and gazed down at her flushed face, her eyes shining in the dim light. 'I would like to take you home with me, but I think I should let you go while I still can.'

'You don't have to...' She searched his eyes, then she smiled mischievously, drawing her fingertips along his clean-shaven chin. 'We don't have to go to the theatre, do we?'

'No, not if you don't want to—if there is something else you would rather do.'

'Well,' she said, moving closer to him, her eyes never leaving his. 'I can think of something that would be far more pleasurable than watching actors prance about on a stage.'

His eyes narrowed and he chuckled softly. 'Are you saying what I think you are? Because if that is the case then I will tell you that I am in need of a bed—with you in it.'

'I'm serious, Maxim. Do you mind? We can go to the theatre any time.'

He grinned. 'I like your priorities. It was not what I anticipated.'

'I am no dewy-eyed innocent who is foolish enough to presume a few kisses and making love are nothing less than a declaration of any kind of commitment—as well you know, Maxim. I don't expect anything of you.' She smiled. 'You don't seem as shocked by my proposal as I would have expected.'

He grinned lopsidedly, looking deep into her gaze with an expression of such tenderness that it made Eve's heart ache in the strangest way. 'Nothing shocks me any more, Eve.'

'I'm relieved to hear that.'

He drew back, holding her gaze. 'Oh?'

'Yes. So I think I would like you to take me home with you. Besides, I haven't seen inside your town house. I would be most interested.'

Maxim couldn't believe what she was saying. He stared down at her. She had it in her to entice and arouse him, and he knew that if he took her to his home now, at once, then he would fall into the soft pit of hot delight she was offering. The need to make love to her had become like a dam, preventing the flow of normal thought and conversation. He loved the feel of her in his arms, enjoyed kissing her and he knew exactly what he wanted.

A small part of him, which was detached from the physical, was amazed and delighted at the strength and determination of her in wanting this. But his male body had wilfully taken over from his careful, sensible male mind. He looked at her for a long moment, thinking she appeared to capture the very essence and allure of a woman who could tempt a man to barter his very soul to own her.

'Then I will be happy for you to see it.'

Instructing the driver to take them back, they soon arrived and entered Maxim's grand mansion in May-fair.

The door was opened by a rotund butler called Travis attired in a black uniform. Maxim told her he had been with the Randall family for years. Eve stood awkwardly in the hall, which was a vision of white marble and pillars, elegant paintings, mirrors and light. Taking her arm, Maxim escorted her into a sitting room. Tastefully furnished in a combination of classical furnishings and breath-taking works of art, it was decorated in soothing shades of ivory and a pale shade of blue. Oriental carpets shimmered with red, gold and blue on the floor. Like the rest of the house, the room possessed a simple elegance. A fire burned in the marble fireplace and fresh flowers were arranged in a Grecian vase on a sideboard.

She moved to the window. The moon was bright in the dark-violet sky, shining in untroubled serenity over the garden.

'Eve.'

There was movement behind her and the voice that spoke her name was deep, warm and loving. She closed her eyes, feeling the dizzy aura of him, unable to resist it. Wanting to savour the sound of it, she didn't turn, although she could imagine his eyes in the moonlight shining with an expression she would like to think he had given to no woman but her.

She heard him come closer, his footsteps almost soundless on the thick carpet, and then he was directly behind her, so close she could feel the warmth of him on her back. Then his arms snaked around her waist. He pulled her back and she sank into him. Holding her to his chest, he buried his face into the curve of her neck, his lips warm, caressing her flesh. Sighing, she began to melt, feeling a languorous magic drift over her.

'Mmm…' He breathed, his teeth nibbling her earlobe. 'You smell of roses.' His arms tightened about her and his voice was husky. 'Do you know…? Have you any idea how much I want you, Eve? Will you not turn round and tell me you feel the same?'

She turned slowly, shivering slightly, for she felt the full force of his masculinity, his vigour, the strong pull of his magnetism which she knew was his need for her, wrap itself about her. His face was all shadow and planes in the candles' glow, his cheekbones taut, his lips slightly parted. He was so tall, so handsome. She felt a hollow ache inside her as he gazed down at her. She lifted her face and he placed his lips on hers, gently, barely discernible.

Raising his head, he took her head between his hands and splayed his fingers over her cheeks, looking into the liquid depths of her eyes. 'You are so incredibly lovely, Eve Lansbury. I wonder if you have any idea just how lovely you are.'

His voice was soft and melodious. Eve stood very still, barely able to breathe, yet she was trembling inside.

'Come to bed with me, Eve.'

'What about the servants? Won't they be shocked

to see you taking a strange woman up to your bed chamber?'

He laughed softly. 'Not one bit. Besides, they have all retired for the night...'

'The butler?'

'Forget about Travis. He is the soul of discretion and will now have retired.'

Taking her hand, he led her back out into the hall and up the curved double staircase to the upper landing. Eve took note of the white marble statues that were set in alcoves along the landing. Maxim opened the door to a large, elegant bed chamber dominated by a large four-poster bed with green and gold velvet hangings.

'Oh, what a lovely room...' Eve breathed, gazing around her with awe.

'I'm glad you think so,' Maxim said, drawing her close. 'But I did not ask you here to impress you with my bed chamber.'

When he took her lips, she offered so eagerly and she moaned with pleasure. His mouth moulded and caressed, savouring, his tongue invading the dewy softness with hot need. It was a wild, wanton kiss. Heat catapulted through her, setting her whole body on fire. She knew her vulnerability and seriously doubted that she could raise a hand to hold him off if she'd wanted to. Did it matter that they weren't wed when his mouth, his hands and his powerful body were demanding things from her that she knew she could give him, things she wanted as badly as he did?

They shed their clothes on the way to the bed, Maxim's eyes devouring every inch of her perfectly proportioned body. Her breasts were small and round and when Maxim kissed them she gave low moans of pleasure. Finding her lips, he kissed her again, long and deep.

'I want you inside me.' Her voice was husky as she sank onto the bed, pulling him down with her. She wanted him desperately and just now nothing mattered but that.

He gathered her into his arms, his silver-light eyes staring into her very soul. The firm, hard muscles of his body pressed against hers, and the exploration of his hands on her flesh, gentle and caressing, his lips devouring and tender, had Eve glowing and purring like a kitten.

A need began to grow in her as his caresses grew bolder. She felt on the threshold of something great, an overwhelming discovery. She shivered as his fingers stroked the swell of her breasts and continued over her flat belly and on to curve of her hips and inner thighs. What he was doing to her felt as though she were being imprisoned in a cocoon of dangerous sensuality. She moaned and fought against the tumult of frayed emotions, but no effort of hers could bring about the quieting of her nerves.

Trapped beneath the exquisite promise of Maxim's aroused body, and the persistence of his mouth, Eve was impatient for him to possess her. For a moment she was assailed by the memory of Matthew and what he had done to her—how rough and careless his handling of her had been, with no intention of pleasing her.

A dark fear pierced her. Had Matthew mentally scarred her, left her unable to respond to a lover's touch? Her mind rebelled and the feel of Maxim's fingers, caressing and arousing, made her body begin to tremble with uncontrollable need. And when Maxim finally entered her his carefully withheld hunger released itself in a frenzy that demanded he possess her fully. Eve cried out, and so did he, but all around them the servants in the elegant mansion slept and the lovers were unheard.

Sated and heavy with contentment, and lost in the blissful and blessed state into which Maxim had sent her, Eve heaved a soft sigh and settled into the sheltering arms of her lover. No man, not even her husband, had ever made her feel the carnal sensations that had surged through her blood. Maxim only had to touch her and she became alive with emotions that were foreign to her. She had thought herself cold and indifferent to the urges that bedevilled other people, but in Maxim's arms she'd discovered that she was as weak and helpless as anyone else at resisting the demands of passion.

How wonderful it was to linger in his arms, to watch the flickering candlelight wash over their naked bodies still entwined. To feel him hold her close, to rest her cheek on his chest and feel his heartbeat, to revel in the warmth of him and the smell of him. To see his eyes fill with a hungry need as he rolled her on to her back and took possession of her once more, and for a while made her forget everything else.

Any doubts she'd had, all the qualms of gnawing shame she'd imagined would torment her, were not there. More unsettling to her was the strange sense of contentment, of rightness she felt, being in Maxim's arms, as if it was where she was meant to be. She thought how little comparison there was between what had just happened to her and the unpleasant experiences with Matthew. It was more than simply that Maxim could touch her heart while Matthew had meant almost nothing to her. The man to whom she had just given herself so spontaneously, with whom she had just shared the most intimate of experiences, had really become her lover in every sense of the word.

They lay quietly together, listening to the sound of passing horses clopping by and carriage wheels on the street outside.

'You are very beautiful, Eve,' Maxim murmured as he trailed his fingers over her flesh, for so she was. The soft folds of the bed sheet was like a sheath of creamy white about her, so pale it was difficult to distinguish where the fabric ended and her flesh began.

'So are you,' she breathed, admiring his splendid, naked body. It was powerful, lean and broad in all the right places, the gleam of his skin darkened by the generous covering of hair on his chest. 'I don't quite know what to say.'

'Why should either of us say anything?' Raising his head from the pillow, he looked down at her, smiling. Her face was soft with that look a woman achieved when she had been well loved, well satisfied. 'You are not regretting what we have just done?'

'Regretting? Indeed, I am not regretful. Just the opposite. You did not take advantage of me, Maxim. I was a willing partner. I have never experienced anything quite like it.'

'What? Not even with…?'

'No,' she was quick to say. 'Never with Matthew. All his passion, he saved for his lover.'

Unexpectedly, Maxim's expression darkened. 'Did he hurt you, Eve? Did he abuse you?'

'No—at least, not in the physical sense.'

She turned her face towards Maxim. It was as if he had seen through the very bones of her head into the secret places of her mind. 'He didn't hit me or anything—but abuse doesn't have to be physical,' she said quietly.

She placed her finger over his lips, silencing him, knowing perfectly well that he was about to mention Matthew, the husband she did not want to think of in the same moment as the one that had given her such happiness. 'My marriage to Matthew is in the past, and belongs there, but one good thing came out of it—Christopher.'

Maxim raised a quizzical brow, drawing his finger gently down the bare flesh of her slender neck, understanding more about what was going on in her mind than she realised. 'And how do you feel now, Eve, now we have made love?'

'I feel quite wonderful. I have you to thank for that. It is no lie. I confess that Matthew made me doubt myself. He always made me feel unattractive and unworthy in some way.'

'And now?'

'All the doubts I expected, all the qualms of shame I imagined I would feel, were not there. More unnerving to me was the strange sense of contentment, of rightness, I felt being in your arms.'

'I am not like Matthew. I hope you found what we did neither distasteful nor undignified, that you found pleasure not pain in my arms. Making love is a time for giving and sharing, not taking.'

Weak from the turbulence of her emotions, Eve rested her head on his chest and felt his heart beating as fast as her own, which meant that he too must have been affected by what they had done. There was something different about him, something indefinably more tender and more authoritative. Confusion making her feel light-headed, she said, 'What we just did—what does it mean?'

She sounded so defeated by the amazing passion they shared that Maxim smiled against her hair. 'That's very simple to answer. It means we are here because we are attracted to each other.' He lifted his hand, grazing her flushed cheek. Gently he explained, 'At this time it doesn't have to mean more than that.'

Maxim's hypnotic gaze held Eve's as his fingertips stroked her cheek seductively, sliding along the line of her jaw to her lips. From the first moment he had taken her in his arms he had known they were a combustible combination, and what had just passed had been the most wildly erotic, satisfying sexual encounter of his life. Whatever Eve had felt had been real and uncontrived and, as he now knew, she'd been totally uninitiated. She might have been married, but it was clear that she was inexperienced. She was the product of her upbringing and her environment, for all that she had taken over the running of The Grange and was prepared to take the occasional risk. Had she never wondered about what she might really want or need?

His passion flared high, his need to possess her once more paramount, to banish all thought of her former husband from her mind, to claim her body and make her his own in every sense. For the short time left before he would have to take her home, he intended to take his time and seduce her, to make sure with his experienced hands and mouth that her climax would be as devastating as his own.

His eyes revelled in their freedom as they feasted hungrily on her naked body stretched out alongside him: her swelling, full, ripe breasts, pink-tipped and tantalising; the inward curve of her narrow waist; the seductive roundness of her hips and the long, lithe grace of her limbs.

Eve was what every man dreamed of, but before tonight he had been unprepared for this vision of incomparable beauty; of the soft, creamy, satin lustre of her skin that contrasted against the darkness of his own. He wanted to look at her, to explore every inch of her, to taste and smell and to satisfy his male curiosity in the soft curves of this woman. He wanted her more than he had wanted any other woman before, to have those inviting hips beneath him and to have those long, lithe legs wrapped around him.

With her hair spread out in shimmering waves across the pillows, he felt her tremble at the intimacy of his touch and nestle closer. Once again, they came together naturally, like two beings forged together by a common bond and, where he had intended to play out his hand with patience, his intention began to wane. He asked himself what he was prepared to offer Eve. Perhaps a few months as his mistress? A few expensive trinkets to ease his conscience when he was finished with her?

No, he sneered at himself. Just how selfish had he become? That wasn't what he wanted. Eve deserved respect and position. She had come to mean too much to him to let her slip away. He would dearly like to make her his wife, which would have wide-ranging ramifications and would have to be considered carefully. He would provide her with the stature and wealth that marriage to him would bring. He would also be a good husband, faithful and generous, he told himself—not only with his money, but with his body too. The memory of what they had just done drifted tantalisingly through his mind. Oh, yes, he thought, he would be more than generous with his body.

'I think you'd better take me home, don't you?' Eve murmured. Rolling onto her stomach and resting on her elbows, she proceeded to place tantalising little kisses on his chest. There was a hint of surprising mischief in her eyes when she looked up at him, eyes which were still drugged in the aftermath of their love-making. 'It's going to be difficult should my sisters ask me what the play was about—you will have to enlighten me in the carriage,' she said, looking at him with an air of drawing him into an intimate conspiracy.

His mind made up that he was going to make this lovely creature his wife, Maxim grinned. 'I'll do my best.'

When Maxim had said goodnight to Eve and was returning to his home, she filled all his thoughts. Immersed for so long in his military career, he had kept his affairs with women at arm's length. But, since leaving the army and meeting Eve, the melting of old barriers had given him back the ability to love, going beyond the boundaries that for so long had been his defence. The thought of returning to Netherthorpe without her made him feel depressed. He thought about what they had just done and how contented he had felt afterwards. When was the last time he had experienced such a sense of rightness and satisfaction with his place in the world? Never.

His love and devotion to Eve were laid wide open, so he knew what he had to do. He could not deny or hide his emotions any longer.

In her own bed later that night, Eve went over every detail of the night of blissful passion they had shared, a night that had been self-scourging, a deliberate act on her part to try and purge herself of what Matthew had done to her. Sated, and heavy with a contentment she had never believed possible, she had settled in the sheltering arms of her lover.

How wonderful it had been to linger in his arms, to watch the flickering candlelight wash over their naked bodies entwined, and feel him hold her close. How wonderful to rest her cheek on his chest and feel his heartbeat, to revel in the warmth of him, the smell of him, and to see his eyes fill with hungry need as he had rolled her on to her back and taken possession of her once more. For a while everything but him had been wiped from her mind.

The following morning, all was hustle and bustle as two of Eve's sisters and their families prepared to leave for their respective homes. Eve had no idea when she would see them again, although she did promise she would visit them some time during the spring. Sarah was to remain in London a while longer so she could spend a few extra days with Eve.

When they had left, Eve accompanied Sarah to the Royal Exchange to do some shopping and to enjoy themselves for a couple of hours or so. When the carriage turned in to Cornhill, they were both in good spirits. They stared with excitement at the immense stone front of the façade of the Exchange, with its high arcades, columns and the clock tower reaching skyward.

Alighting from the carriage, they went through the archway where the arcade square of the Exchange opened up before them. It was filled with merchants, traders and hawkers of wares, mingling with people of all occupations, positions and gentlemen in military uniforms. It was a fashionable place to shop and was used as a rendezvous, much frequented by beaux waiting to meet a lady bent on flirtation.

'What a wonderful place this is,' Eve murmured,

breathing in the different smells that reached her, from roasting chestnuts to hot pies and horse dung. It was a rarity for Eve to come to such a place. She was captivated by the sight, and would have stopped, but Sarah was moving through the yard. Eve hurried after her.

'I think I would like to have a look round the little stalls in the yard first, but the shops upstairs are the best.'

And so they passed a pleasant half-hour browsing among the stalls with Sarah dipping into her silk purse for coins to buy fripperies, placing them in her basket. They mounted the staircase and strolled along the upper gallery. It was thronged with shoppers and Eve found it difficult to keep Sarah within her sights, as she kept wandering off when something of interest caught her eye.

When she disappeared inside a shop to purchase some gloves—telling Eve that she would probably be a while, as she wished to browse—Eve slipped into a shop to purchase some embroidered ribbons and lace to brighten up some of her older dresses. On leaving the shop, Eve saw Elena Devlin strolling towards her, taking a leisurely path along the gallery—the one woman Eve would like to have avoided at all cost.

Her heart began to pound and a cold finger ran down her back. It was as if some unseen presence was warning her to take care. The mere sight of this woman filled her with loathing. Their glances caught and for a moment they looked into each other's eyes, mortal enemies. Eve felt the malevolence oozing out of Elena.

She would never like this woman who had stolen her husband.

'So, Mrs Lansbury. You are enjoying London?'

'I was, Lady Devlin.'

Lady Devlin forced a dry smile. 'Until you encountered me, no doubt.'

'No doubt,' Eve confirmed coldly. 'Will you please move out of my way? I have nothing to say to you.'

'No, I cannot imagine you have. You look surprisingly well. It is clear London suits you.'

'And how would you know that?'

'I don't—and it does not bother me one way or the other in the slightest.'

Eve had no time for simpering, feminine compliments, insincere smiles and subtly disguised cuts. Lady Devlin's eyes were hard and shining, ruthless as those of a cat watching its prey. Eve returned her stare, not at all disconcerted or intimidated.

'I really do not think we have anything to say to each other, Lady Devlin, so if you will excuse me...' She was about to move on when Lady Devlin's next words made her pause.

'You look decidedly smug, Mrs Lansbury—for a woman whose husband was unfaithful to her.'

Eve's eyes widened incredulously. For a moment she was silent, then very quietly she said, 'And you would know all about that, wouldn't you, Lady Devlin?'

Lady Devlin leaned forward, holding her satin reticule in front of her. 'You may think so, if you like. Matthew never stopped seeing me while he was married to you. All the times you thought he was hunting, he was with me. All the nights he wasn't at home, he was with me—in my bed.'

Eve stared at her, a kind of repugnant horror on her face. What was this woman trying to do—bait her, prod her most sensitive emotions, humiliate her with boasting of Matthew's infidelity? Did she wish to see her cringe?

'Did you think I didn't know that? What you didn't know at the time, Lady Devlin, was that you were welcome to him. But what of your own husband? Your propensity to acquire other gentlemen to satisfy your needs and to escort you here and there does not present him in a good light, and he is a greater fool than I thought.'

She and Lady Devlin stood very close, breathing each other's breath, staring into each other's eyes.

'Will you step out of my way to let me pass,' Eve demanded coldly. 'Nothing can possibly be gained by this.'

She glanced down into the square below and saw Edward Randall, dressed in all his vivid finery, engaged in jocular conversation with three young gentlemen. 'I believe your present lover is looking for you. I warn you to have a care. With your husband hovering in the background, I'll wager that nothing can come of the affair.'

She began to push past Lady Devlin, who all at once laughed, a hysterical laugh of anger and nervous repression. 'Just listen to yourself speaking of wagers. You know nothing, do you, Mrs Lansbury, as you parade yourself on the arm of Lord Levisham.' Her eyes narrowed maliciously. 'You thoroughly believe yourself the equal of him, don't you? You are of a different class and ill-equipped to deal with the society he inhabits.'

'And you would know that, Lady Devlin.'

'Of course.' She moved closer, her hostile eyes never leaving Eve's. 'Obviously you are flattered by the attention he showers on you. You think you can keep him, don't you? Well, when I've told you a few facts about your precious Maxim Randall, he will be the last man in the world you want to associate with. You really have no idea what is going on, do you?'

Eve's eyes narrowed. 'What are you talking about?'

'I think all the attention he is showering on you has addled your brain. Your interaction at the theatre told everyone that you are in a relationship with him. London is abuzz with rumours. The two of you have become the subject of much speculation and comment—did you know that?'

'I never listen to rumour, and I do not care. The rumours will soon be forgotten when some new scandal comes along to take their interest.'

'Oh, it will—and soon, you can be sure of that. But the rumour mill has not done with you yet—far from it.'

Eve sensed Lady Devlin had something unpleasant to impart and that she wouldn't like it one bit. 'Kindly explain yourself.'

'With the greatest of pleasure. Edward has long favoured living at Netherthorpe but the Dower House will do for now. Lord Levisham and Edward have made a wager that, should Lord Levisham fail to seduce you before Christmas, then Edward will move into the Dower House.'

Eve went cold. 'A wager? I don't understand.'

'Of course you don't. How could you? This is one wager Lord Levisham wants kept out of White's betting book.'

Lady Devlin's disclosure was like an arrow sent straight to Eve's heart. She felt the blood drain from her face and her eyes had a haunted, almost desperate expression. 'You're lying,' she said quietly, unable to believe what she was hearing.

'Am I? I don't think so. Edward believed his expectations would be fulfilled while you were residing at The Grange—where the seduction of the unsuspecting Mrs Lansbury would be more difficult than here in London. You have clearly developed a *tendre* for Lord Levisham in such a short time.'

'That is none of your business.'

'No, it isn't, but I am doing you a favour in telling you this. My advice to you is to get back to Surrey post haste before the wager becomes public knowledge. In the past, Lord Levisham has flayed the reputation of more pretentiously proud females than can be recalled. You are no different from any of them.'

# Chapter Nine

A wager!

Eve stood like a pillar of stone as she watched Elena Devlin saunter off as if nothing untoward had occurred. She wondered at the strange pain in her heart and realised that, beneath everything, she had learned just how much Maxim had come to mean to her.

She looked down the long, lonely corridor of the future. It was worse than anything she had known, that silent acceptance, thinking of the man she had come to trust so completely and who just as completely had deceived her, had betrayed her. He had only meant to use her, and had done it very cleverly too.

Suddenly the happiness and security she had found with him these past days was gone. Her mind was numb, and she felt physically sick. What Lady Devlin had just divulged hung in the air like a bad smell. No one had insulted her as much as this and it was more than her pride could bear. She had been careless of her emotions to let it get so far. Maxim had used her. She had been a diversion to him, one of those women who fill a need in a man. Deep down she was furious, furious at the injustice done to her. Cold fury engulfed her. Of all the treacherous, underhanded tricks…

Dazed and unable to form any coherent thought, she turned when Sarah came up behind her, wanting nothing more than to escape this place, where she felt everyone was looking at her. Seeing her stricken look, Sarah reached out and took her hand.

'Eve, what is it? You are as white as a ghost. I saw you talking to a woman. Do you know her?'

'Yes, Sarah. It was Elena Devlin.'

'Oh, I see. The woman who Matthew…'

'Yes, Sarah,' Eve said sharply. '*That* woman.'

'What did she say that has upset you so?'

Eve swallowed, shaking her head. 'I—I can't tell you. Not now. I would like to return to the house. I… Oh, Sarah. It's so awful.' The very thought of the extent of the monstrous deceit Maxim had practised made her tremble with such uncontrollable fury that for some moments she thought she was suffering from some kind of seizure.

Without more ado, Sarah took her arm and returned to the carriage, instructing the driver to take them home.

Alone in Eve's bed chamber, Sarah insisted Eve tell her what was wrong.

'Tell me, Eve. Is it so terrible?'

'The worst. I've been such a fool, Sarah. A stupid, gullible fool.'

Rage was rising in a red tide. She hardly knew what

she was doing. She felt half-crazed with pain, anger and humiliation.

'It can't be true,' Eve repeated more than once.

'For goodness' sake, Eve, tell me,' Sarah demanded.

Eve looked at her, her eyes wide with every emotion she was capable of feeling. 'I made a mistake in trusting and allowing myself to feel things for Lord Levisham, like some besotted idiot. From the very start, his easy banter and relaxed charm completely disarmed me. I know men take advantage of women, so how have I allowed myself to fall into that trap?'

'Why? What has he done?'

'He has been playing a game with me. I was his prey, and from the very start he was intent on seducing me, dishonouring me—all for a wager he had made with his cousin. To win his bet, nothing was going to deter him from trying. The plan was that he had to seduce me before Christmas. Should he fail, his cousin would take up residence in the Dower House at Netherthorpe.'

'My goodness! But—how could he do that? I cannot believe it of him, Eve. There may be a perfectly good explanation. He has been so attentive to you since you came to London.'

'For good reason, it would appear. A house, for heaven's sake!' It was more than Eve's lacerated nerves could withstand. He had won the wager and his wretched cousin would know all about it, increasing her humiliation—the kind of humiliation that would increase a thousand-fold should Sarah find out what she had done.

Her face blazed with fury. 'Oh, the humiliation of it, Sarah. And, if he succeeded, what would my life be like, following a tainted liaison with a renowned rake?' Her throat ached with tears. The discovery of Maxim's treachery had destroyed all her illusions. She'd never trust him again, ever. How could she? He would never redeem himself from this. 'Why would Elena Devlin tell me this? It's outrageous.'

'You sound like you're trying to convince yourself,' Sarah said, shaking her head. 'Surely she wouldn't have told you if it wasn't true. Would she?'

'I don't know. I have no idea.' Eve turned away and faced the window, and Sarah reached out to touch her on the shoulder. 'Eve, it will be all right,' she said in a placating voice.

Eve's shoulders began to shake and then she gulped back a tear. 'I hate him. Why did he have to do this to me?'

'Who? Lord Levisham or his cousin?'

'Both of them.'

No longer able to withhold the tears, Eve started to sob. It hurt to think about it. When she did, it only made things worse—if they could possibly get any worse. She shrank from the pain and her tears came in a kind of primal, visceral despair. It was too dreadful for words, as if a part of her that had only recently awakened had gone, a part she would never recover. It had vanished overnight. Her sobs came in waves, engulfing her in an awful torrent of emotion. But after a while her tears subsided.

'How could Maxim do this to me?' she said, her

mouth twisting with anger. 'How could he?' She stood, staring out of the window, her hands clenched into fists by her sides. She felt Sarah beside her.

'I don't know. But listen, we still don't know if that woman was telling the truth.'

Sunlight crept into every corner of the room and Eve longed to be back at The Grange, to be outside walking across the land and into the woods—anywhere but here, away from this awful torrent of emotion that roiled inside her and which she could find no way to halt.

'What am I going to do, Sarah?'

Sarah took her tormented sister in her arms, swallowed up by her distress. 'Darling Eve. You don't have to do anything you don't want to do. You don't have to see him again if you don't want to. It doesn't have to change anything.'

Eve pulled herself away, furiously wiping away the tears with the back of her hand. 'How can you say that? It changes absolutely everything. I never expected anything like this. I never want to see him again.'

'You don't have to if you don't want to,' Sarah finally said. 'Will you tell him what Lady Devlin has divulged?'

'No—no, I won't.' If he tried to lie to her or beg her forgiveness, she would despise him. She wished she could do that. It would make things easier for her if she could turn her love into contempt—for love him she did, agonisingly, hopelessly, to the very bones of her. Her body went limp and she sank onto the bed, as if all the tension was draining from her. Looking up, she gave Sarah a sad, broken kind of smile, as if conceding defeat.

'I wish I had never met him, Sarah.'

'He has come to mean something to you, hasn't he? Is that what you're saying?'

'I don't know what I'm saying.' She needed to explain things to herself as much as to her sister. 'I don't know what I'm doing except that I'm in an awful mess over it. I may not like or admire Elena Devlin but I suppose I have much to be grateful to her for. I have made a lucky escape. When Maxim first appeared in my life, it was the sort of relationship I thought I could do with. Pleasure without involvement—no commitment.'

She gritted her teeth against the tide of pain that slammed into her at the realisation of what he had done to her. 'Maxim Randall could not have made his lack of regard more clear if he had etched it in stone. It's all gone wrong.' She wiped her eyes with her fingers. 'I am shocked, angry. Never again will I allow myself to be taken in by the likes of Maxim Randall.'

'You are neighbours, Eve. It is inevitable that you will meet on occasion. And, not knowing what his cousin has divulged, he is bound to seek you out.'

Eve set her chin, her eyes hardening. 'Then let him. If I want to avenge myself, then I will play him at his own game if necessary, and he will have no idea of it.'

'But you are not like that. The Eve I know would have no time for such foolishness.'

'That was before I married Matthew and I found myself playing second fiddle to his mistress.' She looked at Sarah. 'You knew about his affair, didn't you, Sarah?'

'Yes, Eve. We all did. But we thought it best not to interfere.'

Eve shrugged. 'It wouldn't have made any difference if you had. Nothing would have been achieved by it.' Getting up, she walked to the window and stood looking out, seeing Nessa walking in the garden with Christopher, her beautiful boy with his curly strawberry-blonde hair framing his face and his complexion rosy and clear. He was playing with Sarah's young daughter, and they bounded along the paths in pursuit of each other.

When she turned back to face Sarah, an icy numbness took over, and she was surprised to find she was no longer in the throes of heart-wrenching pain.

'I can tell by your face that you've made a decision, Eve.'

'Yes. Yes I have, Sarah,' she replied, knowing it had been traumatic for Sarah to hear of her life laid bare and to be enraged on her behalf. She relived the encounter with Elena Devlin. Half of her wanted the woman's blood, the other was consumed with shame at her own gullibility and stupidity in trusting Maxim Randall. 'Somehow I don't think Maxim will know Lady Devlin has told me about the wager—and neither will I tell him.'

'Won't you?'

'It is all so sordid, Sarah—and I have my pride. I will be the one to walk away, to move on from this. Knowing about the wager has given me an advantage to outmanoeuvre him.'

'What will you do? You have arranged to go on a carriage drive to Hampstead tomorrow.'

Eve shrugged. 'Yes, I have. I'll write to him—tell him I have to return to Surrey immediately, that some unforeseen problem has arisen that requires my attention.'

Already she began to plan a way to thwart, foil and exasperate the plans of the infuriating lord. With tremendous will, she knew she would have to be strong to withstand a man of his character. Maxim Randall had no claim to being a gentleman in her interpretation of the word, but she knew him to be a proud man, and she intended to trample his pride to pieces. She was strong and resilient and would get over this. She would leave London for Surrey tomorrow.

Early the next morning, Eve sent a brief note to Maxim's town house in Mayfair and spent the rest of the day preparing for her departure. She was impatient to return to The Grange, to put this unfortunate business behind her. Engulfed with anger and emotion, she felt that she had aged a lifetime in the time it had taken her to realise what Maxim had done. Dark feelings swirled about her like smoke, filling the crevices of her mind and creeping into her thoughts. The house suddenly felt deathly quiet. She could hear no familiar sounds from the kitchen as the servants went about their work, no bird song from the outside world. Everything stilled. Only her breathing could be heard.

As if challenged by what Maxim had done to her, she made a deliberate effort to pull herself out of her mood of near despair and to banish self-pity, the sense of loneliness crowding her. When she was back at The Grange, work would once again become a ritual in her life. She would welcome it.

She was on the point of leaving when Maxim arrived at the house, hoping he was in time to see her before she left.

He was shown into the drawing room, where Eve received him alone. Her heart gave a familiar leap of excitement. Much as she wanted to hate him for what he had intended for her, she could not help noticing how alluring he looked—the shade and colour of his eyes, the hard line of his jaw and the harsh slant of his lips. Her deadened sense of unreality was crumbling to allow her raw, aching emotions to be exposed. He only had to appear in her sights for her pulse to pound and her body to tremble in anticipation of his attention. Despite all the reasons not to be, she was in love with him. It was a bitter admission, but there it was. She had to face up to the truth, like the idea or not.

Stiffening her spine, she reminded herself that she was the woman he had intended to desert as soon as he had seduced her. Dear Lord! Only let her have the strength not to show anything, but to act as well as he could when it suited whatever devious purposes he had in mind. She prayed she would eventually have the strength to forget him and that disgusting wager. She must, otherwise she would suffer the bitterness and pain that twisted so hard inside her that she thought she would die of it. This was why she had to put some distance between them, why the only way she could salvage any peace for her future was to leave London, to return home to the life she had mapped out for herself and Christopher.

For a moment, perhaps the last time they would be alone, she let herself look at him, take in the sight of this man who had turned her life inside out. He was dressed immaculately, fastidiously even, his fine lawn shirt beneath his coat beautifully laundered. The cut of his expensive coat set off the powerful width of his shoulders, his long legs strong and shapely in the tailored perfection of his trousers. His hair was smoothly brushed back from his face, his eyes piercing and bright. He stood looking at her and she realised that they had reached a defining moment in their relationship, if a relationship was what they had.

'Maxim!' She wanted to treat him with complete indifference, to be free of him, to take up her life as it had been before Maxim Randall came storming into it, and devote herself to her son. She looked away before she became lost in the dark beauty of his eyes. 'I did not expect to see you. You got my letter?'

He nodded, watching her carefully. 'You have to return home. It must be a serious matter for you to have to leave London with such haste.'

She heard the disappointment in his voice. She'd had many hours in which to build her rage against him. Rage, yes, but far more—a deep, underlying bitterness which stirred beneath the surface. Thankfully she'd had time to grasp the realities now laid before her and she managed to bring a smile to her lips. She would not allow him to see how humiliating, how shaming this was for her. Yet, seeing him now, she knew he wasn't to know how all her senses were crying out for him, how she was slowly dying inside. He had callously set out to dishonour her, and it was all she could do not to humble herself at his feet.

'Yes, it is,' she replied, surprised her voice didn't shake. It was low, furiously controlled. It disguised the venom she would have injected into her words, fuelled by bitter humiliation from the knowledge that she had come to enjoy his attention in recent days.

'You look pale, Eve. Are you unwell?'

'I am quite well, Maxim,' she answered, her manner brusque, causing a flicker of consternation to cross his face.

'I shall miss you. I had hoped you would remain in London a few more days at least.'

'I am anxious to go home,' she said simply.

'And I can't persuade you to say?'

'No, no, you can't. Please excuse me. I'm sorry not to have more time, Maxim, but the coach is waiting. Nessa and Christopher are waiting for me.'

'Then I wish you a safe journey.'

'Thank you. I'm sure it will be. Please excuse me.'

Maxim stepped back as she turned from him and went into the hall, hugging Marian and Sarah, promising to write very soon. He followed Eve outside to the waiting coach, in which a tearful Christopher, who didn't want to leave his young cousin, was bouncing about. Nessa was trying to settle him with a toy soldier

Robert had given him as a parting gift, but she wasn't having much success.

Maxim held out his hand to assist Eve into the coach, but she ignored it and turned away. He felt his jaw suddenly tighten. Women didn't usually turn away from him. What game was she playing? Politeness, formality, detached indifference... She wanted to avoid him, that much was obvious. He stood aside while she spoke again to her sisters. Refusing to be dismissed in so casual a manner, when she would have climbed into the coach his face darkened and he took her arm.

'Eve, a moment, please.' He drew her aside, out of earshot. 'Why are you doing this? Why are you angry with me?'

Her wide-eyed look was one of complete innocence. 'Angry? I am not angry,' she replied with a brittle gaiety.

'After spending so much time together, I thought...'

'Thought what, Maxim?' she asked, bitterly aware that she had allowed herself to be lulled by his charm and her own treacherous emotions. She was trying to harden herself against him, to forget his kisses, his love-making and the way he had held her.

'You told me you had no regrets about what transpired between us. Has something happened to change your mind?'

She met his gaze head-on. 'No, nothing at all. I was a willing participant in what happened between us.'

'And I took what I desired without giving anything.'

'Did I object or complain?'

'No, but I should have known better. You are not

just a bored widow seeking a brief diversion. You are young and vulnerable—you deserve better.'

'Maybe I do, but at present I have pressing matters to take care of. I have my own life at The Grange. Nothing can change that. We enjoyed ourselves, and I thank you for paying me so much attention and taking such good care of me. I most certainly did not expect you to make any kind of commitment to me, if that is what you think.'

'And the times we were alone together? Did that mean anything to you?'

'Of course it did, but it shouldn't have happened. I think we both let the atmosphere of that particular evening go to our heads and we lost control.' She looked up at him, looked away and back again. 'I should have known better than to submit to the charms of a philanderer.'

Maxim arched his eyebrows, riled at being written off so easily, while wondering what in God's name had happened to the beguiling woman he had escorted about London. 'I'm sorry you feel that way, because I think you are the loveliest, most courageous young woman I have ever met.'

Eve felt as if her heart were breaking. His gaze was one of consuming intensity, his mouth all wilful sensuality. 'Please stop it. Your compliments smack of insincerity. This time I have spent in London has been a pleasant interlude, an amusing diversion from my life at The Grange. What happened was nothing but an amusing diversion. It was a sophisticated flirtation—the rule being the one you, an experienced man of the world, usually play by—that no one takes anything seriously. It was nothing more than that.'

He frowned. 'What is this, Eve? Are you afraid of what happened between us?' he asked in a voice of taut calm.

'Afraid? No, of course not. Why should I be? It's just that I'm not on the market for romance or anything else along those lines. Before I know where I am, I might start falling for it and believe you really care.'

'And how do you know that I don't?'

'It's far too soon,' she replied, struggling valiantly to sound flippant.

'Are you saying it meant nothing to you?'

She shrugged. 'Please don't go on, Maxim. I really must be going.'

Maxim's face hardened into an expressionless mask, but his eyes were probing hers like daggers, looking for answers, as if he couldn't really believe this was the same woman who had melted in his arms with such sweet, innocent passion and had yielded her lips to his. Try as he might, he could not fathom a reason for the change in her manner towards him. His disappointment made him carelessly cruel. 'You would do well to remember how you responded to my love-making— willingly, I might add. How much you enjoyed being with me.'

'That was then. This is now. Things change,' she said, doing her utmost to avoid his eyes as a change came over him. In all her life she had never encountered such controlled, purposeful anger.

Maxim stared at her. 'Forgive me if I appear dense, but you gave a fair imitation of enjoying it.'

She smiled. 'And no doubt, after your many conquests, you're surprised to discover there is a female who finds you resistible.'

'I would like to convince you that you can overcome that problem—to persuade you,' he said, his voice dangerously low.

'You will not succeed in doing that. I will not allow it. Face it, Maxim. Any kind of relationship between us would be a disaster.' It seemed to Eve as if his eyes had never looked so deeply grey or so imperviously hard as they did at that moment.

'That depends on what you mean by a relationship.'

'What do you mean by it, Maxim?' she said defensively.

Clearly offended by her outspokenness and the distance she was determined to place between them, he looked at her and stepped back. 'You are right. Maybe it would be a disaster. At this particular point in my life—with someone doing their damnedest to end it—I'm in no position to think much beyond the present. Therefore, a relationship to me is all to do with the here and the now. You must forgive me if I was mistaken and presumptuous. I thought you were different from the rest—fool that I am.'

He spoke with such biting bitterness that it made Eve's heart squeeze in the most awful, inexplicable way. His face was expressionless. His eyes were empty, a glacial grey emptiness that told her nothing of what he felt. He spoke only a few parting words.

'You are impatient to be on your way, so I will detain you longer. You'd best get into the coach. Your son is waiting. Goodbye, Eve. I hope you have a safe journey.'

The regret in his voice touched Eve to the core of her being. She would have turned back but, reminding herself about all he was guilty of, she rebuked herself. When the coach pulled away from the house, she experienced a sharp tug of loss at the realisation that whatever there had been between the Earl of Levisham and her was over.

Her heart ached with the desolation of it and tears stung her eyes. Angrily, she blinked them away. She must cling to the thought that she was extremely fortunate to have found out about that wretched wager before she had made a complete fool of herself. That she had realised the full extent of his profligacy, and that the original rumours had been correct. But it was all so painful and dreadful beyond anything she could have imagined.

His eyes as dark and ominous as the River Thames on a moonless night, Maxim leaned back against the squabs, struggling to make sense of his last exchange with Eve. Truly believing that he was the injured party, he was determined to purge her from his mind. Purging her from his heart would not be so easy. The truth was that, for the short time they had been together, she had filled a gaping emptiness in his life and nothing could blunt the feelings he had for her.

He could not understand why she had gladly climbed

into his bed one minute, melting into his arms with a passion that had surprised and bewitched him, and then for no comprehensible reason had treated him as if he were contemptible, as if she were trying to teach him some well-deserved lesson. She was a woman of gentleness with an aura of unflustered serenity. Yet below that surface was a quiet steeliness. Everything about her was ruled by duty to her home and the love she had for her son.

When his work in London was concluded, and unable to forget Eve, he left for Netherthorpe. Unable to think of anything but Eve, how much he wanted her, how she represented everything he found desirable in a woman, he was determined not to let go of her. When he had taken Edward's wager, she had merely been the tantalising object of his lustful thoughts, and he'd thought of little else but possessing her. But, after giving it careful thought, he'd quickly changed his mind.

Seducing women of Eve's ilk was not his style. The effect she had had on him then had been as unsettling as it was now. He was unable to analyse the raw heat that ran through his veins whenever she was close. Since he had dispensed with his military career and returned to the responsibility of his inheritance, it was his duty to marry and provide an heir, a responsibility of which he had been constantly reminded from the day he'd learned of Andrew's death.

Eve was the woman he wanted. No other. The fact that she had determinedly begun to oppose him—the reason a mystery to him—did not deter him. Had he not felt her body's response when she had shared his bed? He did not have the slightest doubt that he would be able to lure her back into his arms. His decision to make her his wife was one that brooked no further debate.

Eve's return to The Grange brought her relief but little comfort. She would have to cope with every day life even though she longed to have someone beside her, someone she could confide in and trust, even a strong shoulder to lean against and a pair of strong arms to hold her. Coming home was more unsettling than anything she had known since leaving for London, because she now had time to think and to feel. She felt like a fox that had out-run the hounds and found temporary sanctuary in its earth, a brief respite, for she knew her torment would begin again when Maxim returned to Netherthorpe. Living so close, it would be difficult to avoid him.

What he had done disgusted her. He was hardly worth thinking and she must learn to put him out of her mind like every other unpleasant thought that only served to anger her. What she had done could not be undone—although she had certainly learned a lesson that should serve her well in the future.

Agatha and the rest of the servants had missed Eve, and in particular Christopher. The house had been far too quiet without his constant chatter, and they made a huge fuss when they arrived home. Looking forward to Sarah's visit, who had promised to stay for a few days on her way home to Sussex, Eve spent the first days back with Henry, discussing what had transpired in her absence. Agatha lost no time in filling her in about the gossip in Woodgreen, but it was from Henry that Eve learned Sir Oscar was not in the best of health and had taken to his bed while his wife was gallivanting about in London.

She had been back at The Grange for two months when she could no longer ignore the changes in her body or the exhaustion and nausea that racked her body every morning—which in itself was a diagnosis. Initially, the revelation that a new life was growing within her, one in which Maxim had equal share, brought her no joy. A child would only exacerbate the difficulties of the situation. When a fresh wave of nausea swamped her, leaving her spent, the harsh reminder of her position struck her like a hammer blow.

Maxim had impregnated her with an ease she found maddening. Why had she not considered the consequences of going to bed with him? This daze of wretchedness and uncertainty she had blundered into was quite devastating—a shocking outcome to one night of indescribably wonderful love.

With a profitable harvest behind her, Eve decided the farm would run to another horse to work the land. It was a bright day, the first good one after five days' rain. She breathed deeply, filling her lungs, hoping for a trace of autumn. But there was a definite chill in the air, a sign of the winter to come.

She set off with Henry to purchase a horse from a local farmer who had one to sell. Christopher sat between them in the carriage. Arriving at the farm, they made for the stables, where Farmer Humphrey was working. They entered the stable's dim interior, the smell of manure and leather strong, though not un-pleasant. There were several people at work, among them Farmer Humphrey. A man in his thirties, tall, slim, with a ruddy expression and friendly eyes, he was well known to her.

When he saw her with Henry, standing in the door-way, he immediately left what he was doing and strode over to them, smiling a welcome.

'It's good to see you, Mrs Lansbury—and this young man,' he said, ruffling Christopher's hair.

'And you, Mr Humphrey. We are here to look at the horse you have for sale.'

'So I have. It's in the field. Come and take a look. He's three years old—good worker, but he's surplus to requirements.'

Leaving Christopher with one of the farm hands, they went out into the field. The horse was exactly what they were looking for. After making arrangements for Henry to collect it the next day, they walked back to the stables, where they spent a moment chatting to Farmer Humphrey. In the stable Christopher was playing with some puppies, his young voice bubbling with glee. Mr Humphrey promised him he could have one when the pups were old enough to leave their mother.

Eve was unaware of the man who had ridden into the yard and dismounted from his horse and who, on hearing her voice, swung round. From the corner of her eye, she glimpsed a tall man to the side of her and an uncontrollable tremor of dread shot through her. She could have sworn she saw him stiffen with shock, but

in that instant she was absolutely besieged by coward-
ice and kept her head averted, her face hidden behind
the brim of her bonnet.

'Eve!' Maxim's voice rang out.

As she turned her head, their eyes met instantly, and
so abrupt was Maxim's appearance that Eve started,
although she shouldn't have been so surprised, as Mr
Humphrey was one of Maxim's tenant farmers. A
world of feelings flashed across his face—surprise,
disbelief, admiration—but only for a moment. How she
would like to have said she was not in love with him,
that all she felt was physical desire, an animal crav-
ing that affected her body but never her mind. But she
couldn't say that.

A lock of hair tumbled over his eyes. He looked irresistibly attractive, and Eve wanted him to take her in
his arms there and then and tell her what he had done
had all been a mistake. Immediately she pulled herself
together and averted her eyes until her heartbeat had
lessened. She looked back again at his chiselled profile, marvelling at the strength and pride carved into
every feature on the starkly handsome face.

'It's a pleasure seeing you again,' he said with grim
formality.

At the scathing tone of his voice, the fantasy of seeing him remorseful following their bitter parting in
London collapsed the instant she saw his face—it was
hard and forbidding as a rock. Now was not the time
to inform him he was to be a father.

When they had parted, she had not expected to feel
the awful lack of him in her life. For a short while he

had filled every moment of it with his often difficult, sometimes passionate and demanding self. He had angered and amused her, aroused her, made her feel and think—and had hurt, shamed and humiliated her. The wager he had made with his cousin was at the forefront of her mind, and it still burned with the memory of what he had done. She would never forgive him. But what could she do now she was to bear his child?

He stood holding the reins of his horse, watching her through narrowed eyes. His thick hair was tousled, his face one of arrogant handsomeness with its sculpted mouth and striking eyes. But there was cynicism in those eyes and a ruthless set to his jaw. As she searched his features, there was no sign that he had actually held her and made love to her with seductive tenderness. She flinched at the coolness of his eyes as they raked over her.

'How is Christopher?' he enquired.

Eve swallowed and was surprised that she managed to reply without her voice shaking. 'He is very well, thank you—as you will see when he can be drawn away from Mr Humphrey's puppies. And you, Maxim. Are you well?'

She was awarded with a cynical upward tilt of a black brow as he drawled, 'As you can see, I have survived our previous encounter without scars.'

'Mrs Lansbury is here to purchase a horse, m'lord,' Henry said, who had observed the exchange and noticed his employer's unease. 'Our business is over, so if you wish to speak to Farmer Humphrey he is in the stable.'

Eve turned to Henry. 'See if you can drag Christopher away from those pups, will you, Henry?' She turned back to Maxim. 'You—are settling down at Netherthorpe?'

'I am—and, as you see, I haven't been shot.'

Eve paled. 'Have there been more incidents?'

He shook his head. 'No, but the threat remains.'

'The man who died when he fell off your balcony… Could the constables throw any light on his identity?'

He shook his head. 'I have no doubt that the person who wants me dead will soon hire someone else now he has failed to get results.'

Eve looked towards the stable where Mr Humphrey's wife had appeared, holding the hand of a scowling small boy. He was clearly put out at being dragged away from the puppies.

Eve sighed. 'Oh, dear! Mr Humphrey has promised him one of the pups but they're not yet old enough to leave the mother.'

Eve was unprepared for her son's reaction at seeing Maxim. It was as if the puppies no longer existed as he uttered a squeal of delight and his little legs propelled him in Maxim's direction. Maxim laughed and lifted the pink-cheeked child off his feet.

'I am flattered that Christopher remembers me—and he is obviously happy to see me,' Maxim said, swinging him high into the air.

Eve looked at her son. He was indeed smiling at him, and gurgling. Traitor, she thought, scowling at her son. How could he do that? She felt betrayed by her own child. Never had she imagined she could feel

envious of her offspring when Maxim held him close…
But, no, she thought defiantly, she didn't want him to
touch her ever again.

After greeting Lord Levisham, Mrs Humphrey
looked at Eve. 'It's good to see you, Mrs Lansbury. I
meant to call on you to ask if you would be willing to
help out at the annual ball in the assembly rooms this
year. You know how everyone looks forward to it—
especially the young ones. They get so excited when
the bidding starts.'

Mrs Humphrey was a tall, stout woman, one of
three benevolent ladies who were pillars of the community, whose lives revolved around doing charitable
deeds. They worked hard collecting funds from well-
off neighbours in and around Woodgreen. They orga-
nised charity events for the poor throughout the year,
such as bazaars, the events culminating in a charity ball
in the assembly rooms two weeks before Christmas.
It always created an element of excitement as gentlemen were allowed to bid for the lady of their choice
on the dance floor.

'Yes, of course. I'll be there on the night to lend a
hand, and I'll have a word with Agatha, who always
likes to contribute to the refreshments.'

'And you will be present for the bidding, won't you?'

'I wouldn't miss it for the world, Mrs Humphrey.'

'I wager you will attract the attention of more than
one of the local gentry—which happens every year,
even though you decline the gentlemen.'

'I'm not a betting woman, Mrs Humphrey,' she said,
looking pointedly at Maxim. 'What do you say, Lord

Levisham? I imagine you are a betting man? That you like a gamble? Now, please excuse us,' she said, reaching out and prising her wriggling son out of Maxim's arms. 'We must be on our way.'

'Mrs Humphrey,' Maxim said without taking his eyes off Eve's back as Henry drove off, Eve's parting words having brought a curious frown to his brow. 'I assume I am invited to this ball in the assembly rooms next week?'

Mrs Humphrey beamed up at him. 'Why yes, of course you are. You don't need an invitation, Lord Levisham. It would be wonderful if you were to honour us with your presence. It is an event for charity.'

'In which case, you can be assured that I shall make a generous donation.'

## *Chapter Ten*

Sarah arrived with her daughter, to Christopher's absolute delight. Sarah's husband, who had business in the city, had remained in London and was to travel down to Sussex in time for Christmas. With her husband spending more and more of his time in the city, he and Sarah were considering moving out of Sussex and residing closer to London, much to Sarah's delight. But she was adamant that she would not live in the city itself, preferring a more rural place to live.

Observing Eve's pallor and her melancholy mood, Sarah was troubled. On seeing her leave the house one morning to walk alone in the gardens, she followed, finding her seated on a bench, and staring at the black water of a lily pond, her face set in unhappy lines. She sat beside her.

Taking Eve's hand in hers, she gave it a little squeeze, looking with earnest eyes at her sister. 'What's wrong, Eve? You have been in such low spirits since I arrived. Is it The Grange? I know how hard you work. Are you finding it too much for you?'

Eve shook her head slowly, a tear running down her cheek. 'No,' she whispered. 'It's nothing like that.'

'Eve, listen to me. What concerns you, concerns me. Now, tell me.'

Swallowing hard, Eve looked directly into her sister's eyes, feeling an obligation to tell her the truth. 'I am with child, Sarah.'

The silence that followed was heavy between them.

Sarah's features tightened slightly and, although the words were softly spoken, they hit her with the blow of a pugilist. At length, she said, 'I see. And would I be right in assuming the father is Lord Levisham?'

'Yes—yes, you are, Sarah.'

Noting the catch in her voice, and the sudden tears awash in Eve's eyes, Sarah reached out and grasped her hand. 'Don't, Eve. Don't upset yourself.'

'Oh, Sarah. I've been such a fool. I should never have let it happen.'

'We're all entitled to make mistakes—even you. Did—did he force himself on you?'

'No—he would never do that. I—was not unwilling,' she replied, having the grace to lower her eyes as she confessed quietly to the sin she had committed with Maxim.

'Oh, Eve. I should have seen something like this coming. The two of you were close—until you found out about that wretched wager he had made with his cousin.'

'We were. I don't know what to do, Sarah. Can you advise me?'

'How can I not, you unhappy girl? More foolish than wretched,' Sarah murmured, smiling softly. 'You are my beloved sister and I care deeply about what you do. Lord Levisham must be told, Eve. You do realise that, don't you?'

She nodded. 'Yes—and I will. But I love him, Sarah. I never thought I would love anyone as much as I do Maxim. I—I just wanted him to come to me because he loves me—not to do the decent thing by me for the sake of the child.'

'In this instant, the child is all important. You have to find a way to put aside your own feelings of hurt and disappointment in order to secure the best future for your child.'

'Yes, you are right, Sarah. I know you are—and I shall. As to what will happen afterwards when I have told Maxim, well, we shall just have to wait and see.'

Eve was only too pleased to help out at the charitable event in Woodgreen's assembly rooms when she could—it was the least she could do for the needy in and around the town—but with everything she had to do at The Grange her time was limited. She was accompanied by Sarah, who had offered to help, only too happy to lend a hand.

Eve was a well-known figure and on arrival she made a point of speaking to several of the elderly ladies, some of them on the committee in whose hands the responsibility for the whole event rested. The room

was a kaleidoscope of colour, of dazzling dresses, men
in brightly coloured waistcoats of silks and satin and
powdered wigs. The young ladies with dancing curls
looked like butterflies in their floating flounces of colourful silks and lace. Excited with the joy of the occasion, each gazed flirtatiously at the young men, all a
twitter about the bidding to take place after the refreshment break. Eve watched them with a savage envy in
her heart, wishing that for this one evening she could
be as free as they were.

The walls were decked with long ropes of Christmas
greenery, giving out a spicy smell. There was a raised
platform at the end of the room where the musicians
were tuning up their instruments. More people began
to arrive, and the room became warm with bodies and
the many candles in wall sconces and chandeliers suspended from the ceiling, the air smelling of different
colognes, hair pomade and the gentlemen's cheroots.
An adjoining room was laid out with refreshments to
be eaten halfway through the evening.

Suddenly the musicians began to play a rousing
country dance and groups of young people took to the
floor. Eve was aware of admiring glances from several gentlemen known to her. She was alluring, bright
and unpredictable, often engaging and just as often
frostily aloof. Despite having acquired the sobriquet
of 'the ice widow', she drew the attention of the opposite sex almost without benefit of conscious effort,
but her attitude did not encourage them to come too
close. Those who fell victim to her potent magnetism
soon learned to their cost that the fascinating Widow

Lansbury, while accepting their masculine admiration as both her right and pleasure, kept herself beyond their reach.

As the young women swished their skirts and laughed, looking with shining faces at the handsome young men standing about the room, Eve felt no joy as she looked about her. Every woman present was bursting with an excitement and an emotion she did not feel. When the noise of feet stamping on the wooden floor and the cacophony of music and voices became deafening, she went to assist with the refreshments.

When everyone had eaten their fill and left the refreshment room, Eve stood in the doorway and watched as the dancing resumed. Her gaze went to the doorway as more people came to partake of the jollities. She started in recognition of one of them. It was Maxim, with Edward standing a little behind him. Dressed in a suit of midnight-blue velvet, he towered over those who stood near him. Tall, slender-hipped and broad-shouldered, he was as handsome of physique as he was of face. His chiselled profile was touched by the warm light of innumerable candles, and the growing ache in Eve's chest attested to the degree of his handsomeness.

His eyes did a slow sweep of the room, coming to rest on her—a still figure across the room, standing in the shadow of the doorway to the refreshment room. He gave a slow smile of utter assurance, and there was a twinkle in his bold eyes as he stared at her. She was dressed in a gown of sapphire-blue silk spangled with silver, her hair perfectly arranged in curls around her perfectly shaped head.

Edward came to stand by his side. He looked straight at her, and she resisted the urge to duck her head away from his glance. Seeing Maxim here tonight, she turned her thoughts back to her present predicament and cringed inside at the thought of the outcome.

The arrival of the Earl of Levisham with his handsome features and noble mien caused quite a stir, drawing the eye of everyone in the room. Local dignitaries left their wives and made their way to his side, eager to ingratiate themselves with the new Earl of Levisham and to welcome him to this happy event—and hopefully a profitable one when the bidding began. Suddenly everyone was bowing and curtseying, eager to welcome this illustrious visitor.

Eve was aware that his blatant masculinity appealed to the females present. More than one favoured him with indiscreet glances, fluttering lashes and blushing prettily while wafting fans. He returned their interest with a roguish grin. Indeed, Eve realised he accorded the elderly matrons the same treatment as the young ladies. Yet she couldn't help experiencing an ungovernable jealousy at all the attention he was attracting.

Standing in the doorway to the refreshment room—wishing to remain invisible, for she was suddenly reluctant to speak to him—Eve's first instinct was to shrink back. But, remembering all he was guilty of where she was concerned, she stayed where she was.

There was a roll of drums, announcing that the bidding was about to begin. Eve fixed her eyes on what was happening on the platform, feeling Maxim's eyes burning holes into the back of her head. As the people melded into a haze about her, she remembered that unforgettable time she had spent in his bed, and the exquisite ecstasy she had felt when he had made love to every part of her body—teaching her that loving and the act of love itself was something that was felt, because emotion was neither clinical nor pretend. Despite trying not to think of that time, against all logic and reason she continued to yearn for what she could not have.

Much as she wanted to turn her head and look back at him, she straightened her spine, lifted her head and remained facing the front of the room. The chattering throng gathered around the platform where the bidding was to take place. All eyes were on the mayor, who was to act as auctioneer, his arms spread wide.

'The dancing will open with a waltz followed by a reel and a schottische. So, gentlemen, if you wish to lead the dancing with the lady of your choice, you must bargain for her, and I ask you to give generously. The proceeds are to go to local charities—the hospital and the orphanage.'

There was general excitement among the younger members, while the older members passed comment as each gentleman placed his bid for the lady of his choice to tumultuous laughter. There was a loud burst of applause after each bid, laughter and shouts of approval accompanied by many blushes and giggles from the ladies. Some of the more popular ladies attracted the highest bids, one ending when the auctioneer's gavel came down at forty guineas, the highest of the night. Surrounded by a sea of silk and lace, Eve observed the proceedings without being overlooked herself. Out of the corner of her eye she saw Maxim standing towards the back of the room. His shoulder was propped carelessly against a pillar, his arms folded across his chest, and he watched the proceedings through narrowed eyes.

The bidding was coming to an end and gentlemen were already leading the ladies of their choice onto the floor.

'Any more bids, gentlemen? There are more lovely ladies to bid for.'

Eve saw Maxim shrug himself away from the pillar and come to stand in the middle of the room. Casting a look at her, he cocked an eyebrow and his mouth quirked in a smile. He looked ahead at the auctioneer and his voice rang out.

'Two hundred guineas—for Mrs Eve Lansbury.'

A communal gasp was followed by a hush that fell on the whole room. Both the sum and the name of the lady had shocked the crowd. The auctioneer's eyes sought out Eve, who had come erect, her eyes open wide with disbelief.

'Two hundred guineas, Lord Levisham, is indeed a generous sum.'

Two hundred guineas was a sum that could not easily be challenged, so there were no more bids. The gavel came down and the auctioneer grinned broadly at Lord Levisham. 'You've purchased a rare prize, Lord Levisham.'

Maxim nodded, making his way to Eve's side. As he strode nearer, there was something in his measured stride that suggested the implacable approach of fate itself. The musicians began to play a waltz.

He bowed with a grand sweeping gesture and held out his hand to her. 'Shall we?'

Eve would have liked to refuse but, as he had bid so much money to dance with her, she was obliged to accept. The curious waiting to see how she would react pressed in around them, forcing politeness on them both, so that they stood back from their private quarrel to defend themselves from an enemy.

Maxim smiled down at her, taking her hand. She was tempted to snatch it out of his grip, and she would have too, if she hadn't thought it would be noted and give everyone something to talk about. All eyes were on them. His smile was the kind of smile that would melt any woman's heart if she didn't know him for the arrogant, heartless libertine he was. With expert ease, he took her in his arms and swept her onto the floor as the strains of the music filled the room.

Eve's heart had begun to pound with a mixture of so many emotions that she hadn't time to examine or comprehend what was happening at first—or how she suddenly found herself being twirled about the floor with the one man she had hoped never to encounter again. It was only the firm pressure of his hand on the small of her back that forced her to keep moving in time to the music. The rhythm released their tensions and they began to unbend.

'You shouldn't have done that,' she said at length.

'It was the only way I could think of to get you to talk to me.'

'You didn't have to bid two hundred guineas to do that.'

'Why not? The money will be going to a needy cause. Besides, you have been avoiding me.'

'I have not. I am not here to enjoy myself—or to seek your company either. And will you not hold me so tightly? If you were really a gentleman, you would not have forced this dance on me. Besides, there is nothing I have to say to you.'

'You think not? We have a great deal to say to one another. When you left London I was quite put out that I had been rebuffed by you. I have thought about you, Eve—a great deal, as a matter of fact—and now here you are.'

'You are very convincing, and you have a flattering tongue,' Eve uttered scathingly. 'In fact, I could actually believe you are speaking the truth, but then you have undoubtedly had a great deal of practice.'

He raised a brow and gave her a lengthy inspection as he whirled her round the floor. He laughed softly, his hooded eyes full of sardonic amusement as his arm tightened about her waist. 'I've had my moments—as well you know. I am thirty years of age and I have not lived the life of a monk. I'm quite nonchalant about these things.'

'Now, why am I not surprised?' In his arms, Eve felt that in his sublime male arrogance he was more attractive than ever and, despite her protestations, the urgency to be even closer to him was more vivid than before.

Sensing her resistance was beginning to crumble, and regardless of the many eyes watching them with interest as they twirled about the floor, he bent his head so his mouth was close to her ear and said, 'I'm difficult and quite impossible—that I know—but that's because I'm attracted to you. I want you, Eve.'

'Want? There is nothing wrong with wanting, Maxim, but it is a sin to take what is no longer on offer.'

He laughed low in his throat. 'I have been sinning all my life, so there is nothing new there. I'll do my penance later. Did you imagine you had committed some mortal sin because you enjoyed what we did and it made you feel as if you want to experience even more? I don't think so. I do want you. I have from the first moment I laid eyes on you.'

'And you are sure of that?'

'Absolutely. I am quite sincere.'

Feeling divine sensations shoot through her body, Eve closed her eyes. She had good reason to doubt him. From her own personal point of view, she had a score to settle—at least, she had, before she knew she was carrying his child. It changed everything, but she had no intention of making it easy for him. That humiliating wager was still uppermost in her mind. 'You haven't a sincere bone in your body.'

'But I have an overwhelming need for you—and I know you want me,' he told her with a knowing smile.

It dawned on Eve as Maxim's gaze fastened on her lips that he was remembering the night she had spent in his bed. For a man who had suffered such a crushing let down when they had parted company, Maxim seemed disgustingly at ease. Despite the fact that she shook her head, what he'd said was true—she did want him, very badly—but she wouldn't give him the satisfaction of saying so. 'We are in full view of everyone. Please don't look at me like that.'

Maxim's hungry gaze settled on her flushed, entrancing, rebellious face and a smile tugged at his lips. 'You have no idea what I would dare do to you,' he warned with a lazy, suggestive smile. 'And do you have any idea what will happen if I follow my inclinations and kiss you—here, in front of everyone? For a start, we will be talked about, and you will be out of bounds to every respectable male in Woodgreen and beyond.'

Her eyes shot daggers at him. 'I'm out of bounds anyway—of my own volition.'

They remained silent as they negotiated a path through other couples twirling about. She was surprised to see Edward dancing with Lady Devlin, who was resplendent in a dress of peacock-blue and wore an arrangement of matching feathers in her hair.

'You have brought Edward along, I see.'

'He insisted on coming with me—I think Lady Devlin was the attraction. Sir Oscar is not well, I believe.'

'No, apparently not.' She caught Edward's gaze and he smiled, a smile that caused a finger of unease to trace its chilling path down her spine. 'She doesn't appear to be too concerned about him—although, if she were to look towards the entrance, she would see a gentleman who looks remarkably like her husband loitering in the shadows.'

Maxim followed her gaze, seeing the gaunt figure of Sir Oscar leaning on his cane, his expression one of pure unadulterated hatred, as if he were about to commit murder as he watched Edward twirl his laughing wife about the floor. 'You are not mistaken. That's Sir Oscar—with a face like thunder.'

'And not as unconcerned by her dalliances as his wife would like to believe. I think she may have embarrassed him once too often and is about to get her just deserts—and about time too.'

Not until the dance ended and Maxim led her off the floor did he speak. 'For some reason unbeknown to me, Eve,' he said, his voice low and serious, 'I believe you are somehow testing me.' His eyes glinted like hard metal. 'I think this may bear further investigation and we must discuss the matter.'

'I don't think so,' she murmured on a more subdued note, tired of sparring with him, but not yet ready to let him off the hook. 'Let it be, Maxim—at least for tonight. This is neither the time nor the place.'

Reaching out, he gripped her arm as she was about to walk away. His eyes narrowed as they looked pointedly into hers. 'Not so fast. I have another dance to claim from you, don't forget. I paid two hundred guineas for the privilege.'

Eve managed to feign a look of disappointment and mortification. 'You should have consulted me before you did that. I promised Mrs Humphrey I would help out and I have things to do.'

'You cannot escape me so easily, Eve,' Maxim said calmly. 'I am not so easily got rid of—as you must have realised by now.'

Eve's face turned ashen under the careless remark, and she swayed on her feet, feeling faint—a reminder of her condition, but this was neither the time nor place to inform him about that. He steadied her by placing his hand under her elbow and turned her to face him.

'You do remember, don't you?'

Eve stared at him. She felt all the warm and passionate memories well up in her, but at the same time sadness. Dearly as she wanted to tell him she would never forget the magic they had spun in the privacy of his bedroom, that it had been the most wonderful thing that had happened to her in her life, her pride would not allow her to reveal how she felt when she remembered that disgusting wager.

'Remember?' she bit back, jerking her arm from his grasp, her anger giving virulence to her tongue. 'Yes, I remember everything,' she said furiously, remembering how she had enjoyed the things he had done to her, had revelled in it even, before she had known he did not feel anything for her. Now more than ever, she needed her forceful personality to keep her sane for what was to come. 'You have made it impossible for me to forget.' She found his sudden smile infuriating.

'I do seem to have a lasting effect on the ladies I make love to.'

'Don't flatter yourself, Maxim. Now, please go away and let me do what I have to do.'

The smile vanished and his face darkened with annoyance. Eve could almost feel his struggle to hold his temper in check, but before he could reply she had turned her back on him and walked away in the direction of the refreshment room without a backward glance, leaving him to exist in a state of seething frustration.

Maxim saw how heads turned to look at them, half-aware that Eve had slighted him. He should have taught her a lesson by cutting her in public, as if he'd never met her before, or forgotten that he had. But damn his own weakness. On some senseless impulse, he hadn't done that. He'd allowed himself to make that ridiculous bid for her so he could hold her in his arms once more, drawing attention to themselves.

'You are not gaining headwind tonight, Maxim,' a calm voice said next to him. 'I would say Cupid has smitten you,' Edward observed, 'If you have to follow Mrs Lansbury to the local assembly rooms. Wouldn't have thought this would appeal to you.'

Maxim whirled round but stopped when he saw Edward's slumberous eyes watching him and the unthinking response that sprang to his lips died. For Edward was right, he thought angrily. He was bewitched and beguiled by the young widow. In short, for the first time in his life, his heartfelt emotions were overruling his head, and he didn't suffer the affliction well.

'I saw what you did—the two hundred guineas. Way over the top, I thought, but you are the earl after all, and have to set an example. And Mrs Lansbury does shine tonight. She is also an exquisite dancer—and she appears to be avoiding you. Why, I can't imagine. Would I be right in thinking you've had a change of heart and would like to seduce the lady after all?'

'Mind your own damned business, Edward,' Maxim growled.

Edward smiled lazily, not in the least offended by his cousin's offhand remark. 'If I didn't think you were pursuing her, I'd be tempted to make a play for her myself.'

Maxim gave him a bland stare. 'If you value our relationship, Edward, you will forget you made that remark.'

Edward slanted him an amused look. 'You're beginning to sound like a jealous swain, Maxim. Don't tell me your attentions towards Mrs Lansbury are honourable? Good Lord! Perish the thought. I am trying to imagine what the *ton* and the people of Woodgreen will make of the renowned Earl of Levisham, once libertine *par excellence*, should he decide to wed the Widow Lansbury.'

Adopting a bored expression, he glanced towards the refreshment room, where the aforesaid lady was busy clearing away the debris off the tables. 'I always find evenings such as this unbearably flat—don't know why I bothered coming. I think I'll take the delectable Elena back home to her husband.'

'That's a sensible idea,' Maxim ground out ungraciously. 'Although, if you'd taken note half an hour ago, you would have seen Sir Oscar himself. He looked positively ill—and more than a little put out on seeing the two of you together. As far as I am aware, he remained no longer than a few minutes before he left. For myself, since there is nothing to be gained by remaining, I will take my leave and return to Netherthorpe.'

Eve returned to The Grange, shaken by her encounter with Maxim.

'I saw the two of you dancing together, Eve,' Sarah said in the carriage. 'Two hundred guineas was an awfully large amount of money to bid for you. He clearly doesn't want to let you go. Did—did you tell him about the baby?'

'No; no, I did not. It was not the right time. There were too many people. I do realise that it cannot be put off. I will go to Netherthorpe tomorrow.'

Leaving Christopher in Nessa's care, it was a determined Eve who rode to Netherthorpe the next morning. The day was sunny but there was a definite wind chill. Normally Eve would have enjoyed the ride and the freedom from household duties, but today she had too much on her mind about her meeting with Maxim to relax. Listening to Agatha as she'd prepared breakfast, and the gossip the girl from Woodgreen had been quick to impart about the night in the assembly rooms, it was inevitable there would be speculation as to how well Lord Levisham and the widowed Mrs Lansbury knew each other and for how long.

On her arrival, Hoskins opened the door.

'Is Lord Levisham at home?' she asked, stepping inside.

'Not at present, Mrs Lansbury. He had to ride into

Woodgreen. He should be back shortly. Would you care to wait?'

'No—no, I will leave. Perhaps you could inform him of my visit.'

'I will.'

Eve paused when Edward appeared from one of the rooms and strode towards her. He was dressed in a showy jacket, adorned with too much gold braiding for the time of day, she thought. The last person she wanted to encounter just then was Edward. She waited for him to reach her while Hoskins quietly slipped away.

Edward sidled up to her. His eyes, hooded and inscrutable, studied every detail of her appearance. 'Well, Mrs Lansbury. Here you are again. Is it a habit of yours to call on gentlemen in their homes alone? It's most inappropriate. You really can't keep away, can you?'

Eve stiffened in the face of this unexpected and unprovoked attack. She eyed him coldly. 'This is just my second visit to Netherthorpe.'

'And you are here to see Maxim?'

His voice was light and casual, but Eve was not deceived. She felt a darkness descend over the whole room like a shadow and she shivered in the sudden chill. 'Who else would I be here to see? Certainly not you.'

'What a shame he isn't here—which means you will have to come back.'

'If I have to.'

'You know, Maxim may be willing to wine and dine you, and escort you about town to this and that, but you've a long way to go before he will put himself out for you. An acquaintance and a mistress are not the same thing—even though you may not be able to see the difference between them.'

'I see well enough. All women are not such fools as you like to think.'

'I'm not like my cousin and not as easily taken in by fluttering eyelashes. You see, I've met your kind before—full of tricks before you get exactly what you want. I am quite certain that you possess a clever and inventive mind and that you are a calculating adventuress.'

The contempt in his voice made Eve's blood boil and she could not prevent her voice from shaking as she repeated unbelievingly, 'Tricks! My kind! A calculating adventuress! Do you mean to imply that I have attempted to entice him in order to…? Oh! How dare you? If I have learned anything at all about Maxim, he is not the type to be taken advantage of.'

'Then what did you hope to get from it? Money? Which, by all accounts, you are in dire need of. Or did you set your sights higher than that? Marriage, perhaps?' He laughed sneeringly. 'Maxim would never go so far as to do that.'

The cold, contemptuous words were uttered in a tone that was like a slap in the face, and Eve could hear them resounding in her head like a hollow drumbeat. What he was saying was that she was some upstart with pretensions above her station who had wormed her way into Maxim's affections. His rudeness was not to be endured.

'You needn't elucidate further. I get your drift. By what right do you speak to me like this?'

'By what right? My God, lady! Maxim and I are cousins, of the same blood. As well as being forced to leave his military career, he has suffered the loss of his brother. I will not stand by and see him taken advantage of by a scheming widow with a child. Wives in his circles are from the right families, to breed sons and carry family lines and titles. You have nothing to recommend you, nothing to bring with you into a marriage to such an illustrious a man as Maxim. So, whatever aspirations you might have, you are wasting your time here.'

There it was. She might stiffen against his criticism. His advice might be delivered without any compassion for her situation. But Eve could not deny its truth. 'If I was acquainted with such terms of verbal abuse as you seem accustomed to, I would use them, but I doubt there are any words vile enough to describe you, believe me. Whatever my relationship with Maxim might be, it is none of your business.'

Refusing to be intimidated, she took a step closer to him, her chin tilted, her eyes fixed on his. 'You may think what you like. I see some things you may think I don't, too.'

'Oh, do you?' His tone had the subtle sneering contempt she had noticed on their previous encounters.

'Be assured that I pose no threat to Maxim—whereas you, sir, are a different matter. You may pretend you are Maxim's most devoted cousin—but I know better. You, more than anyone else, are aware that Maxim's life is under threat. Whoever it is that is trying to kill him—perhaps he should look closer to home. You will be the next Earl of Levisham, will you not? You have much to gain.' She found herself drawn into his gaze. Here was a lethal ambition that would stop at nothing. That was the moment she knew Edward was capable of engineering Maxim's murder without a qualm.

'You suspect me of trying to murder my cousin?'

'I might.'

He laughed, a thin, unpleasant sound. 'I have never killed anyone in my life, and I never will.'

'Why would you do that when you can pay some-one else to do the deed?' Disgust shook her, but she kept her eyes steady on his, determined not to show fear, not to allow him any hold over her. He would feed on her weakness if he saw the panic on her face. She tried not to step back, but everything in her shrank from him, so she did.

Edward's eyes narrowed, a cruel light glinting in their depths. He took a menacing step towards her. 'You and Maxim may have become close, but I feel I must warn you not to get too comfortable at Nether-thorpe. You would regret it.'

Eve's heart lurched in fear. This didn't sound like a warning. This sounded like a threat. He was capable of anything, she thought with a touch of fear. They stood staring at each other, and neither could pretend any longer. There was frank dislike on both their faces.

Ignoring the danger signals she saw in his eyes, Eve said, 'You are mistaken if you think you can in-timidate me. You have no right to ask anything of me. You are nothing but a scoundrel and a false friend to

Maxim. I am aware of the wager the two of you made. I am disgusted by it. Before I go, I have some advice of my own to impart to you. You think you are clever in your dealings with your cousin, but have a care. He is a soldier with experience of scheming, calculating pathetic men. You are not in the same league as him.'

'In your eyes, maybe not. I can see how marriage to Maxim is desirable to you. Has he seduced you with his body and noble ways?' He laughed softly. 'You are shallow, Mrs Lansbury. It seems a title and fortune can tempt any woman fickle in her affections.'

'If you have any more illuminating observations of the inclinations of Mrs Lansbury, Edward, I suggest you make them to me.'

Maxim stood unobserved in the doorway. In the emotionally charged atmosphere, they had not heard him enter. There was anger in his eyes, all the more deadly because of his icy control. He had not been present to hear Edward's full attack on Eve, but he sensed the uncontrolled violence in Edward's stance. His voice was low, but there was no doubting the note of command.

Eve looked at him. 'I came here to see you, Maxim. If you don't mind, I will leave. I have no wish to stay any longer. The atmosphere, you understand,' she said, looking coldly at Edward, 'Is not to my liking.'

Without another word, with her head held high and with a quiet dignity, she turned and left the house, leaving Edward staring after her with a perplexed, uncertain frown and a furious Maxim striding after her.

## Chapter Eleven

Heading for her horse, Eve realised her mistake in coming to Netherthorpe. Clearly this was not the time for a confrontation with Maxim. She was about to mount her horse when Maxim, having followed her out of the house, called for her to wait. Seeing his fixed expression, she was filled with unease and foreboding.

'A word, if you please, Eve. You are not thinking of leaving?'

'Yes, I think I must. Had I known you would not be here, I would not have come.'

Maxim clamped his hand on her elbow. 'You are here now. It would be a pity to waste your journey. Will you please come back inside?'

'No, thank you. Having just encountered your charming cousin, I have no stomach to face him again.'

'Then come, let's walk away from the house where we will be less likely to be interrupted.'

'Very well, but please let go of my arm.'

He did as she bade and, side by side, they did not

speak until they had reached the garden and a place where they could not be observed from the house.

Eve took note of the judicious set to Maxim's jaw. She waited for him to speak, enduring the icy blast of his gaze. It dawned on her that he was striving to control his anger and she prayed he would gain it before she told him about the child.

'Were you deliberately trying to publicly humiliate me last night?' he demanded suddenly, giving her no time to prepare for the attack. 'Come, Eve,' he continued when she merely stared at him. 'Don't tell me you are stuck for words. You are clearly a woman of many talents, and it would seem one of them is to try and humble me. You didn't succeed, by the way. I am too experienced and too thick-skinned to be baited by you. Why, if you feel compelled to show me you care nothing for me, did you need to prove it in such a petty, small-minded way?'

Maxim's reprimand for her behaviour of the previous night was deserved. But Eve had not refused to dance the second dance with him to shame him or humble him in any way, so how dared he take the high ground after what he was guilty of where she was concerned?

'Don't you dare talk to me about being humbled and humiliated,' she uttered irately. 'You seem to believe this is all about you. What did you expect? It was more than you deserved.'

'Really? I disagree.'

Eve's mouth went dry when he moved closer. She

stepped back. 'Don't you dare touch me. I hate it when you do.'

Maxim's dark brows drew together and, reaching out, he pulled her into his arms. Before she knew what he was about, his mouth swooped down on to hers. She wanted to pull away, but she wanted his kiss more. Her anger quickly melted into searing passion.

When he felt her begin to respond, Maxim raised his head, looked down at her upturned face and smiled sardonically. 'Now tell me you hate it when I touch you. Perhaps next time you decide to humiliate and embarrass me in public you will reconsider.'

Drowning in shame at her inability to control her own treacherous body, with flaming cheeks Eve twisted free of the bewilderment that had gripped her when he had drawn her into his arms.

'You—humiliated? Embarrassed? How dare you say that, you despicable hypocrite?' she fired back and had the satisfaction of seeing shock crack his hard, handsome features. 'From the very beginning you set out to degrade me in the most shameful way of all, and yet you accuse *me* of humiliating you. Believe me, Maxim Randall, what happened to you in the assembly rooms was pretty tame, considering what you had intended for me.'

Maxim cocked a brow dubiously, somewhat amazed by the spirit of her. He reached out to draw her to him. Furiously, she shrugged him off.

'Keep your hands off me. I haven't finished. I'm not too proud to admit that in the beginning I was foolish enough to fall for your charms. It was quite wonderful, the most wonderful and remarkable thing that had ever happened to me. And now…now I have been told about the wager you made with your cousin. I am so ashamed—it was so trite. You are no doubt accustomed to that sort of feminine reaction wherever you go,' she uttered scathingly. 'I succumbed, just like every other unsuspecting woman you take a fancy to—a foolish inclination on my part, not supported by anything other than infatuation and my own imagination, because you felt nothing for me at all. That I knew.'

'The wager? How did you know?'

His shocked expression and the question told Eve she'd made a mistake—that she had almost revealed her secret that she loved him—but she was so angry it no longer mattered.

'I know because I was told.' She flared, looking him in the eyes, ashamed of the feelings she carried for him in her heart. 'I know because Elena Devlin told me the night after we were together. I may be naïve and silly, and many more things you've probably implied to your cousin, but at least she opened my eyes to the fact that you are nothing but a deceitful scoundrel.' Turning from him, she moved to stand away from him.

Comprehension and a hint of dismay dawned on Maxim's face. 'What, exactly, did she tell you?'

The sound of the swiftly indrawn breath seemed loud in the still air between them as Eve whirled to face him, her eyes blazing against the angry flush on her taut face.

'Enough. About the wager you so callously made with your wretched cousin—that if you failed to seduce me by Christmas Edward would be richer by a house. A house, for heaven's sake! Is that all I am worth? How dare you use me for your amusement by pretending to be my friend by using deception and trickery on someone who is too honest—and, yes, naïve, even—to recognise how depraved you are? How you must have laughed to yourself at my stupidity. When I first met you, I saw only a show of civility on the surface—just as easily as you wore your polite manners and title. I knew nothing and understood nothing—even about my own body or the sensations and emotions easily aroused by an unscrupulous seducer.'

'Eve, I am grieved that Lady Devlin told you about the wager, but please believe me when I say I regret even considering it. I give you my word, I never intended to hurt you.'

Her eyes were alight with pain and fury. 'Liar!' she cried contemptuously. 'Your word means nothing to me.'

White-faced with his guilt and remorse, Maxim tried to placate her. 'It was a temporary madness. It was cruel and thoughtless, and I realise you must be deeply hurt.'

'Yes, I am,' she snarled, her eyes blazing with turbulent animosity. 'And there is no excuse. How does it feel to know you won the wager? Are you pleased with yourself? At least you won't have Edward living on your doorstep. What a fool I made of myself. You are a scoundrel, Maxim, and what is true of most scoundrels is doubly so of you—you despicable lecher.' She turned from him and walked away, as if she couldn't bear to look at him.

'Eve…' Maxim began tautly, but she whirled on her heels like a dervish and stalked back to him, her storm-dark eyes pinpointed by tiny red flames reflecting the light of the sun. Did she but know it, she reminded Maxim in that moment of a cornered vixen, all teeth, claws and angry vibrations that he could feel emanating from her.

'Tell me, Maxim, what was I?' she scoffed sneeringly, jabbing her finger into his chest. 'Was I some tender morsel you decided to play with, a simpleton to fill your needs for a night or two? What amusement you must have had playing your sordid little game with me. My one regret is that Elena Devlin didn't tell me before I shared your bed.'

Nothing moved in Maxim's face, but his eyes darkened. Quietly he asked, 'Will you listen to what I have to say?'

'No. I am not interested. I will never be able to forgive you. But you listen to me, Maxim Randall,' she said, her chilled contempt meeting him face to face. 'The harm you have done me will stand between us for ever. There are some issues we will have to talk about—important and necessary issues—but this is not the time. Not when there is so much anger between us and I expect your cousin to appear at any minute.'

With her head held high, she turned, marched out of the garden, headed back to the driveway and mounted her horse. She was down the drive and heading off across the fields before Maxim could gather himself and call her back.

Eve's hostile encounter with Maxim had stoked a burden of emotion inside her. She should have told him about the child, but she hadn't wanted to discuss something so precious to her in an atmosphere of hostility. She firmly believed Maxim didn't feel any remorse at all for what he had done to her. Her mind had always shied away from delving too deeply into what her feelings were for him, but now she had to ask herself.

Despite what he was guilty of where she was concerned, she cared for him deeply—there was no denying that—and she treasured the times they had been together. She could not discard from her mind that exquisite night she had spent in his bed, in his arms and the pleasure and intensity she had experienced before she knew about the wager.

Almost beyond conscious thought, she felt as if all emotion had been drained out of her. She reminded herself that he was a scoundrel, a libertine, and that righteousness was on her side. But, if so, then why did it hurt so much and why was her face wet with tears?

Maxim didn't return to the house immediately when Eve had left him. Weighted down with unbearable guilt, and hating himself with a virulence that almost choked him, he stared into the distance. So that was what all this had been about—that blasted wager. Everything had been made clear, presenting the whole sordid picture in every profane detail. As he watched her leave he was not afraid for himself, but he was tortured by the thought that he could lose her. Imagining it, he felt sick.

He had come to realise that he wanted to spend his life with her. He never again wanted to be separated from her. This was a life-changing thought and he played out the consequences in his mind. He was sure Eve's feelings were similar to his own. Despite the distance she seemed determined to put between them, he thought he could not be mistaken about that. But she had created so many questions for which he had no answers.

He belatedly realised he should never have agreed to the wretched wager in the first place. What had he been thinking? Damn it! He was old enough and experienced enough to have known better, and to have thought of the possible consequences, and he cursed himself for having so recklessly allowed himself to be goaded into yielding to a wildly irrational impulse. He had made a mess of the entire situation and he had no one to blame but himself. Eve's revelation answered so many questions and why she had behaved as she had on leaving London.

Dear Lord, he had hurt her very badly. She must hate him, and with good reason. Knowing this, he felt a pain that was a thousand times worse than any wound he had ever received. If only she had waited and allowed him to explain that he had told Edward the wager was off, that he could have the house since he wanted to renege on the bet. He was going to have to find a

way to tell her, to redeem himself—but would she believe him?

It was not until he was returning to the house that
he wondered what had brought her to Netherthorpe.
It hadn't been about the wager—that had cropped up
incidentally. So why had she come? And what 'important issues' had she been talking about?

Unable to leave things as they were between them,
he was soon riding in the direction she had taken.


Far too tense and overwrought to remain calm, Eve
rode her horse hard. When she was out of sight of the
house, she slowed. It seemed as if everything about
her had become still, almost as if time itself hung
precariously before petering out. The only sound she
could hear was in her head—Edward's condescending,
harshly delivered words echoing cruelly in the darkness of her mind—until suddenly she could hear the
drumming of a horse's hooves coming closer.

Halting her horse in a clearing, she waited for the
rider to emerge from the trees. She wasn't really surprised to see Maxim. Bringing his horse to a halt, he
threw himself out of the saddle and strode towards her.

'Get down, Eve. Please. There is too much between
us for us to part in anger.'

On a sigh, she slipped from the saddle, looking up
at him.

'I couldn't let you leave like that. I've been trying to catch up with you, but you were riding as if the
Devil himself were in pursuit. We cannot leave things
as they are.'

'No, we can't. I'm sorry if I spoke harshly, but my encounter with Edward made me angry.'

'I can understand that and, for what it's worth, I'm sorry. But you must listen to what I have to say.'

'Yes, of course. I am all ears, Maxim. Perhaps you should begin by telling me about the wager—which one of you came out the victor?'

'There was no victor, Eve. I reneged on it.'

Confused, Eve stared at him, a feeling of unease beginning to steal over her. 'I think you'd better explain.'

'I wanted to. As I recall, you didn't want to know. You were so furious with me, I felt my protestations of innocence would fall on deaf ears.'

'You had made me an object of ridicule and I was furious—as anyone would be. Why did you agree to the wager in the first place?'

'Because I wanted you—quite desperately, in fact. I wasn't thinking straight. I never can where you are concerned.'

His words didn't answer her question fully, nor did they remove the hurt. But they did fill her with hope, with warmth and, loving him as she did, she realised for now it would have to do. 'Why did you fold on the wager?'

'Because I had developed a deep regard for you, and I would not dishonour you. True to my word, I honoured the wager when I saw Edward in London. Allowing him to take up residence in the Dower House is proof of that.'

The blood drained from Eve's face and she almost stopped breathing when the implication of what he'd told her hit home. 'I see,' she said tightly. 'And your cousin? Does—does he know…?'

'What? How well we came to know each other?' He shook his head. 'Of course not. What happened between us is no concern of anyone else.'

'Thank goodness,' she murmured, suddenly beginning to feel tired. 'Although it will be a long time, if ever, that I will be able to forgive you for agreeing to the wager in the first place. But did you have to allow him to live in the Dower House?'

'I'll have to discuss it with him further. In all truth, I don't believe I can suffer having him living on my doorstep.' Maxim stroked her cheek with the backs of his fingers. 'You look pale, Eve. Are you unwell?'

'If I am, then it is your fault.'

His body tensed, his jaw tightened and his eyes grew cold. 'My fault? How is it my fault? And what were the issues you referred to before storming off?'

'I am with child, Maxim. Your child,' Eve said quietly. 'Small wonder the ladies you associate with can't forget what you do to them, if you impregnate them the first time you take them to bed.'

Maxim's face became thoughtful, his eyes narrowing speculatively. 'How long have you known?' He stood straight, his hands by his sides, his face impassive— the expression he normally wore to shield his thoughts when troubled or angry. A muscle began to twitch in his cheek.

Eve found the calm of his demeanour to be more infuriating than any display of anger. 'A couple of weeks,' she replied.

'I see. And you are certain?'

'Of course I'm certain. The child is yours, Maxim, so don't you dare try wriggling out of it,' she snapped.

'I would not do that.'

'That's something, at least.' Her face became flushed with emotion.

'Is that what brought you to Netherthorpe today? To tell me about the child?'

'That—and to tell you I knew about that disgusting wager you made with your cousin.'

'I'm sorry. I take full responsibility for what has happened and I am duty-bound to do the honourable thing. Why didn't you tell me before now?'

'You've no idea how much I wanted to tell you, but I couldn't.'

'You need not fear for the future.'

'What are you saying?'

'That we will be married immediately.'

Eve could not believe what she was hearing. He sounded so dispassionate, she was not quite sure if she had received a proposal of marriage or a comment about some inconsequential issue of the day. 'I see.' She took a deep breath. 'And are you quite sure that you want to marry me, Maxim?'

'These are not the most romantic of circumstances under which to propose, and I am more than likely wounding you by discussing the arrangements in such a blunt way, but we have no choice.'

A lump of nameless emotion constricted her throat. He was treating her as if there had been nothing be-tween them, as if they had never shared the intense passion between a man and a woman. She suppressed the intense regret that it was so. She had not yet said she would marry him. So much still remained unspoken between them. *Tell me you love me!* She didn't say the words. She couldn't. Nor could she speak of her love for him.

'That was not what I asked you.'

'My feelings have no bearing on this. There is nothing else to be done. You must be aware of the stigma attached to an illegitimate child, that it will be an object of censure and ridicule throughout its life. Think about it. A woman alone with an illegitimate child is prey to the pitilessness of society.'

'I know. A harsh society that believes the sin is all the woman's, that she is to blame for being in the condition she has brought on herself, and that the child as well as her must be shunned lest it contaminates them—while the man who is equally to blame walks away without a blemish on his name. I would like to say that I will not allow my destiny or that of my child to be dictated by circumstance, society or you—but I cannot.'

Maxim looked at her hard. The expression on his face was difficult to read, but some new darkness seemed to move at the back of his eyes. 'I have an obligation to the child—to you, Eve. We will be married as soon as it can be arranged, for I will not compound any wrong I have done you by abandoning my honour and my duty. It takes two to make a child, and you and I made together the one you are carrying.'

Eve pulled herself erect with as much composure

as her shaking limbs would allow, but the penetrating eyes meeting hers gave her no assurance. 'I know, but that was before that cruel wager you made with your cousin. I was alone and confused and I had to deal with what happened. So, you see, after this you cannot blame me for being angry. I even told myself that I did not want you to be the father of my child.'

His expression changed, becoming harder still, and the tone of his voice became deadly quiet. 'Nevertheless, that is what I am, so let that be an end to it. It may not have been conceived in the kind of circumstances I would have liked, but I will use every means at my disposal to keep its reputation untarnished.'

She nodded her agreement. 'Yes. That is how it must be.'

Turning away from him, she went to her horse. Maxim stood and watched her. For the first time in his life he found it difficult to tell a woman that she was the most alluring and desirable he had ever known. Even when she had told him about the child, when the consequences of his actions were so grave, he wanted her. She had become a passion to him, a beautiful, vibrant woman, and he had hurt her very badly.

Striding after her, he halted her before she could mount. Placing his hands on her shoulders, he turned her to face him, looking at her for a long moment. Even now, when the consequences of what he had done to her were grave, when the future of his heir was all important, he wanted her.

Without warning or hesitation, he bent his head and brushed her parted lips with his own, encouraged when she did not protest. His kiss was slow. He didn't use force but, when the tip of his tongue touched hers, her lips opened a little more without any direction from her or urging from him. Some part of him wanted more, but he simply let his mouth linger a moment longer and then pulled away.

'I have hurt you very badly, Eve. I know that. I suppose it's conceited of me to assume you will marry me, that you would accept our marriage as a matter of course because of the child. But, putting all that aside, I do want to marry you regardless of anything else.' His eyes softened. 'Do not fight me, for I've wanted you from the moment I saw you. I consider marrying you as simply the right and honourable thing to do.'

He lowered his head and kissed her again, bending her head back better to accommodate his lips on hers—soft, gentle and ever so persuasive. Eve was as helpless to stem the rising desire consuming her as she had been when first they'd kissed in London.

'Eve,' he murmured against her mouth. 'What do you say about our marriage? You're a difficult woman to win over.'

Eve's senses were still spinning. She wasn't sure what bothered her more—that he'd dared to kiss her, that he seemed so unaffected by it or that she was beginning to realise that she was no longer able to control her own fate.

'Damn you, Maxim Randall.' She flared, pushing him away and folding her arms over her chest. 'You are right, and I hate you for being right. If I am to give our child the best possible chance in life, then it will need a father—so, yes, I will marry you.'

'Good. That's settled, then.' He put his hands gently on her shoulders and drew her to his chest. 'I have had lovers before, but I would like you to know I have never felt this way about anyone before. You are the only woman I have wanted to marry, Eve,' he murmured, his mouth touching the crown of her head just where the thick, golden hair parted.

'Believe me, my darling. You have nothing to fear. You are a wonderful, brave, incredibly beautiful woman. I never wanted to hurt you. I love you—how could I not? I love you more than anything on earth.'

Eve's breath caught in her throat and, tilting her head back a little, she looked up at him, feeling a glimmer of hope. Maxim loved her? The beginnings of happiness swelled in her heart.

'You never told me.'

'That was because it took me a while to realise it,' he said tenderly. 'And then there was so much going on between us that I was afraid to mention it until I was sure I stood a chance of winning your regard. I do love you. So very much.'

Hearing the gentleness in his voice, Eve drew back to search his rugged face. Sunlight slanting through the bare branches of the trees highlighted his thick hair and increased the sharp clarity of his eyes, making it impossible for her to deny the love she saw there. She took a steadying breath, daring to believe. And, suddenly, all the doubts and fears of the past days and weeks were gone.

'I thought I had lost you,' she whispered, a break in her voice. 'And I couldn't bear it.'

'Well, well,' a voice rang out. 'What a touching scene.'

Maxim and Eve spun round to see Edward pointing a pistol at them.

'What have we here?' Edward jeeringly asked, arrogant in his demeanour, confident with a gun in his hand. 'A love scene—how very touching.'

Maxim stiffened and his cheeks tensed with fury. 'Edward!' he exclaimed, automatically taking Eve's arm and thrusting her behind him. 'What the devil are you doing?'

'I have some unfinished business. I wanted the two of you to be together. This is perfect for what I am about to do.'

Maxim's eyes never wavered from the man he now knew to be the most malignant of enemies, his nemesis, the man he was now certain had murdered his brother. His tall frame was rigid with anger, his voice when he spoke measured with a sinister steadiness.

'So, Edward, we have the truth at last. I understand what all this means, and why you have decided to enact it now, and how you have schemed and manipulated and must have waited for this moment. After two attempts on my life have failed, it appears you've decided to finish me off yourself. I congratulate your bravado at last.' Each word had a bite, and Maxim's eyes were deadly. 'Who'd have thought it of my cousin?'

Edward's smile was icy. 'You never did know me very well, did you, Maxim?'

'That was my mistake. I do now,' Maxim replied with tightly controlled fury. 'I never thought… I never realised… How could I have known, my clever, vindictive cousin, to what ugly lengths you would go? You killed Andrew, didn't you, Edward.'

He shrugged. 'It wasn't difficult. Yes, I partly severed the girth on his horse. It broke during the hunt, throwing him off. When he tried to get up I…'

'Hit him over the head. According to Dr Ennis, it was the blow that killed him.'

Edward raised his head aloofly, his expression carefully controlled with no hint of either guilt or regret. 'I do not deny it. No one was present. If anyone suspected me, then they did not speak out.' He was confident now, a triumphant smile on his lips. 'There was no proof. There was no one to set themselves up as my executioner for a crime they were unable to prove that I committed. I should have been the Earl of Levisham—according to my father, who always professed to have been the first born.'

'So he would have you believe. He was mistaken—like he was in every aspect of his misbegotten life. You should have left well alone. With Andrew out of the way, no doubt all your hopes of me dying in the Peninsular were dashed when I came back to take up my rightful position at Netherthorpe.'

'Yes, something like that. You came back to cheat me out of all this.'

'Netherthorpe was never yours, and yet you have been brooding and seething all this time. The longer

your resentment went on, the more bitter and dangerous you became. You're quite mad, Edward.'

Intent and dangerous, Edward advanced on Maxim,
all trace of patience vanished in his need to finish what
he had started when he'd killed Andrew. The only sign
that he had come close to losing his control showed
in the harshness of his breathing, in the stillness that
held them all in thrall. If Eve had thought he hadn't the
stomach to assassinate Maxim himself, she now knew
she had been mistaken.

'That's right. I am mad, and I have no conscience
for what I am about to do. When your bodies are found,
no one will have reason to suspect me. Two attempts
have been made on your life already—and I was nowhere in sight. Yes, you killed the last assassin—but
it will be assumed he wasn't working alone.'

'And the reason?'

'That will be open to conjecture. As a soldier just
returned from Spain, it would not be unusual for someone to have a gripe against you and be out for revenge.'

Instinctively Maxim's arm snaked behind him to
protect Eve. 'You intend to kill us both?'

'Why not? It would be suicidal to let her go. She
knows too much.'

'Eve is with child—my child. Would you murder
that too?'

Edward's face hardened as he looked towards Eve,
who moved closer to Maxim. 'So, you seduced her after
all. I understand now why you reneged on the wager.
All the more reason to get rid of the three of you.'

Eve had to admire Maxim's cool nerve, which she put down to his military training.

Suddenly one of the horses shifted and snorted, the noise sounding loud in the quietness of the glade. Distracted, Edward whipped round. Maxim took this moment of distraction to leap forward to knock the weapon out of his hand, but Edward held on to it and leapt back. A struggle ensued. Eve watched, her heart in her mouth as the two fell to the ground, locked in a deadly struggle.

She pressed a hand tightly across her mouth as her heart throbbed in sudden dread. She stood irresolutely on the edge of the scene, her eyes darting from one to another of the major players in the drama unfolding before her eyes. Fear rose within her and she could not beat it back. A bright flash of light erupted from the gun and the sound was deafening. The next moment, Edward became still, clutching his chest, blood beginning to seep through his fingers.

Maxim got to his feet and looked down at the man who had wanted him dead, bending over his prostrate form. One of Edward's hands clutched at his chest, blood seeping from between his fingers. He was obviously in a lot of pain, his breathing ragged. The lines around his mouth were deep and his face was pale. He lifted his hand and groped around for his pistol.

'Leave it,' Maxim said. 'You're in no condition to put up a fight. You fool, Edward. Guilty of killing Andrew and your attempts on my life—you have got what you deserve.'

Edward raised his head and glared at him, his gaze

shifting from Maxim to Eve and then back again. 'Damn you, Maxim,' he gasped, his head falling back as the effort proved too much. 'You've finally got it all. This was not how I planned things. And you, Eve Lansbury—with aspirations above yourself.'

'It will very soon be Eve Randall,' Maxim informed him curtly, pulling her close against his side. 'Countess of Levisham. Eve has consented to be my wife.'

'Wife?' Edward snarled. 'Then I damn you—twice, Maxim. You have it all. You really have no idea at the lifetime of misery and humiliation your family have subjected me to over the years—the poor relation, my fate decided when our fathers were born and your father was proclaimed the heir—damn him.'

'As you damned me in your ambitions to remove me as you removed Andrew.'

Edward closed his eyes to hide the pain of his own defeat. 'Don't be smug, Maxim.' And then he laughed, a horrible, grating sound which made a cold shiver run down Eve's spine. 'At least I've cheated the hangman.'

The words came haltingly from between his lips, and when his head fell back they realised there was nothing they could do. There came a sudden death rattle in his throat, and his whole body heaved, as if in a convulsion. Even as Eve gave a little cry of horror, he collapsed.

For a long moment there was silence in the woodland glade as they realised Edward was dead. Eve's face was drawn and white, the ordeal having taken its toll. Maxim held out his arms and she moved into them gladly, almost like a child seeking comfort and reassurance, for she was still prey to the fear she had felt when she'd truly thought Edward was going to shoot them both. Maxim placed his lips gently on the crown of her shining hair, which snaked its way down her back like a silken sheath.

'What a dreadful thing to happen. How are you feeling?' he asked quietly.

'Overwhelmed by a turmoil of emotions. It's a combination of relief, gladness and at the same time a feeling of horror, mingled with some element of surprise—knowing that the man who intended destroying us both is dead himself.' She looked at him, her eyes luminous with tears. 'It was so terrible. I truly believed, Maxim, that we were going to die.'

Maxim's arms tightened around her, for there had been a moment when he had also thought this. 'I know,' he said hoarsely, overcome with emotion.

Eve leaned back in his arms and looked at him. 'This is so awful for you, Maxim, knowing Edward really did kill your brother—that he was also the one trying to kill you.'

'At least we know the truth of it now and we can move on. Dear Lord, how I wish I had looked into Andrew's death sooner. If I had, none of this would have happened.'

'You could not have foreseen what Edward would do. Don't blame yourself. It wasn't your fault. You weren't to know he would go to such drastic lengths.'

'You are very generous, but I cannot be acquitted so lightly, my love.' Looking down at Edward's recumbent form, he sighed. 'What has happened has to be dealt

with. Do you think you could ride to Netherthorpe?
Tell them what has happened and send someone into
Woodgreen for the constable. I'll wait here.'

'Yes—yes, of course. I'll also have someone ride to
The Grange to explain things to Sarah. She'll worry
if I'm late.'

Not until Edward's body had been taken back to the
house and Eve found herself alone with Maxim did
she begin to relax. Darkness would soon be falling,
and they were alone in the elegant drawing room at
Netherthorpe, seated side by side in a window recess.

Taking her hand, Maxim raised it to his lips. 'How
I have agonised over that dreadful wager I made with
Edward. You had every reason to be angry with me
that day, and I should have known better than to do
anything so reckless. My ignorance as to the merits of
your character has caused me to reproach myself many
times. It was cruel and indefensible.'

'Yes, it was, but I beg you not to reproach yourself
further. All that is in the past—let us put it behind us.
Edward can no longer harm us.'

'That's true. Without doubt he was a man driven by
ambition and disillusionment over the past—embittered
and vengeful. I did not realise how fanatical he was in
his desire to take Netherthorpe from me. There is little
he would not do—even murder—to further his goal. He
confessed to killing Andrew. Justice has been done, but
I feel no victory in it. All his hopes were pinned on getting Netherthorpe for himself. I should feel compassion
for his loss, but I cannot find it in my heart to do so.'

'I can understand that. Edward brought fatal harm and too much distress to you to deserve your sympathy.'

'I have always believed in Edward's sincerity. No amount of gossip and scandal could shake me from that belief. No proof of his perfidy—and it has been offered to me—could convince me that he was other than what he seemed. But I now realise that, in all the years I have known him, I have been allowed to see only one side to him, the side he wanted me to see. He created an image of himself of a loving, concerned cousin or, perhaps by a stretch of the imagination, a brother. Thinking of him now, I feel the pull of old loyalties, of the confidences between us, the laughter and adventures we had as boys.'

'He clearly grew up with a grievance towards you and Andrew. Did he not consider a military career like yourself?'

'No, not a bit of it. As an only child he had never done a day's work in his life. The only thing that mattered to him was pleasure—his pleasures many—and becoming the Earl of Levisham. He was agreeable in public to most people if it suited him to be, people who could make his lot in life easier, but I now know that underneath he was quite ruthless and a calculating congenital liar. With his sights set on Netherthorpe, getting rid of Andrew was a calculated risk, but it had worked—until I came home from the Peninsular. I had to be got rid of and then his path to being the Earl of Levisham would be clear.'

'Thank goodness he didn't succeed.' Nestling

against him when he placed his arm about her and drew her close, she said, 'Are you sure you want to marry me, Maxim? You're not just asking me because of the baby?'

'I want *you*,' he said in a tone of tender finality. He took her chin between his thumb and forefinger and lifted it, forcing her to meet his steady gaze as he quietly added, 'And you want me. Ever since that day you left me in London, I've been in purgatory. You have no idea how much I wanted you, how I tormented myself thinking of ways to get you back. You are going to marry me. I am determined.'

'But I am not of your world. We aren't suited.'

'None of that matters,' he whispered, sliding his hand around her narrow waist and moving her closer against him, his tender gesture demonstrating quite clearly that he disagreed with her. 'I adore you, Eve. I have adored you since I first looked up and saw you bending over me when I'd been shot. And that,' he added on a husky note, 'Is no doubt the reason I was willing to go to any lengths, honourable or not, to make you my wife. I love you.'

'Oh, Maxim,' she murmured, her eyes shining with her love. 'You are a wicked rogue, and after the way you have treated me you do not deserve that I should love you, but I do. Very much.'

'Then you agree that we will be married as soon as it can be arranged?'

'Yes,' she whispered. There were tears in her eyes. Tears for the speed of her surrender. Within the protective circle of his arms, she tilted her head. There was nothing she wanted more in life other than to be joined to him for ever. 'I do love you, Maxim. I shall be proud to be your wife.'

## *Epilogue*

It was the day of Maxim's and Eve's marriage. Netherthorpe hadn't seen such a gathering since Maxim's father had died. It was a truly joyous occasion, with family and friends all invited. It was attended by a select few local residents, family and Maxim's friends from London. The weather was cold, and snow threatened, so the feast was laid on in the house for the guests.

Eve's family made themselves at home at The Grange. They were all delighted at the way things had turned out for Eve and were impressed that she was to be the Countess of Levisham—although Eve's pregnancy caused a few raised eyebrows. Sarah was very much in charge, since she and her husband were to take up residence there after the wedding. Eve couldn't be more delighted. The arrangement satisfied all concerned, especially as Sarah had no wish to live in London, yet needed to be close enough to the city so she would not be separated from her husband for long periods.

Not only did this solve the problem of what was to be done with The Grange until Christopher was of age to take on the responsibility himself, but Eve was looking forward to having Sarah close. Christopher was also excited, knowing his young cousin would be on hand to play with.

The wedding breakfast was a light-hearted affair. Having cast off the gloom of Edward's demise and funeral, Eve was a vision of loveliness in a dress of cream silk and as slender as a wand. She moved beside Maxim, tall and extremely handsome in a dark-green velvet suit and ivory embroidered waistcoat, his dark hair brushed smoothly back from his brow. Eve caught her husband's eye and a smile moved across his lean face, his eyes becoming more vivid over the rim of his champagne glass, silently informing her of his impatience for the night to come.

'Marriage obviously agrees with you,' he told her softly when he managed to get her to himself for a brief moment. 'I have never seen you look more delectable than you do at this moment.'

'Don't all brides?' she murmured.

'I only have eyes for the one,' he replied. 'You look quite stunning in that cream dress, but I am impatient to reacquaint myself with what you're wearing under it—or not wearing. I already know it conceals a body destined to stir the lusty instincts of any man.'

Eve laughed up into his face, flushing delightfully. 'Maxim Randall, you are incorrigible. You will see soon enough.'

Sarah was almost as radiant as the bride, losing no time in telling Eve that the next gathering of the family would be for the christening of her child when it was born. As she said this, she was looking adoringly at her young daughter and Christopher tucking into some iced cakes, licking their sticky fingers and giggling together.

'I couldn't be happier at the way things have turned out, Sarah, and to have you living at The Grange is an added bonus. As you know, Maxim is to have it farmed along with Netherthorpe, so you won't be bothered with that—until Christopher is old enough to take responsibility for it.'

'I'm so thrilled for you, Eve. Things couldn't have turned out better. And look at you—Lady Levisham, the Countess of Levisham. I'll never get used to it.'

Eve laughed, hugging her close. 'Neither will I.'

'Oh, I think you'll do very well—with that handsome husband of yours by your side. Never have I seen two people look more in love than you two, and it gladdens my heart.'

Having said farewell to their guests—Sarah having taken Christopher with her to spend the night at The Grange with his young cousin—Maxim and Eve were alone in the room they now shared. They lay side by side on their rumpled bed, Maxim leaning on his elbow and looking down at his wife's face, flushed and pink in the soft glow of light that bathed the room.

When they had closed the door behind them, he had undressed her and laid her down on the soft bed.

When he'd joined her, she had turned and faced him and closed her eyes, letting the warmth of his body against her cool skin wash over her. He had caressed and stroked her and found the core of her so that she sighed and moaned between her kisses. Holding her close, his hard-muscled chest pressed against hers, he had entered her and she'd clung to him. He had been devoured in a searing, scorching flame that had shot through him like a flaming rocket, moving and seeking, their need for each other a hunger beyond sanity. Never had either of them felt such delight.

Having fallen into a light sleep following their love-making, Eve's eyes were closed and Maxim remained unmoving, afraid to break the magic of the moment, pride almost bursting his heart as he looked down at her sleeping face. She was so beautiful that he was mesmerised by her sheer perfection. He could not cease to marvel at the fact that she was his wife, that she belonged to him completely—and that she gave herself to him with a passion and intensity that equalled his own and brought them a wondrous awe.

She stirred and opened her eyes sleepily, smiling up at him, happiness giving her an inner glow that shone through. With a happy sigh of contentment, she nestled closer to him.

'What are you thinking?' she murmured.

'How lucky I am to have such a beautiful and clever wife—and how amiable you have become, my love,' he teased gently. 'There is scarcely a trace of the contrary young woman I came to know in the early days of our acquaintance.'

'Don't be deceived, for she is still there—lurking somewhere in the background. No doubt it will come out in our son or daughter. Do you mind which? Although that is a silly question to ask a man who must have a son and heir to carry on the dynasty.'

'Girl or boy, I don't mind which, providing the child is healthy. But don't forget, my love,' he said, rolling her onto her back and beginning to place gentle kisses on her face, 'That it is not uncommon for the women in my family to produce two babies at a time.'

She pushed him away, looking up at him with shock and seeing a merry twinkle in those dark depths. 'Twins?' she murmured, disbelief evident in her tone. 'Oh, dear! Goodness me! I—I hadn't thought...'

Maxim laughed, gathering her into his arms. 'Then you should, my love, because it is highly probable. Why, I'd wager my...'

Eve immediately silenced him by placing her hand firmly across his smiling lips. 'Don't you dare mention a wager to me, Maxim Randall. Your days of making wagers are well and truly over.'

\* \* \* \* \*

*If you enjoyed this story, be sure to read*
*Helen Dickson's other exciting books!*

Wedded for His Secret Child
Resisting Her Enemy Lord
A Viscount to Save Her Reputation
Enthralled by Her Enemy's Kiss
To Catch a Runaway Bride
Conveniently Wed to a Spy